DATE DUE   JUN 0 6

8-1-06			
OCT 1 8 '06			
GAYLORD			PRINTED IN U.S.A.

Stealing Freedom

Elisa Carbone

Thorndike Press • Waterville, Maine

Recommended for Young Adult Readers.

Newspaper advertisement on page 7 courtesy of Montgomery County Historical Society from the *Montgomery County Sentinel*, December 8, 1855.
Photograph on page 7 courtesy of Montgomery County Historical Society from *The Underground Rail Road* by William Still, 1872.

Published in 2005 by arrangement with Random House Children's Books, a division of Random House, Inc.

The tree indicium is a trademark of Thorndike Press.

The text of this Large Print edition is unabridged.
Other aspects of the book may vary from the original edition.

Set in 16 pt. Plantin by Elena Picard.

Printed in the United States on permanent paper.

Library of Congress Cataloging-in-Publication Data

Carbone, Elisa Lynn.
    Stealing freedom / by Elisa Carbone.
        p. cm.
    Summary: a novel based on the events in the life of a young slave girl from Maryland who endures all kinds of mistreatment and cruelty, including being separated from her family, but who eventually escapes to freedom in Canada.
    ISBN 0-7862-7314-3 (lg. print : sc : alk. paper)
    1. Weems, Anne-Marie — Juvenile fiction. 2. Large type books. [1. Weems, Anne-Marie — Fiction. 2. Slavery — Fiction. 3. Underground railroad — Fiction. 4. African Americans — Fiction. 5. Large type books.] I. Title.
PZ7.C1865Su 2005
    [Fic]—dc22   2004028047

To Miss Ann Maria

This book is based on
the true story of Ann Maria Weems.

$500 REWARD.

RAN away on Sunday night, the 23d
instant, before 12 o'clock, from the
subscriber, residing in Rockville, Montgomery county, Md., my NEGRO GIRL
"Ann Maria Weems," about 15 years
of age; a bright mullatto; some small freckles
on her face; slender person, thick suit of hair,
inclined to be sandy. Her parents are free,
and reside in Washington, D. C. It is evident
she was taken away by some one in a carriage,
probably by a white man, by whom she may
be carried beyond the limits of the State of
Maryland.

I will give the above reward for her apprehension and detention so that I get her again.

sep 29—3t   CHAS. M. PRICE.

One

Unity, Maryland, 1853

"Mamma said we've got to, that's why." Ann Maria fairly dragged her brother up the hill toward the sound of barking dogs.

A cloud enveloped the moon, and the shadows shifted. Addison stopped abruptly, listening. "What's that?" he whispered.

"Your own breathing," she snapped. "Would you come *on?*"

Addison took several more hesitant steps, then stopped again. "If Master Charles catches us, we'll get a whipping. A bad one," he said.

He was trying to scare her into giving it up, she knew. He was the older one, so why was she the braver one? "It's Richard's birthday celebration tonight, and not Master Charles nor Mistress Carol is going to take notice of these scrawny dogs howling at the moon."

"What if they bite my hand off?" Addison still refused to move.

Ann sighed, exasperated. "Mamma has fed these hounds lots of times. Papa, too. You see them missing a hand?"

The moon peeked out again and Ann saw Addison's round eyes, bright and fearful. More gently she said, "Let's just do it quick, so we can get back." The smell of the fried cornmeal mush in her apron made her stomach grumble for its own supper. She broke the slab of mush in two and gave half to Addison.

They crept up the grassy slope. As they approached, the dogs' barking turned to howling. There was the wooden worm fence, the maple tree around which the hounds' chains were wrapped, and beyond them the summer kitchen and the stone house, with warm yellow light shining from the windows.

"Shhh . . . shhh . . . shhh . . ." Ann shushed with each step — shushing either the dogs or her pounding heart, she wasn't sure which.

Two pairs of eyes gleamed as if lit from the inside. The hounds panted now, yelped, and strained against their chains toward the smell of corn and fatback.

Ann ran the last few steps to the fence.

One hound lunged at her, the other at Addison beside her. She thrust the cornmeal mush toward the sharp teeth and glowing eyes, and the next moment the dogs were sniffing the ground for crumbs and she and Addison were wiping dog spit off their shaking hands.

The door of the stone house opened, and in the sliver of light that was the doorway stood Ellie, the Prices' house slave. "They're quiet now, Master Charles. You still want me to have a look?"

The answer from inside must have been "no," because the door closed.

Ann and Addison raced down the hill, their bare feet slapping the well-worn trail. Shimmery light peeked from their own cabin. It came from the one window, from around the ill-fitting door, and from between the logs that lay sideways to form the walls.

They burst inside. "We did it, Mamma!" Addison landed a kiss on his mother's sweaty cheek as she stood in front of the hearth managing one skillet of beet greens and another of frying mush.

"Go wash up, then," their mamma ordered. "Those dogs' mouths are slimy as a slug's belly."

Once Addison was safely outside, Ann

turned to her oldest brother, Augustus. He was carefully whittling a rounded piece of wood for the chair he was building. He frowned at his work.

"He was scared," Ann said matter-of-factly.

Augustus kept whittling. "And you weren't?"

Ann squared her shoulders. "Not like he was."

Augustus shook his head. His curled-up eyelashes might have given his face a gentle look if his eyes had not been so steely hard. "You better start acting like a girl sometime soon," he said, "or no boy is ever going to take a shine to you — especially with those freckles."

Ann glared at him and ran a finger over one cheek. "Mamma says my freckles are nice," she said defiantly. She had seen herself in the looking glass in the Prices' parlor — seen her dark, wide-set eyes and upturned mouth — and she honestly didn't think the freckles were a problem. "And anyway, why would I want to ever hold hands with a boy or any such thing?"

Joseph, her youngest brother, rescued them from further argument. "Were you really not scared?" he asked. He was wriggling on the dinner bench, where he was supposed to keep still. Ann sat with him to continue the story.

"Their eyes were on fire, and when we got close we could feel the heat, just like Mamma's hearth there."

Joseph's mouth twisted as his imagination flew. "If I was there, I'd punch those dogs." He jumped onto the bench and swung a vigorous right hook. "I'd punch them so hard they'd fly up on Master Charles's roof! Then they'd fly all the way to Baltimore!" He hopped off the bench and continued punching the air, his thin arms quick as grasshopper legs.

"Joseph, you sit on that bench where I put you." Mamma brought a huge bowl of steaming greens to the table. "Ann Maria, go tell your father and your sister that no one in their right mind works a garden all night, and it's time for supper."

Ann was thankful for the chance to go outside again. The heat of the day had gathered in the house along with the cooking fire, but outside it was already cool, and a soft wind carried the songs of crickets and cicadas. Nearing their small garden plot, she heard the chink-chink-chink of the hoe and heard her father's deep voice joined with Catharine's high one in a hymn. She approached but said nothing, just watched them and listened.

Her father's tall frame made a dark silhouette. She knew the hands with which he moved the hoe were rough and callused, but they were also gentle when they held her face to tell her something important. Her father's skin was a rich chestnut, her mother's as light as just about any white woman's, and the Weems children were a rainbow assortment of gold and auburn tones.

Catharine's form was a heap on the ground where she sat to weed the rows of beans, scooching herself along without standing up as a way to save her strength. Her tight braids stuck out from her head like dark ribbons. Moonlit nights were Catharine's best times to work in the garden.

"Mamma says it's time to eat," Ann said finally.

"Well, then it must be time to eat," her father replied. He stood the hoe in the garden basket, helped Catharine up with one hand, and reached for Ann with the other. She took his arm and hung on it between steps.

"You think I'm not tired enough, I need to cart you back to the house swinging on my arm like a squirrel?"

Ann giggled, and stopped tiring her father out. She took a quick look at Catharine to see how she was doing. It was a habit she had developed after Mistress Carol first decided Catharine was old enough to work in the fields and put a hoe in her hands. Each time Catharine worked, her rattly chest got more and more rattly as she swung the hoe, until she couldn't breathe at all and she fell to the ground, her lips a scary blue. Ann wasn't sure what got Catharine breathing again — her own screams for Mamma, Mamma's shouts to Heaven, or Catharine's stubborn will — but every time, Catharine gasped and coughed like her chest was a railroad car full of rocks, and started breathing.

Ann thought one time should have been enough to make Mistress Carol decide to put Catharine to work in the house and inn instead. But it took three times, and probably would have taken a fourth if Mamma hadn't volunteered Addison for work in the fields even though he was just a bitty thing at the time.

They stopped outside to wash, then opened the door and were met with heat, filled with the wonderful smell of fried cornmeal mush and greens.

"Leave that door open, John," her

mother told her father. "I'll take the mosquitoes along with the cool air tonight."

They slid onto the benches, heads bowed, and waited.

"Lord God, we thank Thee." John Weems's strong voice rose and fell with the cadence of his prayer. "We thank Thee for the mighty blessing of this food. We thank Thee for the mighty blessing of this home. We thank Thee for the mighty blessing of this family. Amen."

"Amen" echoed all around.

There was, as usual, little talking during the meal. Everyone was too hungry to waste time jabbering between mouthfuls. And there was, as usual, not enough to fill Ann's stomach to where she didn't feel hungry anymore. She reminded herself that Sunday was just a few days away, ran her fingers through the grease in the bottom of the greens bowl and sucked at the last of the flavor.

"Ann Maria Weems, did I raise you to have the manners of a barn cat?" her mother scolded.

"No, ma'am." Ann tucked her greasy hand under the table.

Catharine elbowed her. "You wash, I'll dry tonight."

They rose to clear the table. Joseph, Addison, and Augustus climbed the ladder to the sleeping loft, and her father and mother sat in the two rough-hewn chairs to work: her father on his chair-building and her mother on mending for the Prices.

As she leaned over the wooden washtub, the smell of lye soap filling her nose, Ann's mind went back to a subject it had been working on for several days, ever since Richard announced his upcoming birthday celebration.

"Mamma?"

"Hmmm?" Her mother's lips held a new piece of thread. One solitary candle gave a flickering light for her work and lit up her almond eyes and smooth cheeks.

"How old do you figure I am?" Ann asked.

"I figure you're not a little girl, because you have no braids."

Ann smiled sheepishly. She'd never had the patience to sit still and have her hair braided properly, and her mother and sister finally gave up trying.

"And you're not a woman," her mother continued, "because you asked me this fool question. So you're somewhere in between."

Ann's smile fell. It was not a fool question. White children always knew how old they were. She'd seen adults at the inn ask them, and even the youngest ones would hold up five fingers or three fingers. Richard Price knew what *day* he was born, and it had a name and a number to it.

"I reckon you're about the same age as young Master Richard," her father said. He whacked a chair rail into its hole with a wooden mallet.

Ann swung around. "Really? How do you figure?"

"I heard his folks saying how he was born the year it didn't rain. That's the same year you came into this world."

"Lord, I remember that!" Her mother's voice was suddenly alive. She laid the shirt she was mending in her lap, and wiped beads of perspiration from her cheeks. "Addison wasn't even walking yet, and Ann Maria up and decided to arrive. It was corn-planting time, and I was out in the fields with Addison strapped to my back and Ann Maria sleeping in a basket at my feet, and the dust rising like a cloud of hornets with no rain to keep it down."

Ann kept the movement of her dishwashing a constant plunge, scrub, plunge, hoping that the rhythm would keep the story going.

"And Catharine running between the

rows and coughing in that dust like she'd choke to death on it, and — thank you, Jesus — Augustus just old enough to hold her hand and take her back to the house when her coughing fits got real bad." She shook her head. "We planted, and waited, and it wouldn't rain and it wouldn't rain." Her mother's words slowed, recalling the sameness of day after day with no hope. "And when the crops came in next to nothing, old Master still had his goose for Christmas, and we had the hungriest winter ever. If it wasn't for my milk feeding the two littlest ones, we'd have starved." Her mother fixed her eyes back on the torn shirt and attacked it with needle and thread.

"I was born at corn-planting time?" Ann asked. She loved her mother's stories, but not when they grew sad. When they turned sad, she wanted to put the stories in a sack and heave them into the Patuxent River, so Mamma wouldn't have to remember that part anymore.

"Yes, baby."

The room went quiet except for the splashing of the wash and rinse water, and the faint squeak of Catharine's drying rag on the clean plates.

Two

The first birds hadn't yet begun to sing when Ann awoke the next morning. She sat on the wooden floor of the sleeping loft that served as their bed. Her brothers lay sprawled about, their blankets tangled in wide-flung legs and arms. Catharine lay straight as a tree, her breath rattling softly, her strong jaw and delicate lips relaxed in sleep. There was too much excitement in Ann's blood for her to lie back down: today she would find out her age.

Starting chores early, she reasoned, would give her a chance to slip away to talk to Richard. His birthday celebration had been just up the hill, at the stone house where his older brother, Master Charles — Ann's owner — lived. Richard lived with his parents, Master William and Mistress Mary Elizabeth, in the frame house near the public road. The tavern was on the first floor of the house, and the inn was simply the upstairs bedrooms, which had been vacated by Richard's nine older brothers and sisters when they married and left home. The elder Prices owned all the land and the houses. They also owned Tom and Lizzy and their eight children.

His parents were too tired to give him a birthday celebration, Richard said. He'd heard it all before. They were tired because Mistress Mary Elizabeth had been raising her children for over thirty-five years, and Master William had been running the inn and tavern, albeit with the help of his family, and farming for even longer. Richard said they were also tired of all the folks who hated them just because they were Irish.

Ann climbed down the ladder and tip-toed past her sleeping parents. She carried two buckets to fill at the spring, one for washing and the other for her mother to use to cook cornmeal mush for breakfast. As she trudged back up the hill, the heavy water sloshing, the first bird called out its song, was joined by another, and soon the air was filled with their singing to the brightening sky.

Next, she ran to Master Charles and Mistress Carol's house. She started the fire in the summer kitchen so it would be good and hot by the time Ellie was ready to cook. She scattered corn on the ground for the flock of squawking chickens, filled water buckets for Bob and Sally, the roan gelding and bay mare, sneaked past the hounds without waking them up, and went back to hoeing the peas in the Prices' garden where she'd left off yesterday. Once the Prices awoke, she would empty their chamber pots and fetch their wash water. If she got enough done before breakfast, she could slip away to talk to Richard without being missed. Later, there would be bed linens from the inn to wash, rooms to sweep, lunch to bring to her father and brothers in the tobacco field, and more tending to the animals and the garden.

She liked the movement. Sometimes she wished she had patience, like Catharine and her mother, to sit and shell peas, or snip the ends off green beans, or stitch the fine lace that Mistress Carol liked so much. But for Ann, it was the movement that kept something else quiet — something dark and threatening. The swinging of the hoe, the hoisting of water buckets, the plunge, scrub, plunge of the heavy bed linens against the washboard — it was a comforting rhythm, drowning out a deeper, more ominous one. Even on

Sunday afternoons, Ann had no patience to sit with Catharine and Lizzy's daughter Rachel making cornhusk dolls or taking out last week's braids and putting in new ones for Rachel's little sisters. She had to keep running, down to the pond with Addison, Joseph, and Richard to catch tadpoles in their cupped hands, to chase after squirrels with homemade bows and arrows that never once hit their mark, to dig in the soft earth and pull out squirmy worms. The worms she brought to Augustus, who, with Lizzy's son Henry, had the patience to sit and fish and the good sense, her mother pointed out, to do something on Sunday afternoon that would add to Sunday night's supper.

Catharine found her in the garden. "Ann, you got up so early. Mamma didn't know where you were." Ann's sister shielded her eyes from the sun, which had popped up over the far line of trees.

"Just couldn't sleep anymore, that's all," said Ann. "Do you and Ellie need help?"

"No, but why don't you come along anyway and get yourself out of this sun?" It already felt like one of those days that would make every living thing droop by the end of it.

In the summer kitchen Ellie was slicing

thick slabs of bacon for breakfast at the tavern. She always sliced too much and almost always got yelled at and slapped for it, but it was the only way she and her small son, Benjamin, would get a decent breakfast from the leftovers. Ellie was a hunched-shouldered woman with a way about her that reminded Ann of a dog that tucks in its tail and runs every time you try to get near it. She and Benjamin slept in the loft over the summer kitchen.

Benjamin ran to Catharine, and she swung him up into her arms. She tickled his round belly and he giggled with glee. He had, as everyone could see but no one dared to mention, his father's soft brown curls and clear blue eyes in a face with African features and honey-colored skin. His existence made the childless Mistress Carol so angry she would just as soon kick him as look at him, but from his mother and the other colored folks he got nothing but spoiling.

Catharine sat Benjamin on the table next to where the potatoes lay, ready to be chopped for frying. He swung his short legs and sucked on three fingers.

Suddenly the door opened and Mistress Carol burst in, tall and sturdy in a pale blue dress that matched the veins showing through her neck. "Where is breakfast?" she demanded. "There are two cattlemen at the inn, should have had their herds on the road by now. They've started drinking rum, and they're liable to be here all day at this rate!" Then she turned and saw Benjamin. "Get that filthy child off my table!" she snapped. In two steps she was behind him, and with one swipe of her arm she smacked him hard across the back of the head. Catharine caught the child as he fell off the table, and whisked him out the door as the first wail left his lungs.

"I want breakfast served immediately," Mistress Carol commanded. "I don't care if it's raw!"

"Yes, ma'am," Ellie said, her eyes cast down.

"And you" — she pointed a slender finger at Ann — "were you going to leave the chamber pots all day so the stench would make us ill? In this heat you've got to get up *early* instead of lazing around all morning like I know your kind is fond of. Now *get*." She gave Ann a shove toward the door.

The sound of Benjamin's crying followed Ann all the way into the stone house.

Ann decided she'd have to skip her own

breakfast if she was going to make it to Richard's without being noticed. Not that Mistress Carol was ever in a good mood, but today she was in an especially bad one, and Ann would rather listen to her own stomach growl until noon than be beat about the head by that woman today.

Once the chamber pots had been emptied and cleaned, Ann ran past the tobacco fields and the cornfield to the two-story frame house where Richard lived. The front yard was a circle of dirt and dust because of the frequent traffic of wagons, carriages, horses, and cattle that belonged to folks stopping at the tavern and inn. There, in the dust, under the shade of the big maple, sat Richard with another white boy. Their heads were bent over a circle of marbles.

"Richard," she called as she ran, "I've got to talk to you." She stopped in front of them, panting.

"Who's that?" the other boy asked with a grimace.

Richard looked right at Ann, but with a strange dullness in his eyes. "Just some nigger belongs to my brother."

His coldness hit her like a slap.

"What do you want?" he asked her gruffly.

She stood there, her mouth open slightly, unable to speak. All of a sudden she saw the whole thing as if she were a bird sitting on a branch in the wide, shady maple: two white boys in their homespun shirts and neatly patched britches, sitting in the shade, and her standing there with sweat running down the sides of her face, her dress of the roughest brown burlap hanging on her skinny shoulders like a sack, mud from the garden caked between her toes, and straw from the barn in her hair. This was not the Richard who sneaked off on Sunday afternoons to join her and her brothers to dig and swim and skip rocks across the wide part of the Hawlings River. This was Richard playing with a white friend.

"What do you want, girl?" he demanded again.

"I — I want to know how old you are," she said softly.

Richard hooted, and both boys nearly fell over laughing. "You ran all the way over here to ask me that?" They laughed some more. "Go on back to work," he said, and leaned over the marbles.

Dull stare or not, Ann knew he was the same old Richard inside. She crossed her arms and narrowed her eyes. "I want to know how old you are, because my brother Joseph says he's bigger than you."

Richard hopped to his feet. "That scrawny boy thinks he's bigger than me? You tell him I turned eleven last night."

Ann turned without another word and ran back the way she'd come. She grinned and laughed out loud. Next to the cornfield she stopped and flung her arms open to the blue, steamy sky. "Did you hear that, Lord? I'm eleven years old!"

That evening after supper there was a quiet knock. Then the door opened a crack, and a fat walking stick protruded into the room. Ann looked up from her dishwashing and smiled.

"Uncle Abram!" Joseph cried. He ran to the door, threw it open wide, then jumped up, and hung on his uncle's neck.

"Get down, boy, can't you see I'm a cripple?" Uncle Abram said, laughing.

Behind him came his wife, Aunt Mimi, moving slowly because of her plumpness. Her head was wrapped in faded yellow gingham and she was wagging one finger in disapproval. "He's as crippled as a healthy racehorse, if you ask me," she said.

"Old Master said I was limping so bad, I'd better come see my sister Arabella to get some good doctoring." Uncle Abram laid a hand on one of Ann's mother's cheeks and kissed the other one.

"Is that leg not healed *yet?*" Arabella put aside her mending.

Uncle Abram sat in the chair Ann's father offered him. His thick black hair was bushy all around his head, so that his hat seemed to float atop it. "You're the doctor," he said. "Why don't you tell me?"

Aunt Mimi sat heavily on the dinner bench, and Ann sidled up beside her. "There's nothing wrong with that leg," Aunt Mimi said, wrapping her arm around Ann's shoulders. "He just doesn't want to work, that's all — not for the master and not for me. I have to bring in my own wood, fetch my own water. . . ."

By now Arabella had pulled up Uncle Abram's trouser leg and begun to unwrap the rags that bandaged his calf. The room filled with the faint, warm smell of new skin and old wounds.

Ann, Catharine, and Joseph all bent to take a closer look. The leg was scarred, scabbed, and slightly misshapen, as if the muscles and skin hadn't quite found their rightful places.

Uncle Abram tapped Joseph on the shoulder. "It'll cost you a penny to take a look that close, young man."

Joseph took a step back and grinned. "Tell the story again, Uncle. Tell us how those hounds tore you so bad you could see the white of your leg bone shining under the moon."

"Hush, Joseph." Arabella examined the rags she'd pulled off the leg. "The bandage is clean and I don't see any festering." She pressed gently around the edges of the scabs. "That hurt?" she asked.

"No, ma'am," said Uncle Abram.

Joseph danced from one foot to the other. "Tell us again how the blood spurted when you stabbed the two lead hounds and killed 'em."

Arabella swatted at him. "Joseph, hush now! You've heard that story enough."

They had heard the story several times in the weeks since Uncle Abram had returned: How he'd fashioned himself a knife with the tools and materials he worked with as a blacksmith. How he'd planned to make it all the way to the North, find work, and earn enough money to buy Aunt Mimi's freedom *and* a farm, and build a house. They all knew Uncle Abram's dreams were much too grand for a slave, especially when, after just two days of traveling, he'd been attacked by the slave hunter's hounds. When he'd returned, Master had cussed the hunters he'd hired, because they'd promised to bring Abram back without tearing him, and yet Ann's uncle had returned so bloody and weak that for a while they weren't sure he'd live.

Arabella turned to her brother with a look to silence him. "I don't want these children hearing more tales about running off. You're just a lucky man. No telling what Master would have done to you if the hunters had brought you home instead of you bringing yourself home."

That was the rule on most every farm: Run away, think better of it, and come back on your own, and the punishment would not be severe. But run away and get caught while your nose still pointed north, and the cruelest treatment awaited you at home — a foot chopped off, leg bones broken so they couldn't mend right, or sometimes outright murder, just to discourage anyone else who might be thinking about running off.

Uncle Abram just chuckled. "But I outsmarted them all — killed the hounds, walked on back home myself, and cheated those hunters out of their reward. Never even got locked up, Master was so glad I'd come back on my own."

Arabella clucked her tongue. "You had no business running off like that. Your family is here nearby, and you were leaving us all!"

Uncle Abram's face grew serious for the first time since he'd come in. "I can't abide this life of working for another man's profit, Arabella. Maybe you can, but I can't."

Augustus cleared his throat. He looked steadily at his uncle for a moment, then said, "If you decide to go again, Uncle, take me with you."

The room erupted with emotion.

"That's the very kind of talk I don't want you bringing to this house!" Ann's mother cried.

"If he takes anyone next time, it better be his *wife!*" Aunt Mimi exclaimed. Her cheeks were flushed and she was fanning herself.

"But I don't want Augustus to leave," Joseph complained.

"This family is staying together, *right here*," Ann's father said firmly.

An uneasy quiet settled over the room. Addison touched his mother's arm.

"Mamma?" he asked quietly.

"Yes, baby."

"If we're not going to run, then why are we feeding the dogs?"

Heaviness hung in the air of the tiny cabin. Ann's mother, who always knew what to say, always knew what to do, sat with her eyes cast down, blinking rapidly. Finally, she spoke. "Just in case, baby. That's all. Just in case."

Aunt Mimi managed to change the mood by telling a story about a runaway slave she'd heard about. He was being chased by hunters and hounds, and heard the hunters shouting to the dogs, "Get him, boys! Go get him!" So, when the dogs caught up with him, the slave yelled, "Go get him! Catch him!" The dogs looked at him, wagged their tails, and then ran on ahead, eager to find out who everyone was chasing.

Ann and her family laughed at the story. Then, as both children and adults had begun to yawn, Uncle Abram said they had a long walk home and had better start on it.

Ann's father announced, "Well, before bed *I'm* going out to fetch wood for *my* wife."

Ann jumped up to help.

On their way to the woodpile, she heard Uncle Abram and Aunt Mimi talking as they headed toward home.

"If I start hauling wood and water for

you, Master will think I'm strong enough to run again. Better he thinks I'm like an old lame goat — he hardly even watches me now."

"I'll show you wood and water. . . ." Aunt Mimi's tone was of gentle teasing, and their voices drifted away in the night air.

Ann's father hoisted a small log off the woodpile and handed it to her.

"Papa, is that bad, what Uncle Abram tried to do — steal his freedom like that?" Ann asked.

Her father stopped and stared at her. "He wasn't stealing anything that wasn't rightfully his," he said very softly. "Anyone born a slave gets their freedom stolen the day they're born."

"But what's the difference?" Ann asked.

"Between what?" Her father bent to lift a larger log.

"Between you and the rest of us? You're free, but you still have to work from first light to last light for the Prices so you can have clothes and a house and food."

Her father looked up at the glittering stars, and Ann thought he seemed small under the wide sky. "Baby girl, someday I'll show you what it feels like to be free. We won't have to run, because I'm going

34

to buy your freedom just like my mamma bought her own freedom before I was born. Soon as I've got the money saved up, I'll show this whole family what it feels like to be free." He straightened his back. "There's no other feeling in the world like it. I work just like you, but the master *pays* me with the food and clothes. And on Sunday, folks pay me with money. How do you think we got the seeds for our garden?" He handed Ann one more piece of wood and balanced several large logs on his shoulder.

"Most folks get just cornmeal and fatback all year. And no garden," said Ann.

Her father nodded. "And the master can't whip me like I was his horse, either. I work for him, but he doesn't own me. And he can't sell me off from my family. I'm staying right here." He smiled down at her as they walked toward the cabin.

"But he can still sell us away from you, right, Papa?"

"Aw, Master Charles wouldn't do that, baby girl. Ellie still has her Benjamin, and Tom and Lizzy have all eight of their young ones. The Prices aren't the kind of people to go breaking up a family."

"But he can still whip us, right, Papa? Like he did Augustus when he let the oxen loose by accident?" She shuddered, remembering the blood dripping down Augustus's back, running down his legs to his heels before Master Charles finally stopped swinging the whip.

Her father set his jaw and was silent. And in that silence Ann heard it: the rhythm she'd been drowning out all day. It said, "Look out, look out, look out . . ."

Three

Sunday. Today there would be enough to eat.

Ann itched from her Saturday night bath with the strong soap her mother had just made from rendered lard and ashes from the hearth. She squirmed a bit as she helped tie bits of white lace into Catharine's braids.

"You look lovely, Catharine," Arabella said. "And to think Mistress Carol threw that lace in with the kindling."

First there would be church, then food. Ann thought she would likely enjoy church more if her mind wasn't so distracted by the thoughts of food, but church came first and there was no arguing.

Church wasn't a building. The law said black folks weren't allowed to have a church meeting without a white person to oversee everything. So church was a clearing in the woods near the slave ceme-

37

tery, where tall trees protected them from sun and gentle rain. It was aunts and uncles and friends come from the neighboring farms. If anyone were to discover them, it just looked like a picnic.

Church wasn't the preaching of some white minister telling them how the Bible says slaves should obey their masters. That's what Ann heard when Master Charles hired a visiting Methodist minister to hold services for the local slaves. No, their church was singing and chanting and sometimes shouting, letting their prayers move from their hearts to their throats and rise up to God until the clearing was filled like a cathedral with rich deep notes and clear high notes and all of them intertwining until the blend felt like pure joy, pure light, and Ann felt immersed in love. And when the singing and intertwining voices died down, because the Spirit had moved and it was time to bask in the afterglow, the little clearing felt like a grander place than any cathedral. Someone might still be humming softly, and others whispering, "Thank you, Lord," and calls came here and there from the few birds that had dared to stay and join in that ocean of song.

And with the magic still clinging to the

branches, church *did* turn into a picnic, as the men built fires and fried fish in big iron skillets, the women sliced tomatoes and cucumbers and cabbages, and the children ran to fetch watermelons that had been placed in the creekbed to turn ice-cold. It was the one day of the week they didn't eat corn mush and fatback for three meals.

Ann loved the singing, and she loved the eating, and she loved seeing all the neighbors, cousins, aunts, and uncles.

"Ann Maria, you grew since last week." Aunt Mimi gathered her into a bosom that smelled like lye soap and fresh fried tomatoes.

Ann gave her aunt a quick squeeze. "I'm going to pick huckleberries with Addison and Joseph," she said, and turned to run off with her brothers.

"Ann Maria." Aunt Mimi's voice was insistent. "Come sit with me a moment."

Ann settled on a large stump next to her aunt. "Where's Uncle Abram?" she asked.

"He's talking to your mother and father."

Across the clearing, Ann saw her favorite uncle deep in discussion with her parents. Her mother had her apron twisted in her hands and was wringing the life out of it.

"What's the matter, Aunt Mimi? Is his leg bad again?" Ann asked.

"Nothing's wrong, baby. It's just right." She smoothed Ann's hair back away from her face. "Let me get a good look at you." She cupped Ann's chin in her hand. "You're getting so pretty, child. Someday I'm going to make you a calico dress. What color do you want?"

Ann's eyes grew wide. She'd only ever worn dresses made of slave cloth, which was just as dirty brown and rough as the sacks Master Charles's hybrid seed corn came in. She looked from her aunt's face to the sky above her. "Blue," she said.

"Someday I'll make you that blue dress," said Aunt Mimi. "Someday."

The way she said "someday" sounded sad, and Ann knew that the dress was only a dream, the way Uncle Abram's farm and house and freedom were only dreams.

"Ann, we're leaving — you coming or not?" Joseph called to her from where he and Addison were on their way into the woods.

"Now you say hello to your uncle Abram before you run pick those berries, you hear?" Aunt Mimi ordered.

Ann said, "I will," but when Addison called, " 'Bye, Ann. We won't save any berries for you!" she resolved to see her uncle later and ran to catch up with her brothers.

The huckleberry bushes formed a thick covering on the forest floor. They were filled with green berries, and an occasional ripe purple one. Ann had eaten so much of the other good things, she was glad to eat just a few berries rather than the handfuls they would find later in the summer.

"Pssst."

"What do you want, Addison?" Ann asked without looking up from her berry search.

"Wasn't me," said Addison.

"Wasn't me, either," said Joseph, his mouth already purple.

"Pssst!"

The three of them stood and listened.

"It came from over there." Addison pointed toward a place where thick vines formed a curtain and dappled sunlight shifted.

Suddenly the curtain erupted with a shriek and a dark form lunged out at them. Ann jumped, Addison shouted, and they both ran. They tripped over each other and fell in a heap in the huckleberry bushes.

The next thing they heard was Joseph's voice. "Richard, you are one sorry excuse for an Indian."

Richard was laughing so hard his feathered headdress had fallen down over one ear. "You're nothing but a bunch of scaredy-cats!"

"You didn't scare me one bit," said Joseph. He stood with his arms crossed, right where he'd been standing when they'd stopped to listen.

"Did too. I saw your face — all big eyes and mouth hanging open."

"That's because I couldn't believe how ugly you look in those feathers," Joseph shot back.

Ann and Addison brushed themselves off. "Come on, Richard," said Addison. "Hush up and pick some berries with us."

Any other Sunday, teasing like this would blow over and they would soon find themselves wading in the Hawlings, trying to catch minnows in their cupped hands. But today Richard was in a fighting mood.

"I'm not picking berries until Joseph admits he was scared." Richard carefully folded his headdress and stuffed it into his back pocket.

"You might as well go on home, then," said Joseph, and he crouched down to continue his berry picking.

Ann expected Richard to pull out a bag of marbles or a slingshot or any of the other toys he had and they hadn't. But he didn't pull out a toy. He stepped up to Joseph and kicked him hard in the ribs.

"You think you're so tough?" Richard taunted. "I hear you think you're bigger than me. Prove it."

Ann cringed.

Joseph drew himself up to his full height, a couple of inches shorter than Richard. "I am tougher than you and braver than you every day of the year," Joseph declared.

Richard shoved him in the chest. "You are not. You're a yellow belly."

"Joseph, leave him —" Ann began, but it was too late.

It started as shoving, back and forth; then Richard swung his fist squarely into Joseph's jaw. Joseph staggered, felt his lip, and spat out blood. Then, like a racehorse out of the starting gate, he lit into Richard with his fists, pummeling his face, his stomach, his ribs. Richard punched back, but Joseph was too quick, and Richard was soon doubled over, protecting himself.

Ann watched in horror. She wasn't sure what made her hesitate — possibly the strange pleasure of watching Richard get what she thought he deserved — but she knew it must be stopped. She rushed at Joseph, grasped him by the shoulders, and yanked him backward. They fell to the ground together.

Addison came up behind Richard. "Come on, Richard. It's hot. Let's all go swimming and cool down." Addison's voice was as calm as he could make it.

Richard was crying, and blood trickled out of his nose. "I'll show you who's bigger," he sobbed. He turned and ran through the woods.

"What a coward," said Joseph, brushing the leaves off his clothes.

Ann's stomach was in a tight knot, and she saw the look of fear on Addison's face. Was Joseph just incredibly brave? Or was he too young to understand, too young to remember what they'd done to Augustus for letting the oxen loose by *accident?*

"We better get back to the others," said Addison quickly.

They walked through the forest, silent except for Joseph's occasional comments about the fight. "He kicked me when I wasn't even looking! What a yellow belly!" and "He's got no more strength than Rachel's baby sisters. I'll call him Tiny Richie from now on."

By the time they got to the clearing, Ann's stomach felt as if an entire flock of geese had been let loose in it. Her father had already left to work for Mrs. Griffith, who paid him for his time, and many of the children and other adults had already gone fishing or gone home. Her mother was gathering plates with Catharine and wiping them with sand and leaves.

"Mamma! Catharine!" Ann ran to them, ready to blurt out the whole story, but her mother spoke first.

"Ann Maria, you help us with these things. We're going on home. I've got sewing to tend to." She didn't even look up from her plate cleaning to see Joseph's bruised jaw.

It wasn't like Arabella to give up the one day she could chat and laugh with family and friends to go back home and work. But Ann didn't question. She helped gather the skillet, plates, and spoons they'd brought and balanced the heavy carrying basket on her hip as they began the walk home. The boys ran ahead and Ann hung back with Catharine.

"Why doesn't Mamma want to stay?" she asked her sister in a low voice.

Catharine shook her head. "I don't know. Everybody has long faces, and nobody is telling us children a word about it."

Ann frowned, wondering. There had been a few folks missing today — a couple of the oldest neighbors hadn't come, and

Lizzy had stayed home with Alice, the baby. "Maybe someone is sick and they don't want to worry us," she suggested.

Catharine nodded. "Maybe."

Suddenly Ann stopped short. "I've got to go back. I didn't get to see Uncle Abram."

"Aunt Mimi and Uncle Abram left a long time ago," said Catharine.

Ann pouted.

"You'll see them next Sunday," Catharine said in answer to her pout. "Come on."

By the time they reached their cabin, Master Charles was already in the front yard, and their mother was trying to calm him down.

"He's just a child, Master Charles. You let me take care of him. I'll whip him good and teach him some manners." Her voice held a false calmness covering a layer of fear.

It was obvious that Master Charles had observed the Sabbath as he usually did, by drinking enough rum to make his actions as unpredictable as a storm.

"I'll be the one to teach him. Bring him out here." Charles Price stood in the low sunlight, wavering slightly, a horsewhip in his hands. His startlingly blue eyes were bloodshot and ill-focused, and his curling brown hair was matted with perspiration.

"Now, Master Charles, let me get you a cool drink of water and you have a seat in the shade here. I'll take care of my son Joseph, and he'll never dream of laying a hand on Master Richard ever again. You'll see." Arabella tried again to soothe him, but Master Charles threw down the whip, shoved her aside, and opened the door to the cabin himself. He emerged dragging Addison and Joseph by the necks of their shirts. The boys stumbled as they were yanked along. Addison was crying. Catharine slipped by them into the cabin.

"Which one is it?" Master Charles demanded.

For the first time Ann saw Richard, huddled next to a tree, pale as buttermilk. He did not answer his brother.

"I said, Which one is it? Answer me or I'll whip them both!" he bellowed.

Richard pointed feebly at Joseph.

Master Charles threw Addison to the ground and yanked Joseph's shirt off, tearing it. Then he pulled him over to the tree. "Tie him up," he ordered Richard.

"He can just apologize," Richard said in a tiny, quavering voice. "I didn't —"

"I said, Tie him up!" Master Charles

shouted. He grew red in the face. "No nigger of mine is going to raise his hand to a white child and get away with it."

Richard clutched the tree as if it were the only thing holding him up, and did not move. Master Charles tied Joseph to the tree himself.

Ann dropped to her knees. The rhythm pounded in her head: *Helpless, helpless, helpless . . .*

Crack.

The leather whip sliced Joseph's tender back. Joseph's body jolted, but he didn't cry out.

Crack.

A second welt opened. Blood trickled down.

Crack.

Joseph's legs shook. Blood seeped onto his trousers. Still, he was silent.

Crack.

"Stop!" Ann heard the shout. She realized it was her own voice when everyone turned to stare at her. Suddenly horrified that she'd dared to challenge her master, she felt faint. But Master Charles had stopped swinging the whip, so she kept talking. "It's *my* fault," she said loudly. "Whip me, not Joseph. I lied to Richard. I . . ."

But the exertion in the heat must have been too much for the drunken Charles Price. He gazed at her dumbfounded for a moment, then staggered a few steps, fell down on all fours, and vomited.

Boldly, Ann untied the rope that held Joseph to the tree. She looped his arm over her shoulders and helped him across the yard. Catharine rushed out of the cabin carrying a pot of heated water, cloudy with salt.

"Lay him down so I can pour this over the wounds," said Catharine.

Ann helped him down. Catharine poured. Then, and only then, did Joseph scream.

Four

"No good ever came out of a lie, baby girl."

Ann had cried so many tears into her father's rough shirt, she didn't think she had any left.

"Now, you didn't make Master Richard start that fight with Joseph, and you didn't make Joseph fight him back, and you didn't make Master Charles pick up that whip. So I want you to stop this crying, you hear?" He held her face and she nodded.

She went to say good night to Joseph. Tonight he would share the pile of rags their parents slept on in front of the hearth downstairs, instead of climbing the ladder to sleep on the wooden floor of the loft.

"I guess I proved to that old Richard I'm tougher than he is," said Joseph, lying on his belly with his chin propped on his fists.

Ann touched his cheek. When had her baby brother become so rock hard? "You are *dang* tough, Joseph S. Weems," she said. "But I wish you'd leave Richard alone from now on."

Joseph made a face. "I can manage myself with Richard and Charles and William and the whole lot of them."

His words sent a chill through her. To speak of Master Charles or Master William by only their first names was an offense worth at least twenty lashes from the horsewhip. "Shush, Joseph. You don't need more trouble. I am painfully sorry for this trouble I caused you, but please don't bring more on yourself."

"Don't worry about me," he said. He tried to turn on his side, but winced, groaned, and flopped back over on his belly.

"You'll feel better in the morning," she promised him.

Mistress Carol insisted that the flower beds around the tavern be kept weeded, watered, trimmed and generally better taken care of than even the oxen. She couldn't control the mud in the front yard, but she could protect the flowers next to the house, which she believed would attract customers to the inn and tavern. Ann thought the free-flowing rum and ale, along with a hot dinner for fifty cents for a gentleman and thirty-three and a third cents for a gentleman's servant was plenty to attract people to the tavern. And she thought that a long day on the red, dusty road from Annapolis or Baltimore was enough to cause anyone passing in the evening to want a place to stable their horses and livestock and stay the night. Nevertheless, the flowers, Mistress Carol demanded, must be perfect.

Sitting in the shade of the tall magnolia, Ann pulled out weeds and snipped off dead marigold blossoms. The windows to the house were closed to the midday heat, and the voices inside droned in a murmur.

Suddenly the window above her head was flung open, and she had to press herself against the wall of the house to avoid a dribble of slimy brown liquid dumped from a spittoon. The voices were instantly clear.

"I have no peace in my home. I must do *something*." That was Master Charles.

"You can't sell off one without the other." That was Master William's voice. "If you do, they'll run — especially now, with those two from up the road gone off."

"Then I'll sell Ellie. That would help pay the debt, and the boy is too young to run."

"Son, I know it would pain you to sell the boy, but the only way to make peace with your wife is to send them both away."

There was a loud snap and the window closed on their conversation.

Ann sat motionless in the flower bed. Should she go tell Ellie? Tell her to run with Benjamin before she got sold away from him? The thought made her queasy. She didn't want to think about anyone running, especially running and getting caught. And Ellie was neither brave enough nor strong enough to run. Better to trust that Master Charles would listen to his father and sell Ellie and Benjamin together. She would miss them, but that would be best.

At home that evening, Ann told her mother what she had heard.

"And he thinks that wife of his will be less of a witch as soon as he sends them away?" her mother scoffed. "Women don't forget so easily. That man has a lifetime of anger from her to live with." She stirred the cornmeal so violently, sprinkles of it flew out of the bowl. "Ellie is a good woman, and I'd hate to see her go, but if she gets away from Master Charles, she'll rest easier at night, for sure."

Ann pulled two ants out of the pile of

turnip greens she'd just picked.

"What else did you hear, Ann Maria?" her mother asked.

"Nothing much else. Just that Master Charles has some debt he has to pay — that's why he wants to sell Ellie and Benjamin."

Her mother stopped stirring and looked worried. "What kind of debt? Did they say if it was big?"

Ann shook her head. "He said that the sale would help pay for it, that's all. Oh — and that two slaves have run off. Do you think it's anyone we know?"

Her mother sank onto the dinner bench and held her head in her hands. "Lord, you've got to protect them," she whispered.

Ann stepped behind her mother and wrapped her arms around her neck. "We know them, Mamma?" she asked softly.

"It's your aunt Mimi and uncle Abram."

Ann's throat tightened. She buried her face against her mother's neck. "Mamma?" she said in a small voice.

"Yes, baby."

"I never got to say good-bye."

Five

Every night before supper they prayed for Uncle Abram and Aunt Mimi's safety. And every day that there was no news of their capture felt like a victory. Uncle Abram had promised Ann's parents that somehow he'd send word when they were safely in the North. So they waited, happy to hear no bad news and anxious to hear good news.

Joseph's wounds healed and left raised scars. Joseph didn't lose any of his spirit. He just gained a hotter temper.

Somehow, too, something healed between them and Richard. It wasn't that Richard apologized — he would never have done that. He did, however, start giving them things. First he gave Joseph the Indian headdress. It was just a bunch of crow feathers sewn onto a leather strap from an old horse harness, but he said it would look better on Joseph than on him. Then he gave Ann his two favorite marbles. Ann didn't see how he could tell the difference between one marble and another, since they were all made of the same creamy white clay, but nevertheless Richard claimed those two were his favorites. Ann saw the gifts as the closest thing to an apology Richard could muster, and began to let herself forgive him.

The first tinges of crimson crept into the maple leaves, and the evenings grew cool. Ann's father and brothers worked long hours harvesting the tobacco and hanging the huge leaves to dry in heavy bunches in the tobacco barns.

The pumpkins in the garden turned from green to orange, and when Mrs. Griffith paid her father in molasses instead of coins one Sunday, Ann's mother happily picked one of the pumpkins, chopped it up, boiled it, and turned it into the most delicious pumpkin pudding Ann had ever tasted. That is, until the Sunday Richard brought a gift of pumpkin pudding for Ann, Addison, and Joseph to share with him while sitting on sun-warmed rocks next to the Patuxent River. He'd stuffed it into the leather bag that normally held his marble collection, and since he'd not stolen any spoons along with the pudding, the only way to eat it was to tip their heads back and squeeze bits of it into their mouths.

Ann's first taste was so delicious she closed her eyes to keep the flavor swimming on her tongue for as long as possible.

"Is it good?" asked Richard hopefully.

"Mmm-hmmm," Ann answered, while waiting eagerly for the pudding to be passed to her again.

Addison licked his fingers. "What's in it that tastes so good?" he asked.

Richard shrugged. "Just pudding, I guess." He dangled one foot over the side of the rock he was sitting on and swung it.

Joseph shook his head. "No. There's something in it I've never tasted before."

Addison and Ann agreed.

Richard sniffed the nearly empty sack. "It just smells like nutmeg and cloves and cinnamon — like any other pumpkin pudding."

The three Weems children exchanged glances. Certainly Ann had heard Mistress Carol talk about how she needed more nutmeg from the market, or tell Ellie not to use too much cloves and cinnamon in the hot cider, but she'd never actually *tasted* any of those things.

Joseph stuck out his chin and gave Richard a challenging stare. "I don't believe you."

Richard's eyes widened. "What do you mean? What else would there be in pumpkin pudding?"

Joseph's stare refused to waver. "I think he's trying to poison us." He turned to Addison. "Don't you think that's what he's doing?"

"What?" Richard's cheeks turned pink and he sat up straighter.

"I believe you're right, Joseph," said Addison. "I think he's decided to kill us once and for all."

Ann gave her brothers a puzzled look, but Addison nudged her and she began to catch on.

Richard was shaking his head vigorously. "I ate it right along with you! There's no poison in there."

"Oh, you *looked* like you were eating it, but there wasn't any more gone when you passed the sack to me than when Addison handed it to you," said Joseph.

"I wouldn't poison you!" Richard shouted, his voice cracking.

"He'll have to prove it, then," said Ann decisively.

Her brothers agreed.

"How? I'll prove it. Just tell me how," Richard begged.

"If you bring us some of the spices —

the nutmeg, cinnamon, and cloves — and if they smell and taste just like the ones in the pudding, then we'll know you didn't add any poison," Ann told him.

Richard's eyes shifted. "My mother will whip my backside so I won't sit for a month if she catches me taking her spices."

The three Weemses were unimpressed.

"Oh, all right." Richard leaned over and rinsed his marble bag in the river. "I guess if I pinched the pudding I can pinch some spices."

Ann, Joseph, and Addison lay back on the rocks, sunning themselves, while Richard ran the mile back to his house. As soon as he was out of earshot, Ann let out the giggle she'd been suppressing.

"And have you figured out what we'll tell Mamma?" she asked Joseph.

Joseph stretched and smiled, his head resting comfortably on his folded arms. "Another present from Richard. And that's the truth."

When Richard returned, they sniffed and inspected the dark, aromatic powders he brought folded in brown paper. Ann even dipped her finger in one of the packages for a taste, but found the spice bitter without molasses to accompany it. With serious faces, they finally agreed that

Richard had not, in fact, been trying to poison them. Richard was relieved, and the brown paper packages disappeared discreetly into the cuff of Addison's britches before the four of them moved on to their next activity, which was heaving large stones into the river to see who could make the biggest splash.

Their mother clucked her tongue when they gave her the gift. "That poor child has a weight of guilt on his shoulders," she said.

"He *should* have a weight of guilt," said Augustus. He gave the chair he was working on a whack with his hammer. "And he's not a poor child. He's a wealthy white boy who will inherit all the land he'll ever need without having to work for it."

Arabella carefully placed the brown packages into the wooden box where her husband's hard-earned coins were deposited each Sunday evening. "We'll save it for Thanks Giving," she said quietly.

"We'll have land someday, too," said Joseph.

"Hmph." Augustus grunted his disbelief.

"Papa says once he buys our freedom he'll start saving to buy land so we can do our own farming and we won't have to work for anybody," Joseph persisted.

The look on Augustus's face was a mixture of anger and pity. "Joseph, you might as well know this right now. Master Charles is never going to let Papa buy our freedom. Haven't you seen how every year when Papa has more money saved, Master Charles says, 'The price of slaves went up again, John. Maybe by next year you'll have enough.' That's because the first person Papa will buy is Mamma, and then she won't give him any more slave children."

"Hush, Augustus," said Arabella. "I don't want to hear you children arguing."

Ann wanted to tell Augustus how he was wrong, how Papa would keep his promise of buying freedom for each one of them. But in her heart she felt the truth of her brother's words.

The stony silence was interrupted by her father bursting in the door.

"They made it!" His smile was wide and his eyes glistened. He hugged his wife. "They made it, Arabella."

"Thank the Lord!" Ann's mother exclaimed.

"Children," her father announced, "you no longer have an uncle Abram."

Ann's stomach lurched at her father's words, but the joy on his face kept her from panicking.

John lowered his voice to almost a whisper. "For safety, your uncle has changed his name. He's no longer Abram Young. He's now William Bradley. He and your Aunt Mimi — Mrs. Bradley now — are living free in New York."

Six

It happened several weeks before Thanks Giving. A cold rain had been falling for three days straight, and the dirt floor of their cabin was muddy as a riverbed. When the wind blew hard, even the table and dinner benches received a sprinkling of rain through the gaps between the logs, and had to be dried off before each meal.

Ann, her mother, Catharine, and Ellie had been busy for weeks in the Prices' kitchen canning everything from pole beans to applesauce. Her father and brothers had been spending their days harvesting the Indian corn, picking apples in the orchard, tending to the fall plowing, and keeping the fires burning in the tobacco houses so the huge leaves could dry despite the rain. During the dark evenings, Ann and her father and brothers had redug the hole behind their cabin. In it, between fat layers of straw, they'd placed cabbages, potatoes, and winter squash from their garden to keep for the next few months. They'd covered the hole snugly with planks of wood to stop hungry raccoons and opossums from having a feast.

It happened just as the canning was almost done, the corncribs were full of dry corn, and the last of the black walnuts had been scavenged off the forest floor ahead of the squirrels. Ann awoke in the dark to the sound of her mother starting breakfast downstairs. She shivered and pulled her thin, rough blanket over her head. Even her ears were cold. She dreaded the thought of going out back to wash.

Two things Ann could not understand about winter: why she had to wash, and why she had to wrap her feet in rags. If it were left up to her, she would stay dirty and barefoot. Washing only made her colder, and the foot wrapping, meant to warm her, took away the freedom to feel the soft parts and the hard parts of the earth on the soles of her feet and toes. But her mother insisted on washing and rags, and there was no arguing.

Behind the cabin, Ann used a stick to break the fragile layer of ice that had formed on the wash bucket overnight. She washed her face and neck quickly, the cold water taking her breath away. She was thankful she would be working indoors instead of guiding a plow in the freezing drizzle all day. Her brothers had already had chilblains on their fingers.

Inside the cabin, the fire and the bubbling pot of cornmeal mush had warmed the room and steamed up the window. The family ate together, with yawns and eye-rubbing taking the place of conversation.

Ann shook the dried mud out of her foot rags and tied them snugly around her feet. Then she wrapped her shoulders in her woolen shawl and, with Catharine and her mother, started up the hill to the stone house. That was when it happened.

Actually, it had happened sometime earlier that morning, but that's when they found out. As they crested the hill, they heard a familiar cry.

"Poor Benjamin," said Catharine. "His mother is so busy these days she hardly has time to hold him."

But Ann noticed something strange about Benjamin's crying. It was more tired, more forlorn than usual — as if it had been going on for longer.

When they reached the summer kitchen and opened the door, there stood Benjamin, sobbing and shuddering in a pool of urine. There was no fire, no warmth, no candlelight to brighten the gray morning. And there was no Ellie. They called her name, and Ann climbed the ladder to the loft to see if she was ill and still in bed. She wasn't.

Arabella folded the weeping Benjamin into her arms, and he quieted. Catharine started the fire, and Ann mopped up the floor.

"Where's your mamma?" Arabella asked when Benjamin was calm and sucking on three fingers. He shook his head and buried his face in her bosom, as if to block out the question.

Ann's heart pounded in her ears. She threw open the door and raced to the barn. The horses were gone. So was Master Charles's carriage.

She ran back to the kitchen, wanting to shout in anger.

Arabella held up one hand to silence Ann, and shook her head. She rocked back and forth, singing softly. There was nothing more to say. Nothing more to do, except welcome Benjamin into their own family and hold him when he cried.

That evening Ann offered to help her father and Augustus carry the chairs they'd built to Mr. McGowan's store to be sold. She needed the movement, and needed to be away from Benjamin's whimpering. Augustus walked on ahead, and Ann kept pace with her father, a chair balanced across her shoulders.

The chilly breeze made her cheeks tingle, and her thoughts felt muddled. Her father had told her the Prices would never break up a family, and yet they had. And there was nothing any of them could do about it.

"Benjamin still has the love he needs — you know that don't you, baby girl?" her father said. "He'll be all right." His words were encouraging, but even in the dark Ann could see the pain in his face. He was simply ferreting out the good parts and striving to be thankful for them — something he always did, and which was normally a comfort to Ann. This time it only infuriated her more.

She grasped the rungs of the chair so tightly it hurt, as if she could strangle some justice out of the unfeeling wood. "It's not fair," she said, her jaw stiff.

"Ann Maria, what is fair is up to the Good Lord, not to us," her father said softly.

"But they do bad things — awful

things — and they never get punished!" Ann cried.

"Baby girl, they have built their lives with the wrong things they do. Master Charles has got debts and drunkenness, a barren wife who's angry as a rabid dog, and fields going sour from too much tobacco growing. They have their punishment every day."

Ann scowled, thinking. Her father's breath and her own made billowy puffs of steam in the cold night air. It was true. The Prices had soft beds, a warm house, and all the food they wanted, but there was no joy in their home.

Her father continued. "I can tell you that Miss Ellie got herself free from that lecherous Master Charles today, and young Benjamin will be spoiled rotten by your mamma and big sister. And come Christmas, if she's not been sold too far south, Ellie will be back to see her boy."

They walked the rest of the way to McGowan's store in silence.

When they arrived back home, a wonderful aroma came drifting from the tiny cabin. Inside, Joseph was giving Benjamin a ride on his shoulders, and Benjamin was squealing with delight. On the table sat a steaming pumpkin pudding, filling the room with the unmistakable scent of nutmeg, cinnamon, and cloves.

Ann knew that the purpose of the pudding was to entertain Benjamin, to help ease the great hole of grief in his heart. How strange, she thought, to celebrate this day by using the spices meant for Thanks Giving. It was upside down, to honor the day a child lost his mother and a mother lost her child.

But as Ann sat with her head bowed and listened to her father's prayer of thanks for the mighty blessings of the food, their home, and their family, she realized that no amount of fancy food or clothes or land could make her happier than the love of her family made her at that moment. So maybe it wasn't upside down, after all. It was just an early Thanks Giving.

Seven

Benjamin cried a little less and laughed a little more each day. When he asked about his mother, their answer was always the same: "She'll come see you at Christmas if she can." And so, Benjamin's daily question soon became "Is it Christmas today?"

Ann was always impatient for Christmas to arrive, and this year Benjamin's impatience added to her own. Christmas was, without a doubt, the very best time of the year. In fact, it was the only time of the year, other than Independence Day and Good Friday, when they didn't have to work six days a week. And Christmas wasn't just a one-day holiday. It was a whole week off from work, stretching all the way until New Year's Day. Some slaves got permission to travel to visit family during that week, and so the Weemses were expecting quite a bit of company.

Soon after Thanks Giving they began to

get ready. They saved apples gathered from the orchard floor and hoarded black walnuts. Arabella kept throwaway scraps from a red dress she'd made for Mistress Carol, and used them to make hair ribbons for Ann and Catharine. Benjamin wanted one, too, but Arabella told him that boys don't wear hair ribbons, and she made him a red bow tie instead.

Up in the loft, which they now shared with Benjamin, they spent their last few sleepy moments at night discussing the delicacies — biscuits, real bread, and maybe even cakes — their mother would make with the peck of wheat flour and quart of molasses Master Charles would give them Christmas morning. They also wagered bets on which item of livestock they would receive for their Christmas dinner.

"He's stingy as an old crow. I say he gives us one scrawny chicken like he did last year," said Augustus.

"I want a hog. A big fat hog to roast in the fire pit," said Joseph dreamily.

"I'd rather have a turkey," said Catharine. "We eat fatback all year — why do you want to eat more pig on Christmas?" She jabbed Joseph in the ribs with her toes.

"At Elton farm they roasted a whole ox

last year," Addison chimed in.

"That's because it broke its neck," said Ann. "They won't have an ox this year, for sure."

They were quiet for a moment, pondering the possibilities.

"What do you want for Christmas dinner, Benjamin?" Ann asked. His choice sleeping place was between her and Catharine, and he had been gently kicking her thigh during the entire discussion.

"Stars," he said simply.

"Stars?" Ann propped herself up on her elbows, but it was too dark in the windowless loft for her to detect Benjamin's expression. The older boys snickered. "You want to *eat* stars?" she asked.

"Yes," he answered.

Ann could *feel* Catharine grinning, and by now Joseph was giggling. "Why?" she asked him.

Benjamin stopped kicking. "So I can fly to where my mamma is."

Ann pulled him close to her and wrapped her blanket over his to keep him extra warm. "That's a good idea, Benjamin," she said in his ear.

As she drifted off to sleep, she imagined that she floated up into the inky black winter sky and flew free with the stars.

★ ★ ★

Their cousins, Hannah and David, arrived from Rockville on Christmas morning, and the relatives from farther away were there by noon. They'd all started walking the night before. They came carrying sacks of potatoes and turnips, baskets of eggs, kegs of molasses, and limp chickens dangling by their feet from carrying poles. They brought all of the special food they'd been given by their own masters, along with plates and spoons, blankets and banjos to add to the celebration, and so as not to be a burden on Ann's family for the week during which they would share their home.

In the midst of these happy arrivals Ann looked up the hill to see Richard watching, his mouth slightly open. She felt her anger flare. This was *her* time, *her* family. He had no right to watch as if their merriment were on display for him. She strode up to confront him.

"What do you want?" she demanded.

Richard startled, as if she'd awakened him. "Uh — Merry Christmas," he said, blushing.

Ann crossed her arms over her chest. "Merry Christmas," she returned, with only a sliver of warmth.

"My brother says come on up and get your presents. We're leaving for my sister's house in a little while, so he said come soon." As he spoke, his gaze kept shifting back to the scene in front of Ann's cabin, where aunts exclaimed over children grown so much in the past year, and uncles laughed loudly, slapping each other on the back.

At first Ann wanted to grasp his head and turn it away. Then she found herself blinking in disbelief as she recognized the emotion in his eyes. He was looking at the scene not with disdain or even curiosity, but with longing.

"I'll go get my father," she said, now eyeing him with curiosity.

Richard nodded, and turned to climb the hill. He was wearing his Sunday best and looked cleaner than Ann had ever seen him. She surmised that the soap he'd been scrubbed with was about as strong as her mamma's soap, because as he walked he scratched, first his neck, then his armpit, then his rump.

Ann ran to her cabin, where her family was crowding inside to warm up.

"Papa." She tugged on her father's sleeve. "Master Charles says come get our presents."

"Then let's go," he said, and invited her along to help carry things.

At the stone house they found Master Charles hitching the horses to the carriage in preparation for the trip to his sister's house.

"Here, let me do that for you, Master Charles," her father said, and took the reins from him to finish the job.

Master Charles willingly stepped back from the carriage and brushed himself off. He, too, was dressed in his Sunday best and, surprisingly, looked sober.

"John," Master Charles began, with an air of defensiveness about him, "it wasn't a very good harvest this year, as you well know."

"No, Master, it wasn't." Her father nudged the bit into the mare's mouth.

"I'd wanted to be able to give your family a couple of turkeys this year — I know those boys of yours are shooting up like cornstalks."

"Yes, sir, Master Charles, they certainly are."

"But," Master Charles continued as he picked horsehair off his black wool trousers, "I can't afford the turkeys. I'm sure you understand."

"Yes, sir, Master, I understand." Her father patted the mare on her neck and she nibbled at his shirt.

"But I do have that old sheep that went lame. She won't be the most tender meat for your Christmas dinner, but she'll provide you with more than you can eat."

"Thank you, Master. Thank you kindly." Her father bowed slightly.

Mistress Carol came out of the house, a long wool cloak covering the red Christmas dress Ann's mother had made for her. "It's time to go. We don't want to be late," she said briskly. To Ann she said, "I've left a sack of flour and a jug of molasses in the pantry for your mother. Go get them — *one* sack and *one* jug. I don't want to find anything else missing when I return." She began to step up into the carriage, then turned as if she'd forgotten something. She opened a small leather purse. "Since it's the season for Christian giving, here." She selected several coins and held them out for Ann to take.

The coins felt cold in Ann's hand — five copper one-cent pieces, large and heavy.

"Share them with your brothers and sister," said Mistress Carol.

"Thank you, ma'am," Ann said softly.

Her father carried the sheep over his shoulders, and Ann balanced the sack of flour on one hip and the jug of molasses on the other. The coins she clutched in one hand. She wondered, as they came down the hill toward the little cabin, if they looked anything like the Wise Men who came bearing gifts for the Christ child.

Ann was thankful that butchering the sheep was her father's job. She busied herself helping to stoke the fire in the fire pit, until a thick bed of glowing coals warmed the gray winter day. The chickens, plucked and gutted, and the sheep, skinned and gutted, were then thrown onto the coals to cook.

Master Charles would have written them passes so that they could travel to visit relatives, but Ann was happy to have the relatives come to them. That way, their home was filled with laughter and music, dancing and the smells of good things to eat, and these things lingered after Christmas, the memories clinging to the beams of the cabin.

They ate, crowded around the table or gathered in front of the hearth. When no one could eat another bite, her uncles brought out banjos and harmonicas, and her cousin David beat out the rhythms of the music on his chest and thighs as if his body were a drum. Catharine danced with

Benjamin in her arms, her bare feet slapping the dirt floor, her crimson hair ribbon and Benjamin's bow tie bright as blood, with Benjamin clapping and laughing, until Catharine's breath caught in her throat and Arabella made her sit to rest.

When it was time for the children to go to bed, Benjamin asked, for the hundredth time, "When will my mamma get here?"

Ann had already heard enough bits of conversation to know that no one had heard from Ellie. That most certainly meant she'd been sold into the Deep South — Alabama, or maybe Mississippi. Too far south to send word back from, and too far away to walk home for a Christmas visit.

Ann watched as her mother sank into a chair and sat Benjamin on her knees, facing her. Arabella sighed, dreading what she had to say.

"Your mamma can't come this Christmas," she said quietly.

Benjamin's face crumpled. He closed his eyes, and his cry came out as a hum from between clenched teeth.

"You will see her again, Benjamin," Arabella was saying. "She will wait for you in heaven, and I promise you will see her there." But her voice was flat, deadened by the knowledge that a future in heaven was little comfort to a child so young.

Ann lifted Benjamin from her mother's knees and let his tears soak into the shoulder of her dress. She helped him climb the ladder to the loft and held him as he cried himself to sleep.

The loft was crowded, with six young cousins now sharing the sleeping quarters. Ann lay awake even after the other children were sound asleep. She listened to the conversation in the room below, where the older cousins and adults gathered in front of the fire. Their talk was alive with news of her uncle Abram — now Uncle William — and Aunt Mimi and their new baby daughter. It was her cousin David, who sometimes worked at the docks in Georgetown, who'd gotten the news from a ship captain from New York — a man for whom Uncle William had sometimes worked, loading and unloading his ship in the New York harbor.

"They had to go," she heard David say. "Master found out they were in New York, and a slave catcher was on his way to hunt them down."

"They say it's horrible cold up there in Canada West," said an elderly aunt. "Can't plant until July and you've got to harvest in August before it frosts!"

"Mmm-hmm," chimed in an uncle. "In January, if you open your mouth, the spit'll freeze."

Ann heard Hannah's laugh above the others. "Uncle William and Aunt Mimi will do just fine," she said. "Uncle still has his dream of owning land. Maybe in Canada he'll be able to."

There was a murmur of agreement. Ann wondered what Canada must be like. Was it really as cold as they said? She pictured Uncle Abram with his hair frosted white with snow and ice. And what must it be like to be free — really free, in a country where slave catchers weren't even allowed to hunt fugitives? She felt a tug at her heart — love for her aunt and uncle, and feeling how much she missed them. She went to sleep imagining them sawing and hammering, building the house her uncle had always dreamed of.

Eight

After the new year came hiring-out time. Master William decided he needed the cash hiring out would bring him more than he needed the help of Lizzy's son Henry, so Henry was sent to live and work at the Dorsey farm. It was plenty close enough for him to walk home on Sundays, so Lizzy and Tom and all Henry's little sisters and even little Evan didn't cry too hard when he left.

Outside it was cold. The ground was frozen, the trees bare, and the fields brown and sad-looking. Fewer people stopped at the inn these days, but there was still work to be done: corn to be shelled and carted to the gristmill up the road in Tridelphia, tobacco to be pressed and weighed and loaded into barrels. There was finally time to patch and mend their well-worn clothes, and to push lumps of mud into the gaps in the walls of their cabin to help keep out the cold. And, of course, the Prices' horses and oxen, chickens, sheep, and pigs needed more care than ever now that there was nothing for them to graze on or forage for.

Benjamin stopped asking about his mother and began to call Ann's mother "Mamma." Arabella said the Lord just made the little ones like that, so when their mamma died or got sold far away they wouldn't waste away from the pain of it. Ann often wondered how Ellie was faring. She was sure Ellie hadn't forgotten her son as quickly as he had seemed to forget her.

Benjamin was never far from Arabella. He went with her to the tavern when there was dinner or breakfast to cook for customers, and he crawled up on her lap in the evenings when she sat in front of the fire to sew. Sometimes Arabella laid down her sewing and played patty-cake with Benjamin, or cuddled him, or told him Brer Rabbit stories.

As Ann watched them one evening, she realized that Benjamin was about the same age her baby brother would have been had he lived. She tried to imagine that it was he who sat on her mother's lap, grown to a young boy and strong. But quickly her mind went back to the night, four winters ago, when her infant brother burned hot with fever. And how, despite a night of prayer and cloths soaked in honeysuckle tea pressed to his delicate limbs, Ann awoke to find her baby brother cold and stiff in her mother's arms. She remembered how they'd buried him. "Thank the Lord, now he'll never be a slave," her mother had said, her voice dry as crackling leaves. And her father had sobbed as he shoveled dirt into the hole, covering the tiny box that held his son.

Yet here was Benjamin, filling her mother's lap. And now that he lived with them, he was much safer from the back of Mistress Carol's hand. Ann smiled at herself. She must be becoming like her father, she thought: able to find the hidden blessings in the middle of the sad things in life.

Sundays were quieter now. It was too cold to meet in the clearing, so smaller groups gathered in various cabins and said their prayers quietly so as not to be caught worshiping without a white person present. Sunday afternoons were spent indoors, in front of the fire, listening to stories — unless, of course, there was snow.

That one particular Sunday the snow began to fall during the night, and by morning it lay thick and quiet. When Ann went out back to wash, she gathered a handful of snow from the top of the wash bucket, rubbed it over her face and neck, and dried herself with the stiff rag hanging above the bucket. If her mother insisted on washing today, this seemed an appropriate way to do it.

With the snow falling so heavily, they dared not venture to another farm for worship, so they shared their prayers in front of the hearth. Ann could hardly sit still, she was so anxious to get back outside. Joseph and Addison were easily coaxed to join her, and after some prodding even Augustus put on his jacket and came out.

The four of them ran down the hill toward the pond, which was frozen quite solid and now had several inches of snow on top. Ann ran along on the ice, her rag-wrapped feet making huge prints in the fluffy snow. Then she stopped abruptly and slid across the ice. She hollered at the joy of it. Her brothers imitated her, running and skittering across the pond on their feet, their knees, and their bellies. Soon, despite their threadbare clothing, their faces were bright with sweat. Ann didn't even mind it when a snowball hit her squarely in the back of the neck. She wheeled around to find Richard gathering another handful to throw.

Richard had the advantage of leather

boots, several sizes too big but easier to run in than rags, and gloves to keep his hands from freezing. But the Weems children had the advantage of four on one. So it was Richard, plastered white and breathless after a snowball fight that rivaled the Battle of Bunker Hill, who begged for mercy.

They sat together to rest, and Richard said innocently, "You folks must be happy to be leaving this boring place."

Ann exchanged a curious glance with Augustus.

Richard didn't wait for a response, but kept on talking. "I wish I was moving to Rockville. My pa said almost *four hundred* people live there! They have the county fair in September, and people come from all over just to see it. They've got a courthouse, and they've even got a *jail*."

"Who's moving to Rockville?" Augustus asked.

Richard stared hard at Augustus, then at Addison, then at Joseph, then at Ann. They each watched him, wondering why he looked so confused. "*You* are!" he blurted out. "Didn't my brother tell you?"

Ann's eyes widened. Certainly, one need only have walked by Master Charles once or twice in the past month to overhear him complaining about his debts, and how farming was no way to make a living, and how he was ready to try something else. But Ann had never suspected he would move away from Unity to do it.

"Are you telling us a story?" Augustus scowled at Richard.

"I'm telling you the truth!" Richard insisted. "I heard my brother say, plain as day, he's fixing to sell the last of the harvest and the animals, and move to Rockville."

Ann found herself grinning at the news. Rockville!

"Do they really have a jail there?" Joseph wanted to know.

"And the county fair — can anyone go, or just the white folks?" Addison asked.

Ann elbowed Addison. "That's the fair Hannah and David went to last year. Of course anyone can go."

Richard answered their questions and told them about the fine houses on Montgomery Avenue and on Washington Street; houses that stood so close to each other, folks could look into each other's windows. He told how he'd driven in a carriage near enough the jailhouse to see it, though he didn't know if there was a prisoner inside at the time.

The discussion with Richard, and later with her family, fueled a growing excitement in Ann. The county fair, as she'd heard about it from her cousins, sounded like the most wonderful experience imaginable. She would be sad to leave Unity, but moving to Rockville would be a grand adventure. Ann had a whole week of dreaming, from that snowy Sunday until the next warm, muddy Saturday. She imagined her mother being allowed to make her own jam, with her name on the jar, to enter in the women's cooking competition at the fair. She imagined Augustus entering the plowing races and winning first prize for Master Charles. She imagined going to the market for Mistress Carol and walking on the streets next to the fine houses. She had a week of dreaming and hoping and planning before everything changed.

Master Charles was in a horrid state all week, shouting orders, threatening with the whip, and forcing her father and brothers to work from before dawn until after sunset with hardly five minutes to take their meals. He drove them to shell mountains of corn, press and weigh piles of tobacco, and load all this, along with many sacks of wheat, into his own wagon and his father's. It was as if he was determined to sell off all of his harvest on one market day and leave nothing for them to eat for the rest of the winter.

Very early Saturday morning, with the stars still shining in the sky, Lizzy's husband, Tom, knocked on their door and said Master Charles wanted the boys to come help unload the sacks and barrels at market. They were headed to Baltimore with the two wagons and could not be expected to arrive home before very late that night. Tom promised to have Joseph and Addison ride with him in Master William's wagon, and to keep an eye on them while they were in Baltimore. Augustus would ride with Master Charles and was old enough to watch out for himself. Arabella worried at the thought of her young boys spending the day in such a large, unpredictable city. Tom just laughed and said Baltimore wasn't anything but a small town that liked to put on airs.

There was no time to cook breakfast, but Tom said he had a big enough slab of cold cornmeal mush to share with the boys. Ann rubbed her eyes as she watched Tom lead the sleepy crew up the hill to the barn. Most of the snow from last Sunday had melted, and the ground was an ugly mix of dirty snow and slushy earth. It was exactly the kind of mix that likes to suck wagon wheels into it, and make a trip to Baltimore and back take two or three days instead of one. Ann was glad her brothers had taken their blankets with them.

It was a scene Ann would never forget: Tom with his arm around Joseph, Addison and Augustus trudging next to them, the four heads bobbing as they made their way up the hill in the moonlight, shoulders hunched under the blankets that minutes before had covered their sleeping forms.

Saturday night, it was the mud they blamed it on. "Those wagons were weighed down so heavy, they probably had to push them all the way to Baltimore," said her father. "We'll see them sometime in the morning, I reckon."

Sunday at church, Lizzy was worried, too; and they blamed it on the rain clouds that threatened. "I suppose Master Charles had best get himself a room at an inn," said Arabella. "If it rains and those roads get any muddier, they'll get stuck for sure."

When Monday dawned sunny and dry, and the mud crusted over and cracked, they searched for something else to blame. "Maybe they broke a wheel . . ." her father began, then trailed off.

By evening Ann's mother had begun a nervous pacing, the way she did when her insides told her something was wrong.

"Mamma, come sit," said Catharine. "They're with Tom and Master Charles. They'll be all right."

But Arabella wouldn't sit, and it turned dark without anyone going to bed. When they heard the knock at the door, they stumbled over one another to get to it. Tom stood on their doorstep, his clothes caked with mud, his face streaked with tears.

"Where are they?" her father demanded, his voice choked into a growl.

"Gone . . . Sold . . . to Alabama." The words sliced Ann's heart.

As Ann's father crumpled to his knees, Arabella's voice rose in a wail — one word, "No!" drawn out like the cry of wind through dead trees.

Nine

No blessings.

Ann could find no hidden blessings in the loss of her brothers — not in the empty places beside her in the sleeping loft, not in her mother's stricken face, not in the defeated way her father held his shoulders, and not in the silence that surrounded every mealtime because each of them was too heartsick to speak.

As she went about her work, the rhythm of it was heavy and dull. It was as though someone else's hands washed the linens, curried and brushed the horses, and chopped turnips for dinner at the tavern. At night she, Catharine, and Benjamin held hands as they fell asleep, as if the others might disappear before morning.

Sometimes they talked about her brothers the way those left living talk about the dead. "Remember how Addison used to pucker up his face and look like old

Aunt Stella when he ate sour cherries?" her mother would ask. Or, "Remember how Augustus used to tease Lizzy's Rachel and make her blush?"

And sometimes they were angry. Ann's mother would spit out words about how Master Charles had no right. Her father would pound the rungs into the chairs he built with such vengeance that, more than once, he split the wood. And Ann found herself, in her mind's eye, wielding a horsewhip to open up bloody slices on Master Charles's pale, freckled back.

Then, just as the lengthening days and warmer nights inspired the first spring peepers to begin their noisemaking, Ann's father stopped mourning and started making plans. At breakfast one morning he pushed back his chair. "At seventy-five cents a Sunday working for Mrs. Griffith, I'll be in my grave before I've saved enough to buy this family," he said. "I'm going to talk to Cousin David. He helped Uncle Abram and Aunt Mimi to find freedom, and Lord willing he'll be able to help us."

He told Master Charles he'd work for him Sunday to make up for today, and left to walk to Rockville. Ann, her mother, and Catharine waited up for him. When he returned late that night, he was weary but filled with hope. "There are folks who can help us," he said.

He told them about free blacks and white people, many of them Quakers, who had formed "Vigilance Committees." They helped fugitives travel north and also worked to raise money to buy slaves for freedom. If he went to the Vigilance Committee in New York, the folks who had helped Uncle Abram and Aunt Mimi, and told them about their family's case, he was sure they would help. "If Master Charles won't let this family be together in slavery," he said, "then we'll join it back together in freedom."

Freedom. Legally. Without fear of capture. Ann was almost afraid to believe it could be true.

In Rockville, John had gone to the courthouse and secured a permit that would allow him to leave Montgomery County and return, as long as he did so within thirty days. If he did not return within thirty days, he wouldn't be allowed to come back into Montgomery County at all. There was no time to waste.

Arabella and Catharine cooked a new batch of cornmeal mush while Ann filled gourds with water. John took the money box down from its shelf and emptied the contents into a rag, which he then tied securely and placed under his shirt. He would walk to Baltimore, and then buy a train ticket to New York. Ann and Catharine both gave him the pennies they'd received at Christmas. He tried to refuse, but Catharine gave him an impatient look and asked, "What could we possibly want more than our own and our brothers' freedom?"

Under his shirt he also slipped his freedman's papers. Even more precious than the coins, they must stay well hidden. It was too easy — and too common — for a thief to steal and burn free papers, and sell the free person into slavery with no one there to object.

When the cornmeal mush had cooled, Catharine bundled slices of it in clean cloths for him to carry. They hugged him and kissed him and wished him well. Arabella asked what she should say to Master Charles when he found out in the morning that John was gone.

"Tell him I've gone to see friends," John said. "And that I figured since he no longer needed the help of my sons, he must not be in need of my help, either."

Ann knew her mother would never say such a brazen thing to Master Charles, but it made her feel good to hear the strength in her father's words. She gave him one last embrace, and breathed deeply of the smell of fire that clung to his shirt. Then he disappeared into the night.

"Catharine, quickly, bring me your soiled rags!" Ann's mother watched something outside the window — something that made her jaw grind.

"I'll wash them myself, Mamma," said Catharine. "I always do —"

"No, you won't. Bring them to me! Ann Maria, fill the washtub, *hurry!*"

Ann and her sister scurried to obey. The washtub lay upside down next to the house, draining from Saturday night baths. Ann turned it over. Then she fetched the water she'd carried from the spring that morning and poured it in. Her mother rushed out of the house and dumped the rags into the basin. As she swirled them around, the water turned a deep, clear crimson.

"Good afternoon, Mistress Carol," Ann's mother called with a strained cheerfulness.

Ann looked up to see the mistress picking her way down the muddy path in the slanting late-afternoon sunlight.

"You caught me washing my soiled rags while my husband is away," Arabella said loudly.

Mistress Carol eyed the dark water, then stared hard at Arabella. She cleared her throat and spoke. "I've come to tell you a whole host of cattlemen have arrived at the tavern and I want you to make supper immediately." Then she turned and trudged back up the hill, placing her feet gingerly on each step as if disgusted by the rich, moist earth and newly sprouted spring weeds.

When the mistress was out of earshot, the complaining started.

"That's not fair, Mamma. Those people shouldn't be traveling on the Sabbath."

"You're supposed to work six days for them, not seven."

And from Benjamin, "Who will cook our supper?"

But Ann's mother ignored their comments. "That greedy witch," she growled. "She's sticking her nose in my business, asking me isn't it time I had another child, watching my belly like a vulture." Sweat broke out on her face.

"Come inside, Mamma," said Catharine, taking her hand and leading her.

She and Ann helped Arabella to a chair.

Ann rinsed a clean rag in cold water and wiped her mother's brow. Benjamin stood next to Arabella and patted her knee. "Don't be sad, Mamma," he said.

Arabella's hands shook. "She won't take this one from me. Not to the auction block, and not to a fever from this cold, leaky shack."

Ann and Catharine stared at each other, surprised. Then Catharine shook her head as a sign for them to continue comforting their mother rather than take the time to be shocked by her announcement.

Ann wiped her mother's arms with the cool rag. "It'll be all right, Mamma," she said. "Papa will be home soon, and he'll bring help."

After Ann, along with her mother, Catharine, Lizzy, and Rachel, had broken the Sabbath by cooking supper for the largest, dirtiest, most foul-talking group of cattlemen who had ever passed through the tavern, she found Richard sitting on the stone wall outside. He was whittling a small Y-shaped branch, which he could barely see because dusk was quickly turning to night.

"Evening," he said, not looking up.

Ann shifted her weight, not sure if she wanted to talk with him or go on home.

Ever since her brothers had left, Ann had preferred to stay close to her family, and Sunday afternoons playing with Richard had abruptly ended.

"It's a new slingshot," he said, referring to his handiwork.

Ann merely grunted.

They were silent for a while, save for the sound of Richard's knife scraping against the hard wood. Ann traced a circle in the dirt with her big toe.

"It's almost done." Richard held up the slingshot for her to see.

Ann nodded, said good night, and left him to his work.

Ten

Ann's father arrived home looking thinner and older, but with a whirlwind of good news that took Ann's breath away. He'd met with the Reverend Charles Bennett Ray, a colored minister from New York, who was the director of the New York State Vigilance Committee. Reverend Ray was so moved by the story about Ann's brothers that he'd already begun to raise money to buy their freedom — and to buy freedom for the rest of the family, as well. Ray had also written to another colored minister, the Reverend Henry Highland Garnet, who was living in Scotland, asking him to raise money in Britain for the Weems family. Her father promised to include Benjamin in the purchase if they possibly could. Ann marveled at the thought of people she'd never met, living in faraway cities, giving money toward her freedom. And she marveled at the thought of freedom actually becoming hers.

Then, as if the news really had been something out of a dream, their days settled into the normal rhythm of their work, sunup to sundown. John was expected to work for Master Charles each day until long past dark, and on Sundays, to make up for the weeks he'd spent away.

It was corn-planting time, and Ann decided she was twelve. Though the weather was warm and the earth soft, and though Tom and Lizzy and most of their children were busy plowing and planting Master William's fields, Ann and her family were busy mostly with packing. All of Mistress Carol's dishes had to be wrapped and placed in crates. Everything from tablecloths to cutlery, mirrors to dresses, had to be packaged neatly for the move. Ann's father worked loading the last of the grain and helping Master Charles herd the animals to market to be sold off.

For Ann, getting a chance to work in the Prices' house could have been pleasant. There weren't nearly as many flies, mosquitoes, or spiders as in her family's cabin, and the windows let in a good bit of light along with the spring breezes. It could have been pleasant, if it hadn't been for Mistress Carol.

Ann wondered why, if the woman was so

afraid of her precious possessions getting broken, she didn't simply pack them herself. She spent her days fretting, giving orders, and reprimanding. And when the packing was done wrong, in her opinion, she made Ann, her mother, and Catharine do it all over again. Ann was relieved when there were guests at the inn and they could leave the packing in order to cook and serve the meals. She also welcomed the chance to bring the midday meal to her father, and always took Benjamin with her. The little boy was spending his days sitting on the floor of Mistress Carol's kitchen with strict orders to keep quiet and not touch anything. More than once he'd been slapped by the mistress for touching the china or putting one of her hats on his head.

One day, as Ann carried a basket of food for her father in one hand and held on to Benjamin with the other, he pulled away from her, fascinated by a flock of birds eating spilled grain near the barn. He ran at them, his arms outstretched. They flew into the air, then swarmed back down to eat. He giggled and ran at them again. They repeated their performance.

"Benjamin, come on. Papa is hungry — we have to take him his dinner."

"No," Benjamin whined. "I want to see the birds."

Ann sighed. If she waited with him, she'd be scolded for being late. But she couldn't bear to drag him away — his days in Mistress Carol's kitchen were so grim.

"Will you stay right here?" she asked him. "You won't wander off?"

Benjamin nodded his promise.

Ann glanced around. The hounds were securely chained and sleeping in the shade. The horses were in their stalls, and he was far enough from the house that Mistress Carol wouldn't hear his giggles.

"I'll be back very soon," she told him, and hurried to where her father was running corn through the corn sheller. She didn't talk with him for more than a moment, but still, as she made her way back toward the barns, she was afraid Benjamin had been alone too long. As she neared the place where she'd left him, the sound of Master Charles's voice made her heart sink. She crept to the edge of a stone wall and peeked out. Master Charles was leading the mare, Sally, and he had Benjamin by the hand.

"Oh, Lord," she whispered. "What is he going to do to him?"

Blaming herself, she tried to think

quickly of what to do. Step out boldly and grab Benjamin before Master Charles could hurt him? Run back to the house to get her mother to come? Scream at Master Charles to stop?

But before she could move, Master Charles did an astounding thing. He lifted Benjamin up onto Sally's saddle.

"She's a very gentle mare, you see?" He was talking to Benjamin in a kinder voice than Ann had ever heard him use with anyone. "When you get a little older, I'll teach you to ride her on your own."

From her hiding place, Ann saw Benjamin smiling, though his blue eyes were wide with uncertainty at being atop a large horse.

Master Charles led Sally, with her very young rider, away toward the cornfield. The last thing she heard him say was "We'll go show Master William what a little man you are."

Ann walked slowly back to the stone house. When her mother whispered "Where is Benjamin?" Ann mouthed the words "With Master Charles," pointing toward the barns. Arabella frowned at her, but Ann assured her he was fine.

So it was not a great surprise when, several days later, as Ann, Catharine, and their mother sat wrapping canning jars in old newspapers, they overheard a vicious fight between Mistress Carol and Master Charles.

"I've been shamed in front of all of Unity — hasn't that been enough?" Mistress Carol spat.

"Stick to your household chores." Master Charles sounded bored by his wife's pain. "You know nothing of business, and this is a business decision."

"A business decision?" The mistress's voice rose to a screech. "I know what kind of decision it is, and I'll not have you making it at my expense!"

"He's too young to work. In five years he'll fetch a handsome price, but —"

"I will not be shamed in front of all of Rockville! I'll kill him first. *Then* how much will he be worth to you?"

They heard a door slam, and there was silence. Ann grasped Catharine's hand and they both looked at Benjamin, who had fallen asleep on the floor. Their mother began to sing softly.

The very next Saturday morning, Master Charles loaded up his wagon with the last of the chickens, five barrels of tobacco, two sacks of wheat, and his son, and took them all to Baltimore to be sold.

Eleven

"We had no right to keep him with us forever," said Ann's mother. "Maybe he'll find his mamma now . . . someday."

Their house was even more empty with Benjamin gone. Ann tried to comfort herself by imagining that he'd been sold to a farm near where Ellie was living and that word would spread about a new arrival — a young mulatto boy with eyes like blue china. Ellie would walk to find him one Sunday and visit him every Sunday after that. Ann had heard stories of that kind of thing, and she prayed it would happen to Benjamin and Ellie.

With the improvement in the weather, many people now passed through the inn. Ann's mother used an extra apron to hide her growing belly, but her desperation grew along with the child inside her.

Late one evening, Ann's family sat huddled around the dying fire. The glowing coals gave a reddish light to their faces, and they spoke in hushed tones.

"Where is the help they promised?" Arabella asked. She didn't sound angry or impatient, just despairing. "We've got to get away from here. Before they sell our girls away from us, before they find out about the one I'm carrying and put a price on his head. Before they break this family into so many pieces we'll never find each other again."

Her husband rubbed her hands between his own. "Reverend Ray said he would work as fast as he could," he said. But his eyes, too, looked as though he was giving up hope.

It was as if the heavens heard her parents' despair and said, "Enough." Three days later Jacob Bigelow came to their cabin.

He was a white man, not particularly tall, though he did bump his head on the door frame because he forgot to duck. He had great bushy sideburns and wiry eyebrows, and wore spectacles that magnified his eyes and gave his face a slightly froglike look. He rubbed his chin a lot. He called Ann's father and mother Mr. Weems and Mrs. Weems and called Ann and Catharine "Miss."

Rubbing his chin, Mr. Bigelow explained what he'd come to do. "I've been sent by the Vigilance Committee to offer money for all three of you — good prices that I believe Mr. Price should accept." He shifted in his chair and it creaked under his weight. "You will become my property — but, I promise you, I only own slaves for a short time. I will draw up manumission papers — as an attorney for the Washington Gas Light Company, I'm able to do that sort of thing in my spare time. Once the papers are signed, you will become free people."

Ann's stomach did a little flip. It sounded so wonderful and so simple. There would be no running through the woods at night, no fear of being caught and punished. She hoped it would happen before too many years passed.

"Where can we live?" Arabella asked. "We'll have nowhere to stay once we don't work for Master Charles anymore."

Mr. Bigelow nodded, as though he'd already thought it all through. "I live in Washington City, and I'll be happy to help you get settled there. I will sign for you for rooms to rent, and I have friends at the docks in Georgetown who can offer you a job, Mr. Weems."

"Thank you. Thank you, sir," Ann's father fidgeted nervously. "But . . . what about my boys?" he asked.

"We have been working to find them," said Mr. Bigelow. "There's still no word, but the Vigilance Committee won't give up easily. Once the rest of you are free, you'll be able to help."

Ann's father grasped her mother's hand and squeezed it.

Rising to leave, Mr. Bigelow asked, "So, are we all in agreement?"

Ann, her mother and father, and Catharine each emphatically agreed to the plan.

"Good," said Mr. Bigelow. "Then I will go immediately to Mr. Price to make the offers."

Excitement shot through Ann's limbs. It was to happen *today?* Right now?

It was a Saturday. They'd stopped work early, as was usual for a Saturday, and because the days were long springtime days, the sun still hung in the sky. Suddenly the cabin didn't seem large enough to hold her joy. Ann ran out into the cool air and twirled around, her arms flung wide. Catharine joined her, and Ann, breathless, threw her arms around her sister. "Let's go listen," she whispered.

Catharine hesitated, but then agreed.

They ran quietly up the hill. The windows of the stone house were open, so they only needed to place themselves under the correct one. They followed the sound of voices, then pressed themselves against the cool stone wall, holding their breath to keep from giggling.

"I hear you're getting out of farming," Mr. Bigelow was saying.

"If the price of a sack of guano wasn't fat enough to choke an ox, I might have been able to make my land fertile again. How do you figure they can charge so much for a pile of putrid bird dung?" said Master Charles.

"I reckon it's the shipping, halfway around the world from Peru," said Bigelow.

"I reckon you're right."

Bigelow began again. "I hear you're selling off your farmhands. I'd like to make you an offer on the rest of the Weems family."

"Now, I hadn't planned on selling them all off. My wife will still need help around the house."

"I'm prepared to make you a fine offer. It should help with any debts you still have from running the farm."

Master Charles cleared his throat. Ann

grasped Catharine's hand and squeezed it hard. A breeze stirred the branches of the maple so that it tossed like a horse's mane against the clear sky.

"A thousand dollars for the mother. Sixteen hundred for the older girl, and five hundred for the younger one."

Ann pouted and scowled at Catharine.

Catharine shook her head. "It's not a compliment to us nor an insult to you, Ann," she whispered. "It's only that . . ." Her voice trailed off.

"It's only *what?*" Ann whispered too loudly.

"Shhh," Catharine admonished. They sat like statues for a moment to make sure no one had heard. Inside, the negotiations continued. "I'll have to consider if my wife can do without her seamstress — but it's true, I do have more debts to pay off."

Ann poked Catharine in the arm, still demanding an explanation.

"It's just that —" Catharine blushed as she continued. "You can't have babies yet, and Mamma and I both can. Babies they can *sell.*"

Ann felt suddenly dizzy and sick to her stomach. She wished she hadn't come to listen as she and her mother and sister were sorted out and priced like cattle.

"Let's go," she whispered, and tugged on Catharine's hand.

"It's all right, Ann," said Catharine. "We're going to be free soon, and none of that will matter. We'll just be girls." She stroked Ann's cheek.

But as they rose to leave, Ann saw her sister's face go slack as Master Charles's words drifted from the window: "All right, then. Twenty-six hundred it is. My wife will have to get used to only one extra pair of hands to help around the house."

"Mr. Price, won't you please reconsider —"

"Mr. Bigelow —" Master Charles sounded angry. "I have made up my mind, and I don't enjoy being argued with. I will not leave my wife without household help. If you don't want the mother and the older girl, then I suggest you leave."

"No!" Catharine said, too loudly, "He can't do that!"

Ann choked on her own breath. It couldn't be. They must have heard wrong.

Two heads appeared at the window. Master Charles pointed at Catharine. "You," he said, "go tell your mother and father you're leaving." Then, to Mr. Bigelow beside him, he said, "I want you to take your property and go. I'll not have them crying and wailing around here all night."

Catharine grasped Ann's hand and started to run. Ann stumbled, keeping up with her.

"Mamma! Papa!" Catharine cried as they neared the cabin. "Don't let them do it!" She fell into Arabella's arms. "They're going to make us go away and leave Ann here."

Their father placed one hand on Catharine's head and looked up at Ann. Ann stopped short of the group of three, huddled together. She felt as if she were sinking, dropping away from them.

"This is not what I asked for," her father said angrily. "I want to join this family together, not break it apart!" He marched up the hill and met Jacob Bigelow, who was on his way down. Ann watched as they gestured. They seemed to be arguing.

Catharine came to her. "Papa won't let them do it," she said. "He'll tell them we won't leave you."

But Ann already felt it. The fabric of her family had been ripped again, and she was the piece that was being torn off.

Her father's shoulders drooped with despair when he returned down the hill. "Oh, baby girl," was all he could say as he enveloped her in a hug that seemed to want to blot out the rest of the world. She felt his body shake and knew it was too late to take back anything that had been decided that afternoon. Ann held him tightly and tried to memorize the feel of his arms and chest.

"Are we leaving, John?" her mother asked quietly. "Am I losing another child?"

"No!" Ann's father released her and tightened his fists. "We'll get her back as surely as we'll get the boys."

Ann felt herself sink further away. She was as lost as her brothers in Alabama. She felt her mother's embrace and vowed to remember the softness of it. She tried to press back tears, but they flowed down her cheeks.

"Can't you stop them?" Catharine begged of their father.

Jacob Bigelow answered for him. "Your master took my offer very quickly, Miss Catharine. It was likely he already planned to sell you and your mother before the move to Rockville. If I leave you here with your sister, your fate can only be worse."

At that moment Master Charles came down the hill, shouting that he'd heard enough weeping for one day. He stood between Ann and her family, his arms crossed, and ordered them to pack and leave at once. "And I don't want you coming to find us in Rockville, is that clear? I will send her to you at Christmas, but if I see *any* of you" — he looked hard, first at Mr. Bigelow and then at her father — "prowling around my home in Rockville, I will have you promptly arrested."

"And what will be the charge?" Mr. Bigelow demanded.

Master Charles grew red in the face at this challenge. "For them, traveling without a permit. A nigger's travel permit makes excellent kindling, didn't you know?"

"And for me?" Mr. Bigelow lifted his chin.

Master Charles narrowed his eyes. "A gift of two dollars to the sheriff will inspire charges, I'm sure."

Ann stood, clinging to the same tree Richard had hidden behind the day Joseph got whipped. From there she watched them pack. Their few possessions — cooking pot, ladle, candlesticks, chairs, blankets, and rags — were moved out of the cabin and loaded onto Mr. Bigelow's wagon. And then Ann's family was loaded in, one precious person at a time. No one dared try to speak to her or touch her again, but their eyes remained locked on hers as the wagon rolled up the hill. The sunset was a brilliant orange, with pink and lavender clouds, and a cool wind that chilled the backs of her knees.

Mistress Carol had come to watch, too. "Get your blanket," she said to Ann. "I want you to sleep in the kitchen tonight so you can have breakfast ready early."

Whether Mistress Carol made that demand for her own convenience, or because she knew that spending the night in the empty cabin would have torn Ann's heart into jagged pieces, Ann did not know. But she obediently wrapped her blanket around her shoulders and walked up the hill from her cabin for the last time.

And so, when the day to move to Rockville finally arrived, Ann sat alone in the wagon atop the crates she and her mother and sister had packed. She had a brand-new slingshot in her hand, a gift from Richard, and a wound in her heart so deep she felt it would never heal.

Twelve

Sleep. Sleep was the only thing that brought her peace.

Ann moved through her days as if she were dragging a sack of rocks with each step. There was no rhythm now, nothing to "look out, look out, look out" for. All the worst had happened.

Mistress Carol demanded that a late garden be planted in the yard behind their rented frame house in Rockville. She wanted all of her belongings unpacked carefully, and the canned goods carried down to the dark, musty basement. And she expected the clothes and linens to be washed regularly, three meals cooked on time, and the small kitchen to be swept every day. Mistress Carol was used to the help of several women around the house, and seemed to think that Ann could do all of the work she used to share with her mother and sister. She complained constantly that if her husband wasn't so greedy he would have left her with some *real* household help instead of this ignorant child.

Not only was the work too much for one person, especially one person slowed by heavy sadness, but in addition, Ann was not a very good cook. Burned porridge, oversalted stew, and meat as tough and stringy as a horse harness became common in the Prices' kitchen. She'd always been a helper in the kitchen in Unity, but never had full responsibility for the meal.

All of Ann's offenses — her slowness, her mistakes, her ruining of precious food — made Mistress Carol as angry as a wet cat. She kept a short, fat stick next to the hearth, and used it regularly. "Wake up! Were you planning to sleep all day?" And down came the stick on Ann's head. "Watch that pot, you lazy wench! You burn it, and that's all you'll have to eat for three days." A blow landed across Ann's shoulders.

Some days her shoulders and arms were so sore from the beating, she felt as though she'd been tumbled in a corn sheller. And her head had lumps that made it difficult to find a comfortable way to sleep on the kitchen floor — which, now that there were no slave quarters, had become her bed. Ann took the punishment in silence, too deadened inside to much care.

The first Sunday Ann was in Rockville, and every Sunday after that, her cousin Hannah came to call. Sometimes David came with her. Hannah was a few years older than Augustus, with long, straight hair she kept in a bright red head wrap most of the time. David was a little older than Hannah, with dark, serious eyes and strong shoulders from hard work.

Her cousins' request was always the same: "Come on, now, Ann Maria. Come to St. Mary's with us. Church will do you good. And afterward we'll go visiting."

But Ann would shake her head, her eyelids heavy. Sunday was the one day she could escape into sleep for all the hours she was required to be alive. No promise of church singing or visiting could tempt her to give up that escape.

She would go to the edge of their yard and lie down under a tree. There, with flies and gnats keeping her company, she would drift off into dreams of sunny days in Unity, of skipping rocks with her brothers, cooking with her mother and Catharine, or gardening with her father while Benjamin played in the dirt nearby. The only thing that woke her from time to time was the ringing of the bell at St. Mary's Catholic Church up the hill.

One Sunday the bell woke her with a start and, try as she might, she could not sink back into sleep. There was a warm drizzle falling, and the dampness of her clothes made her skin itch. She sighed and sat up. The bell stopped, and it was quiet except for the late-summer chirpings of crickets and cicadas.

The service at St. Mary's was over. Soon Hannah and David and the other slaves and free blacks would be going to their afternoon gatherings. Likewise, the white worshipers would be leaving for their own Sunday dinners. Hannah had explained to Ann how St. Mary's was the only church in Rockville where whites and blacks worshiped together, though the whites sat in the pews in the main part of the church and the blacks sat in a tier in the back, up high where no one from down below could see them.

Ann was curious about the church. Too clammy and itchy to sleep anymore, she rose and walked up the hill.

By now, the churchyard was empty. The small white brick building stood quietly. Tall, wide oaks protected the gravestones from the soft rain. Ann ran her hand over one stone. It was rough and caught on her skin.

Suddenly she heard voices. She ran to the edge of the graveyard and lay down in the tall grass. She watched as a white man dressed in religious robes led a white couple into the graveyard.

"Thank you very much, Father Dougherty," said the woman. "I know there must not be many people who make this request."

"I'm happy to do it, Mrs. Fitzgerald," said the priest.

"I figure I'll be resting here soon enough," said the other man. "Might as well be sure I like the location."

"Michael, please don't talk that way," said the woman. "There's no reason to have one foot in the grave already."

"Don't worry, Cecilia. You won't bury me until I'm good and ready."

"Here it is," said the priest.

They talked a little more about how nice the grave sites were, close to the church, under the shade of the grand trees. Mr. Fitzgerald teased his wife about how she'd be joining him there someday, and she shushed him.

When they left, Ann stood up from the

grass and brushed herself off. Something about their conversation had fascinated her. They'd talked about death as "resting." Hadn't that become her one respite from the heaviness of her life? Rest. Sleep.

She glanced over the small collection of gravestones and suddenly felt jealous of the peaceful souls lying under the damp grass. They never had to wake up to sadness or grief or blows from a mistress's stick. She kneeled in front of a headstone and traced the engraving with her fingers. She knew nothing of letters, but the numbers she could read: 1852. The person below her had been dead only two years. What did it feel like to never have to wake up? What did it feel like to rest peacefully . . . forever?

Ann lowered herself to the ground and stretched out on her back with the top of her head against the headstone. She was lying, she realized, just a few feet above the corpse. Could she, too, feel the peace of death? She folded her arms over her chest, to make her body look like those she'd seen at funerals. She lifted her face to the gray sky and closed her eyes. Then she made her breathing as small as she could, and imagined that she was finding eternal rest . . . rest in peace.

She didn't hear the creeping footsteps and she didn't hear the pounding heart. But Ann did hear the terrified scream.

She leaped up from her imagined grave and raced out of the churchyard, quick as a rabbit. She glanced back only once, to catch a glimpse of chestnut arms and legs sticking out of a dress as shapeless and colorless as her own.

Thirteen

The county fair — the event that at one time had made Ann yearn to move to Rockville — came in September and was gone before she even roused in herself enough interest to peer through the gates of the fairgrounds.

On the first chilly night in October the field mice decided it was too cold outside. Ann fell asleep listening to them scurry around the kitchen looking for food. In the morning, when there were holes in the flour sacks and tooth marks in the salt pork, Mistress Carol applied the stick to Ann's shoulders, shouting that if she was sleeping right next to the larder she could at least keep the rodents from ruining their food stores.

In November the banging in the cellar started, with two very dirty, thin-nosed men arriving each morning with hammers and saws, planks of wood and clanking metal. Shortly after that, Master Charles left on a Monday and returned Tuesday night with a sleeping child.

Wednesday morning, Ann was awakened by a small bare foot pushing at her stomach. She groaned and opened one eye.

"I want something to eat." A skinny white girl stood looking down at her. Her nightgown was patched and stained, and there was a thin white crust around one side of her mouth.

Ann sat up and rubbed her eyes. It was still dark outside, and the kitchen was lit only by the moon. Ann sighed, rose from the floor, and went to fill a pot with water to make porridge. So this was Miss Sarah. She was a niece of Mistress Carol's; her mother had died, and so she'd come to live with her aunt Carol and uncle Charles.

The girl positioned herself on a chair at the kitchen table and watched Ann as she prepared breakfast. Her legs were too short to touch the floor, and she swung them. Her face had a pitifully sad look to it. Ann guessed that it was the loss of her mother that had made her eyes sink into dark hollows and her mouth tense at the edges.

"Aunty says you'll do everything I want," she said, and brushed her stringy brown hair away from her face.

Ann had been informed of the same fact. "Yes, miss," she said.

"Miss *Sarah*," the girl corrected. "And I want a glass of water."

Ann brought her the water and, when it was cooked, the porridge. The sky outside began to lighten, and the first carriage went by on the dirt road in front of the house.

"You have to walk me to school."

"Yes, Miss Sarah," said Ann sleepily.

"So put your dress on!" Sarah ordered her.

Ann looked down at her coarse brown shift. "This is my dress," she said quietly. "I don't have a nightgown."

Miss Sarah sniffed.

The school was not far from the house, but it was the farthest Ann had ventured since she'd come to Rockville. The town itself was small, just a collection of houses and farms with a few shops and churches on dirt roads with dirt sidewalks. The muddiest places on the sidewalks had been covered over with boards, for which Ann was very thankful because the thick frosty mud made her bare feet ache. She knew her mother would not approve of the fact that she had not yet wrapped her feet this winter.

The schoolhouse was one room of white-washed pine boards. When Sarah opened the door, they were greeted by a warm blast of air and a stern-looking young man in a gray suit. Both he and Sarah ignored Ann and closed the door in her face.

Ann stood on the front step. In the moment when the door was open, she'd seen the room: wooden seats with several children already sitting, girls on the right and boys on the left. She'd never seen a school before. Unity didn't have one, so Richard had been tutored in reading and numbers by his mother, and he'd hated every minute of it. But Miss Sarah had seemed happy to be going. Ann decided to ask her about it when she walked her home that afternoon.

"Teacher says I'm in the third grade." Sarah tossed her head proudly as she handed Ann a worn gray book and a slate to carry home for her.

"Does that mean you know how to read?" Ann asked as they walked.

"Of course I can read. My mamma taught me that. I can do numbers, too."

"So can I," said Ann.

Sarah's eyes grew wide. "You can read?" she demanded angrily.

"No," said Ann. "I can do numbers. My father is a freeman and he worked for pay, so he knows how to figure coins. He taught me."

Sarah crossed her arms over her chest. "It's a good thing nobody taught you to read," she declared. "It's the worst thing in the world to teach a slave to read."

They walked in silence for a while. Ann had certainly heard how it was against the law to teach a slave to read. But this was the first time she'd heard it while holding a book in her hands.

Just before they got to their house, she opened Sarah's primer to the first page. "If you read so well, what's this?" she asked, pointing.

"That's an 'A,' 'ah,' and that's a 'B.' It sounds like 'buh.' "

"And this one?" Ann turned the page.

Sarah yanked the book out of Ann's hands and glared at her. "Do you want me sent to jail?" she snapped. She marched on ahead and up the front walk to the house.

Ann went immediately to the kitchen to begin preparing supper. She'd been trying very hard to do well in her cooking, to watch the pots so that nothing burned, to use the right amounts of water, salt, and herbs. And for the most part, she'd been successful both in cooking well and in avoiding Mistress Carol's stick. She went outside to the pump and brought in a bucketful of water to start a stew. She placed a chunk of salt pork in a pot and hung it over the fire to sear. Then she fetched potatoes and turnips from the larder and sat down at the table to peel them.

From the living room she could hear Sarah talking with Mistress Carol, telling her about her day at school. As Ann peeled and chopped, she listened. Outside it grew dark, but inside there was the fire and lit candles. There was a cheerfulness in Mistress Carol's voice that Ann had never heard before. She even heard her laugh once or twice.

"Tomorrow I'll braid your hair and put ribbons in it," Mistress Carol said.

"Really?" Sarah clapped her hands. "Oh, please do it now, so I can see."

Ann crossed the kitchen to flip over the piece of salt pork and glanced into the living room. Sarah stood in front of Mistress Carol smiling as her aunt wove her hair into two skinny braids. Sarah held two red ribbons ready to tie at the ends.

Ann stopped and stared. The sight of the red ribbons brought a rush of memory, of her own cabin, the smells of cornmeal mush and fatback, the laughter of her brothers, and her mother's fingers working swiftly braiding Catharine's ebony hair with red ribbons rescued from the Prices' kindling box.

Mistress Carol gave Sarah a kiss on the cheek and a warm hug. Ann suddenly felt the coldness around her own cheeks and arms. There had been no one to kiss, no one to hug, for so many months now. The ache she'd held down for so long began to rise up. She covered her mouth, biting her hand to hold back a sob. It was too late.

She ran out the back door into the frosty air and let the tears come. She closed her eyes tightly and tried to feel, again, the softness of her mother's arms around her, the strength of her father's hug. She'd sworn that she'd never forget, but her memories of them were fading — she couldn't hold on.

She let out a hoarse sob and tried to picture her brothers' faces. But all she could see were the backs of their heads, bobbing as they walked away from her that last dark, muddy morning.

"Come back!" she cried out loud, begging the memories, at least, to stay.

One memory flashed with a vengeance:

Master Charles standing, arms crossed, between her and her parents and Catharine, forbidding them to visit her. "Thief." Her voice tightened with anger around the word. Had he not robbed her of everything she'd ever loved? She clenched her teeth and fists. "Thieves — both of them!" How could they do this to her and her family? How could they sell her brothers, send Benjamin off without a mother, and keep her here as a prisoner, not even allowed to visit her parents and Catharine? She wanted to thrash, to throw something, to hit something *hard*.

The smell of burning salt pork reached her in the backyard. She wiped her face on the hem of her dress and marched up the back steps to the kitchen. Mistress Carol was already there, pouring water into the pot, making great clouds of steam rise into the air.

"You stupid girl! Another precious piece of meat ruined!" Mistress Carol reached for her beating stick.

But Ann was closer. She grabbed the stick in both hands and, with all her might, slammed it against the bricks of the hearth. With a loud crack the stick broke in two. Her hands still shaking with fury, Ann picked up the two halves and threw them into the fire. Then she turned her angry face to Mistress Carol.

Mistress Carol stood there, shocked. Her hands hung limp at her sides and her mouth opened and closed, but nothing came out.

A long moment of silence stretched between them. It was Sarah, frightened and timid, who broke the silence. She tugged at her aunt's dress. "Aunt Carol?" she said, keeping her eyes fixed on Ann.

Mistress Carol looked as if she'd been startled from a trance. "Yes, dear," she said vaguely.

"I have to go to the privy and I don't want to go alone. It's dark out."

Mistress Carol took Sarah's hand, seeming to forget what had just happened, and led her to the back door. Just before they went outside, she turned and addressed Ann, taking on an air of exaggerated authority. "Get a new piece of meat, and see to it that you have supper ready on time. And clean that pot thoroughly — I don't want the stew tasting of burned meat."

After they'd left, Ann stared down at her shaking hands. Where had she found the courage to challenge her mistress, she wondered? Nervously, she ran her hands through her hair, remembering the way Mistress Carol's mouth had opened and closed with nothing to say. So the mistress was not as powerful and unyielding as she seemed. In fact, now with young Sarah to care for and protect from things that might upset her, Mistress Carol might well be less cruel. Ann watched the fire crackle merrily, burning the beating stick. Then she went into the larder to cut a new chunk of salt pork.

Fourteen

Miss Sarah did like to get up early. She was in the habit, each morning, of shoving Ann with her foot to wake her up, the way one might rouse a sleeping dog. It was another of the things Ann was fed up with.

One morning, Ann was already awake when Sarah arrived. She opened her eyes a slit. When Sarah lifted her foot to shove, Ann grabbed it and pulled. Sarah fell squarely on her rump. Her face turned bright red, but she picked herself up and swung her foot way back, ready to kick. Ann snatched Sarah's foot in mid-arc and yanked. Sarah landed even harder. Her eyes filled with tears. She flailed at Ann with her fists. Ann grasped her skinny wrists and wrestled them to her sides.

"Do you want breakfast, Miss Sarah?" she asked her.

Sarah bit her bottom lip, scowled, and nodded.

Ann let go of her wrists. "Then just say so, and I'll hear you and wake up," she said.

That was the last time Sarah tried to wake her with a foot.

Outside, the town of Rockville was settling into the dark days of winter. Smoke curled from every chimney, and the first light snow fell. But inside, Ann felt herself coming back to life. It was as if her thoughts and body had been clouded by a thick fog since she'd come to Rockville, and only now was the fog clearing. And the first thing she wanted to do was go to church with Hannah and David.

"Just do what everyone else does," said Hannah that first Sunday. Ann sat in the balcony, crowded in with the other slaves and free blacks. The smell of wet wool mixed with the incense Father Dougherty burned on the altar below. The low winter light gave a soft glow to the pastel greens, pinks, and blues of the stained-glass windows lining each side of St. Mary's. Ann copied Hannah as the churchgoers kneeled, stood, and crossed themselves.

Because Father Dougherty performed the service in a language Ann could not understand (Latin, Hannah explained), she simply closed her eyes and allowed the lilting of his voice, the responses of the worshipers, and the pungent smell of incense to carry her thoughts to a peaceful place. She remembered times with her mother and father, Catharine and her brothers, and little Benjamin, and though tears ran down her cheeks and splashed onto her woolen shawl, she felt a sweet calmness inside.

She could have stayed in that delicious place forever, it seemed, but a commotion behind her distracted her.

"That's who I saw. I know it is," a girl whispered.

"You're crazy, Edmonia. Now hush," came a man's quiet voice.

"I'm getting out of here. It's a curse!"

Ann turned to see who was whispering. A young man was looking directly at her. He had bronze skin, round, bright eyes, and a full lower lip that made him look as if he were pouting. When he saw her glance at him, he broke into a grin. The little girl next to him hid her face against his sleeve and tugged urgently at his arm.

It was time to stand, and Ann turned around to face forward.

"Edmonia, be *still*," she heard a woman say.

Father Dougherty gave the blessing, and when all the amens were said, Ann followed Hannah and David down the narrow stairway and outside into the cold sunshine.

"You come on over for Sunday dinner, Ann Maria," said David.

But before Ann could accept the invitation, the young man from the balcony came toward her, dragging the little girl.

"You leave me be, Alfred! It's a curse — now you let go my arm or I'll bite you!"

"Edmonia, we're going to talk to her and you'll see she's flesh and blood."

"Noooooo!"

Edmonia flailed like a chicken stuck in a fence while Alfred held on to her. "I'm Alfred Homer," the young man told Ann over the noise of Edmonia's cries, "and my friend here would like to talk to you." As he said the word "talk," he yanked Edmonia sternly.

The little girl hid her face against Alfred's chest. She stopped struggling and said nothing.

Ann assumed the girl was a halfwit and Alfred was trying to teach her some manners. "Good morning, Edmonia," she said politely.

Edmonia didn't answer.

136

"She thinks you're an apparition," said Alfred in a hoarse whisper, as if the girl plastered against his chest couldn't hear him. "She's got a mind full of stories. Says she saw you dead in the graveyard a while back."

Ann gasped. So this was who saw her.

"She doesn't mean you any insult by it," Alfred continued, "I just want to show her you're no apparition and she didn't see you in any graveyard."

Ann looked away, ashamed. "She *did* see me in the graveyard," she said softly.

Edmonia started to wail. Alfred whistled.

"But I'm not dead!" Ann shouted over the wailing.

Edmonia peeked at Ann with one eye.

"I'm flesh and blood, just like you, and I am sorely sorry that I scared you."

The little girl peeked with both eyes. "You *looked* dead," she said.

Ann squirmed. "I know," she admitted. "But I was just . . . sad."

"Ann Maria, are you coming?" Hannah called as she and David started toward home.

"Yes," Ann answered. She reached out her hand for Edmonia. "Here, see? This is no ghost hand."

Edmonia examined Ann's hand and touched it gingerly. She smiled.

Alfred was smiling, too. "I'm pleased to meet you, Miss Ann Maria . . ."

"Weems," said Ann.

Alfred nodded, and Ann ran to catch up with her cousins.

Fifteen

Each morning Ann walked Sarah to school, and each morning she caught a glimpse of the schoolroom before the door shut in her face. Sometimes she stood outside under one of the windows, trying to hear what the teacher was saying. But the windows were closed tight against the cold, and the teacher's voice was usually too muffled for her to understand much.

Ann's spirit was buoyed by the fact that Christmas was only weeks away. She had not forgotten Master Charles's promise that he would write her a travel pass to visit her parents.

One particularly cold day, a carriage was parked in front of the Prices' house when Ann returned from walking Sarah to school. She hurried up the steps. If there was to be company for the noon meal, she'd better start cooking right away.

Inside, she heard loud voices coming

from Master Charles's study.

"Seven hundred is the most I can offer, Mr. Price."

"I will accept nothing less than sixteen hundred. And now that my niece has grown attached to her, even sixteen hundred may not be enough."

The door to the study opened, and Ann froze, caught eavesdropping in the hallway.

"Mr. Bigelow, I will thank you to leave my house, as you were instructed not to come here in the first place."

When the two men saw Ann, they stopped in mid-stride. Then Jacob Bigelow smiled at her and attempted to act as if there were nothing strange about the situation at all.

"Good morning, Miss Ann Maria," he said, bowing slightly.

Ann stared hard at Mr. Bigelow. She had not yet decided within herself whether the man had brought blessings or trouble to her family. To her, certainly, he'd brought trouble.

"Your parents send their love," he said. "Your sister and new baby brother send love as well, and we have *not* given up trying to buy your freedom from your master."

Ann startled, both at the news and at

how glad she was, suddenly, that Jacob Bigelow had come to call.

"I'll not have you talking to her!" Master Charles blocked them from each other and began to push Mr. Bigelow toward the front door.

Mr. Bigelow was forced into backing up, but he continued talking in a jovial tone: "Your father said to have your cousin David bring you at Christmastime. They are living at 422 New Jersey Avenue."

"Stop it! Stop this, I say!" Master Charles was red in the face and waving his arms to try to block Mr. Bigelow's words.

Ann stood, enraptured.

"Your father has a good job unloading boats on the docks in Georgetown. Your mother takes in sewing. Catharine is attending school and minds the children of a neighbor in the afternoons. . . ." By now Mr. Bigelow was having to shout to be heard, he'd been pushed so far out the door.

"Stop this, or I will send for the sheriff at once!" Master Charles gave him a hard shove, and Mr. Bigelow nearly fell down the front steps. Master Charles came back inside, slammed the door, then scowled down at Ann for a moment before returning to his study.

Ann ran to the door and flung it open. Mr. Bigelow was climbing up into his carriage.

"What is his name?" she called.

"Whose?" Bigelow asked.

"My new brother's."

"John Junior, after your father. His first son born into freedom." He took the reins in his hands. "Shall I send them your love?" he called.

"Yes!" Ann laughed and waved as Mr. Bigelow tipped his hat to her and drove off.

Ann started as a firm hand gripped her shoulder. Master Charles pulled her back inside. He shut the door again and blocked it with folded arms and a stern glare.

Ann lowered her head and retreated to the kitchen. But nothing could wilt her joy. As she shoveled ashes out of the hearth and swept the kitchen, she smiled and hummed. New Jersey Avenue, number 422. She would not forget it.

And that afternoon when she stood outside the schoolhouse waiting to retrieve Miss Sarah, she thought to herself, *Lucky, lucky Catharine.*

Sixteen

The first group of them arrived just before Christmas. Ann's own hopes had already been dashed: Master Charles had refused to write her a pass to visit her family over the holidays. He said he didn't trust "that abolitionist Bigelow" and would not let her out of his sight.

That was when they came, with their own dashed hopes. They were connected to each other by chains around their necks. Some, with every step, left the snow tinged with blood from cracked and torn feet.

Master Charles spoke with the white man who'd led them there. Money exchanged hands. And then the group of two men, a woman, and one young girl — who looked to be a little older than Ann — was herded into the cellar through the outside flap doors.

"I don't like this, Charles," Mistress

Carol said that evening as Ann served supper.

"Once again, my dear, you know nothing of business. Clients must be able to contact me here as well as in Baltimore."

"I know what the ladies in this town think about your *business*," Mistress Carol said. She wiped her mouth, but after her napkin had passed the look of contempt was still there.

Master Charles laughed harshly. "Of course. They own slaves, and they trust their husbands to buy them, but they hate the one who sells them. What hypocrites!"

There was uncomfortable silence at the dinner table. Sarah ate quietly, her eyes on her plate, and Ann returned to the kitchen.

She'd heard Master Charles speak of his "business"; she knew he traveled to Baltimore almost every week, and often to Alexandria. But she had not suspected what was now apparent: he had become a slave trader.

After dinner Mistress Carol folded some bread into a napkin and told Ann to take it to the cellar, along with a bucket of water. Ann opened the cellar door, balancing the bread and bucket in one hand and a candle in the other. As she stepped down the dark stairway, her shadow moved on the wall like a ghostly dancer. The cellar smelled of mildew and rotting potatoes.

She heard whispers coming from the back corner, then "Shhh," then silence. She lifted the candle above her head and saw, first, the feet. Some were bare, some wrapped in rags, but all were shackled around the ankles with chains.

Ann blinked and shook her head, not wanting to believe what she saw. The thin-nosed workmen had not been repairing broken steps or mending a crumbling foundation. They had attached chains and shackles to the walls, and in the corner they'd installed a whipping post. She stood motionless. The group sat on the cold, damp floor without a single blanket among them.

"What've you got there? It smells good," one of the men said finally.

Ann dropped to her knees and began to break the bread into four portions. "It's not much," she said. "Tomorrow I'll bring you a good breakfast, whether they tell me to or not."

"Much obliged, miss," said the woman, her mouth full of bread. Her face was broad under a white head wrap. "This here is Richmond, and Theophilus, and this is Martha, and I'm Nancy," she said, and then set into a frightful fit of coughing. Ann offered her a dipper full of water and it eased her cough.

"Do they feed you decent here?" asked Theophilus. His hat was pulled down low, and he looked as if he'd be tall and lanky if he stood.

"Most times," Ann answered.

"That's good," said Richmond. "My old master, down in North Carolina, name of Jesse Moore, didn't hardly feed us. He's as bad as they come — couldn't be any worse to be alive." He stuffed his mouth hungrily. He reminded Ann of Joseph, with his bright eyes and quick movements. Sickeningly, she realized that all three of her brothers might have been chained in dark basements like this one on their way south.

"My master wasn't too bad," Theophilus was saying, "but he hired me out to Master Houston. Master Houston was a hard man. If you didn't eat breakfast before daybreak, he'd drive you out in the field to work all day with no breakfast at all."

Ann saw that the bread had nearly disappeared in two mouthfuls. She wished she'd thought to save part of her own supper to smuggle to them.

"Master Cahell, he fed us good," said Nancy. She pulled her shawl more tightly around her shoulders. "And I grew sweet potatoes and fried them up on Sundays."

They passed the bucket of water, and each used the ladle to drink.

Nancy leaned forward and glanced around furtively. "Anybody here ever run away?"

Richmond gave a quick laugh. "I runned once, a few years back. With a master like Jesse Moore, a man can hardly not think of running. He cured me of it good, though." He rubbed his feet and winced.

"How long'd you stay away?" Theophilus asked.

Richmond grinned. "Four months. Best four months of my life. I lived in the swamp and ate better on squirrels and berries than I ever ate at Master Moore's place." He leaned his head back against the wall, remembering. "And I was *free*."

"What happened?" Ann asked, not sure she wanted to know.

Richmond shrugged. "The hunters finally catched me. When Master Moore got hold of me, he whipped me a hundred lashes. My back was tore up, and the blood running, and he took his knife and slit both my feet clear to the bone, here and here." He pointed to the underside of his arch and the back of his ankle, above the heel. In the dim light Ann could see raised scars. Her belly quivered at the thought of the pain.

Richmond continued, "Then he took that old knife and stabbed me with it, in my arms, my legs, my chest, my stomach. The blood was running everywhere, and do you know what that man did? He sent me to the barn to shuck a pile of corn!"

"Lord have mercy!" Nancy cried. "It's a miracle you lived."

Theophilus nodded solemnly. "A miracle," he echoed.

"I'm glad he sold me," said Richmond. "Can't hardly be a man worse than Master Moore."

Ann felt queasy and shaken. "I hope you get a better master," she said very softly.

"I do, too, miss," said Richmond. "I do, too."

Theophilus nodded and helped himself to more water. "I hear if we get sold in Maryland or Virginia it's easy to go north from here," he said.

Nancy shook her head. "I've lived in Virginia all my life, and wasn't nothing easy to get away from there."

"But I hear sometimes folks can help you," said Theophilus. "Quakers and such."

"Mmm-hmm," said Nancy. She raised her eyebrows and puckered her lips. "And sometimes those folks get theirselves in *big* trouble. Did you hear about that white man, name of Seth Concklin, tried to help a family from Alabama to freedom?" No one had, so she continued: "He was carrying them on a boat up the river toward Canada. They got all the way to Indiana. That's where the slave catchers got 'em. The family, they told the authorities they'd been kidnapped and they got sent back to their master in Alabama without any trouble. But do you know what they did to the white man?"

Everyone shook their heads.

Nancy lowered her voice. "They found him floating in the river with his hands and feet in chains and his skull crushed."

"Lord!" Ann whispered. She felt the blood drain from her face. "They didn't even give him a trial?"

Theophilus tapped the tips of his fingers together. "Sounds to me like they gave him his trial, his verdict, and his sentence all right there on the riverbank."

"And his grave," Nancy added sadly.

The candle flickered and hissed. Footsteps clattered on the floor over their heads, and Ann wondered if someone would be calling her soon.

Nancy sighed heavily. "Well, I am not glad to leave my old master, and I would not have run away, either. I'd have given anything to be able to stay with my mother and brother and my husband and my baby." Her voice broke and she held one hand over her mouth for a moment. "But as soon as Master Cahell died, the mistress got it in her mind to start selling, and with me being so sickly and no good in the fields, she decided she'd rather not have me around to feed." She sniffled and wiped her nose on her shawl.

Ann felt a tightness in her chest. *I've left my whole family, too,* she wanted to say. But she was afraid if she tried to speak she would only cry.

Martha had not yet spoken. She sat listening, her eyes fearful, her thin fingers laced around her knees.

"What about you, Miss Martha?" asked Theophilus. "Did your old master treat you all right?"

"I have no 'old master,' " said Martha quietly. "I have always been free, living in Downingtown, Pennsylvania."

A hush came over the huddled group.

"Why are you here, then?" asked Ann.

"Three white men came to my house in

the night. They lifted me from my bed and carried me out. I screamed and screamed, and my father fought them, but they threw him to the ground and took me away in a carriage. They sold me to the man who brought me here. I tried to tell him I'd been kidnapped, but he said he'd paid good money for me, and it didn't matter."

"How horrible!" Ann exclaimed.

"That ain't right," said Richmond.

"It's against the law," said Nancy.

"And not a one of us can help her," said Theophilus. "Unless a white person testifies, it doesn't matter what crime a black person, slave or free, has seen."

The door to the cellar creaked and Sarah's timid voice came from the top of the steps. "Aunt Carol says it's time for you to put me to bed."

Ann rose quickly and picked up the candle. Then, thoughtfully, she placed the candle back on the dirt floor. She had no blankets, no meat, no key to unlock their chains, and no hopeful words for them. The least she could do was leave them with light.

Later that night, as Ann fell asleep, through the floorboards she heard Martha weeping.

Seventeen

Nancy, Theophilus, Richmond, and Martha left the next morning. Master Charles loaded them into his wagon the way he used to load sheep when he still had the farm. Under the folds of their clothes they carried the extra bread Ann had smuggled to them. And she'd promised to pray for them. She could do no more than that.

She offered up prayers for her own life, too: That soon Master Charles would relent and allow her to visit her family. Maybe for the Independence Day holiday. Maybe for Christmas next year. That Jacob Bigelow would return, despite Master Charles's threats, to bring her more news of her family. And that one day Master Charles would say yes to Mr. Bigelow's offer to buy her from him.

But for now, there was *this* Christmas.

"You will spend the holidays with us, won't you, Miss Ann Maria?" Alfred shifted from one freezing bare foot to the other and blew into his hands. Around them, the other churchgoers hurried toward the warmth of their homes. The naked limbs of St. Mary's oaks stretched out overhead.

Ann squinted up at him, into the low December sunshine. His face was earnest, and the sparkle in his eyes reminded her of Joseph. He couldn't be much older than Augustus, she thought. "I won't be going anywhere else," she said. Her lack of a holiday traveling pass was something all the colored folks from the church had heard about.

"Aw, come on, Miss Ann Maria. It won't be so bad. You'll have fun with us — we'll be your family."

Ann smiled at his generous offer.

Alfred flashed her a grin and ran to catch up with Edmonia, Thomas, Elizabeth, and the other slaves from Dr. Anderson's place. Here in Rockville, so many of the slaves lived in their owners' houses, sleeping in attics and cellars and on kitchen floors, that there were very few choices of slave cabins in which to celebrate the Christmas holidays in peace and privacy. Dr. Anderson was both a doctor and a farmer; he held eight slaves, and provided slave quarters a distance away from his own home. Here was where Ann and Hannah and David were all invited to feast and enjoy themselves during their holiday week.

"I think Alfred has taken a liking to you," said Hannah, putting her arm around Ann.

"Me? Naw," said Ann. Still, she felt herself blush.

"What do you think, David?" Hannah poked her brother. "Has Alfred taken a shine to Ann Maria?"

David snorted. "Alfred's got no time for girls. He never has, and he never will."

Hannah rolled her eyes. "Men don't know *anything*," she whispered to Ann.

On the last day before the school holidays, Ann stood outside the schoolhouse, waiting to walk Sarah home. She wondered what Catharine's schoolhouse looked like. Did boys sit on one side and girls on the other? Did Catharine have her own slate and chalk, and even her own primer? Ann moved closer to the door, straining to hear what was going on inside. With her ear pressed to the white-painted door, the schoolmaster's voice became clear.

"You must not neglect your lessons during the holiday," he was saying. "You must study every day so that you will not all have become imbeciles by the time you return. Do you understand?"

"Yes, Teacher," the children answered in unison.

"If you have younger brothers and sisters," he continued, "teach them what you have learned. The best way to learn something is to teach it."

"Yes, Teacher," came the response.

"All right, then. You may go."

Ann quickly moved away from the door. But in the moments she'd spent eavesdropping, the seed of an idea had been planted.

"Teacher says I'm a very smart young lady," said Sarah, swinging her braids as she walked.

"Mmm-hmmm," said Ann.

"And he told Nathaniel that he's the stupidest one in the class," she continued proudly.

"That can happen to anyone," said Ann.

Sarah gave her a sideways look. "It can not."

Ann shook her head. "What do you think will happen if the other children study their lessons over the holiday, and you just play with your paper dolls? Even old Nathaniel will be smarter than you when you go back to school."

Sarah scowled. "He will not!" she objected.

"He might be," said Ann.

A flicker of worry passed over Sarah's face. "Then I'll study more than anybody," she said with conviction.

"But your teacher said — I mean, it's supposed to be good to *teach* somebody else, not just study," said Ann.

"But my little brother is still with my papa, so I can't teach him. I have no one to teach."

Ann took a breath. "You could teach me — but not teach me to read," she said quickly, before Sarah could object. "There's no law against teaching letters. You could teach me my letters, and that would keep you smart." Ann crossed her fingers, waiting for Sarah's response.

Sarah eyed her suspiciously. "Just your letters. I wouldn't teach you any reading at all, right?"

"Right," Ann assured her.

Sarah looked at her gravely. "You'll have to do all your lessons perfectly, or I'll rap your knuckles, just like Teacher does."

Ann returned the grave look and nodded.

"We'll work at it every day, and by the time school starts again I'll be the smartest one in the class!" Sarah took off running down the frozen dirt sidewalk.

Ann wanted to shout out her exuberance. Instead, she walked briskly after Sarah, her face placid, as if she had not just launched a most exciting plan.

Christmas Day the smells were the same: a turkey and several chickens roasting over an open fire pit, and pan bread baking indoors. The sounds were similar: David on his banjo and Thomas on his harmonica making their lively music fill the tiny cabin. But the feelings were very different. Last year Ann had been so happy, with her whole family together, and all the cousins and aunts and uncles making her own cabin ring with music and laughter. This year she felt like an outsider looking on, wishing she were in Washington City instead.

"Evening, Miss Ann Maria." Alfred scooted up next to her where she sat on a bench.

"Alfred, come help me flip this turkey over before it burns crispy!" Elizabeth called from outside.

Alfred held up one finger. "I'll be right back," he told Ann.

"Ann Maria, help me fetch more water. These folks will be powerful thirsty once we start eating." Hannah pulled her up from her seat.

Outside, the smells of fire and cooking meat swirled in the chilly air. Ann followed Hannah to the pump.

"You see, Alfred does have his eye on you," said Hannah with one raised eyebrow.

"He only said hello," Ann objected.

"We'll see if he does more than say hello when we go back," Hannah challenged with a smile.

They each carried a bucket of sloshing water back to the cabin. Inside, more musicians had joined in, and Edmonia was dancing around the center of the floor with little Eliza on her hip.

"How did you disappear so fast?" Alfred asked when he found her. "I was beginning to think maybe Edmonia was right about you being an apparition!"

Ann tipped her head down and smiled.

"You're still in time for a dance." He said it with a question in his eyes, and waited for her to accept or reject his offer.

Ann glanced quickly at Hannah for advice.

"Oh, go *on*." Hannah gave her a gentle shove.

Alfred took one of her hands in his and slipped his other hand around the small of her back. He drew her into steps and circles and the rhythm of the song, until they were both out of breath and laughing, and Ann felt dizzy and light-headed.

The dizziness could have been because of all the circles. Or maybe it was because they hadn't eaten yet and she was very hungry. But it might also have been because Alfred's face and eyes and breath so close to hers, and his hands, holding her in the dance, made her heart beat faster than anyone's heart should beat, really.

Sarah always waited until Mistress Carol had gone to do the marketing or visit with the ladies in town. Then she would interrupt whatever Ann was working at and say, "Hurry up now, it's time for school."

Ann gladly left the floor half scrubbed or the fireplace half shoveled out, wiped her hands on her apron, and joined Sarah and her primer. Sarah was a mean schoolteacher. She kept a ruler handy, and if Ann gave a wrong answer, she rapped her sharply on the back of the hands. It stung, but the hardest thing for Ann was to keep from laughing as scrawny, pale little Sarah worked to sound just like her own short-tempered schoolmaster.

Sarah taught her her letters, the sound each one makes alone, and the sounds two or three make together. Ann practiced the sounds out loud, and drew the letters on Sarah's slate with a piece of gray chalk.

By the time the school holiday was ready to end, Ann had mastered the alphabet. She promptly complained to Mistress Carol that she was suffering from the cold, sleeping as she did on the drafty floor. She asked if she might line her bed with Master Charles's discarded copies of the *Baltimore Sun* newspaper. The mistress agreed.

At night, after everyone had gone to sleep, Ann lit one solitary candle. By sounding out the letters and joining the sounds together to make words, she began her painstaking study of reading. She was awestruck when the print, which before had been just black marks, began to take on meaning.

Wanted — The advertiser, who is a Protestant, with a wife and no children, wants a situation as a gardener and farmer.

Wanted — Cooks, Chamber maids, Nurses, and girls for General Housework. Catholics and Protestant. Apply at Mrs. Clancy's.

Wanted — One hundred able bodied young men (unmarried) between the ages of 18 and 35 years, for the United States Dragoons and Mounted Riders, to go to Oregon, New Mexico and Texas.

Eighteen

The cold winter months should have felt dead and dreary. The days were short and dark, and last year's garden lay muddy, with shriveled brown vines hanging from toppled stakes. But Ann had, each frozen, bleak day, a strange and stubborn feeling of springtime. Perhaps it was because of her newfound ability to read, which improved every night as she worked with the newspapers. Reading gave her a sense of freedom, as if she'd discovered a doorway into a new world, and because no one knew she could read, the doorway was her own secret.

The feeling of springtime might also have had something to do with Alfred. He had begun to meet her whenever he could on her walks between the Prices' house and the schoolhouse. Master Anderson trusted him with marketing and running errands, and whenever Alfred could manage to make their paths cross, he did.

Sometimes he would arrive at her side, breathless, with just a few moments to spare, to give her a handful of the mushrooms he'd found growing in the barn or to tell her the sorrel mare was going to foal in the spring. Other days he would walk leisurely with her, carrying a package from the post office or a sack of grain from the feed store. He always began by asking how she was faring that day. Then he would ask her about Unity and her family. Ann told him about sliding around the frozen pond with her brothers the winter before, and Alfred laughed out loud. "We'll have to try that on the Rock Creek — if it ever freezes," he said.

She told him about gardening with her father and Catharine, and how they grew pole beans as fat as a man's finger. Alfred said, come spring, he'd show her where to buy the best seeds for her garden. And he said he'd bring her up some manure, too, seeing how the Prices had no cows or chickens.

By the time Ann had told Alfred all about her family — every one of the funny stories, and most of the sad ones — she began to feel as if he'd been there in Unity with them, as if he were one of them. She smiled when she thought of how, before

Christmas, he'd said, "We'll be your family."

Ann wasn't exactly sure what gave her this unexplainable feeling of springtime right smack in the middle of winter, but she suspected that reading and walks with Alfred both had something to do with it.

Finally, real springtime came and the earth turned warm and soft. Ann went with Alfred to the Braddocks' store and exchanged the coins Mistress Carol had given her for an armful of small packages of seeds.

"Are you going to dig up that whole yard?" Alfred asked, his eyebrows raised.

"Most of it," Ann said proudly.

She was very happy to be putting in a real garden, not just a late garden like last year. She turned the sod over in great clumps and greeted the wriggly earthworms. She dropped the seeds into neat rows and covered them carefully. And when she hoed the ground into little piles and placed three or four corn kernels in the center of each mound, she whispered, "I'm thirteen years old now."

Alfred whistled when she told him. "Thirteen. I suspect you'll be getting married soon."

"I will not!" Ann was horrified.

"Don't be mad at me, Miss Ann Maria. Mistress Anderson was just saying how she married the master when she was fifteen and how they'll find the right husband for Miss Julia now that she's turned fifteen. That's what made me think it."

Sarah tugged on Ann to hurry up. The day was sunny and smelled of newly plowed earth.

"Fifteen is different from thirteen," Ann said simply.

Alfred nodded. "I can wait," he said.

Ann stopped walking and stared at him.

"Come on, Ann," whined Sarah. "You can't get married anyway, so stop jabbering about it."

Ann wasn't sure whom she was angrier with — Alfred for suggesting she get married, or Sarah for reminding her that by law she couldn't — but she felt like smacking both of them.

"We could get married," Alfred objected, "if we both got permission from our masters."

"Not in a church, you couldn't," said Sarah. "And you wouldn't be allowed to live together. Not like me. I'm going to have a long white gown, and my papa will find me a rich man to marry —"

"Stop it!" Ann shouted. "Stop talking, both of you." Her voice trembled. "I'm *not* getting married. I'm thirteen. I don't want to hear any more about it."

Alfred excused himself abruptly, saying he'd better get on to the post office. Sarah and Ann walked the rest of the way home without saying anything more about weddings.

It was over a week before Alfred ventured into the schoolyard to see Ann again. He carried a sack of groceries which, Ann suspected, Mistress Anderson was waiting for. Sarah had gotten involved in a game of tag with several other children, and since Mistress Carol was always happy to have Sarah out of the way in the afternoons, Ann had decided to stay and let her play.

"Miss Ann Maria, do you intend to hit me if I try to sit with you?" Alfred asked, giving her a sheepish look.

Ann tried to make her face cross, but a small smile broke through. "Just once or twice," she said.

Alfred put the sack down and joined her on the grass. "I want to apologize for what I said when I saw you last. I had no right to speak of marriage so soon." He kept his eyes cast down.

Ann felt herself blush. What did he mean, "so soon"? Did he really have thoughts about marrying her? She'd convinced herself that the other day he had simply been joking with her, and then arguing with Sarah over laws and principles.

"But I hope," Alfred continued, "that when you turn fifteen, maybe we can talk about it again."

Ann's eyes bugged out and she turned her head away to hide her astonishment. So David was wrong about Alfred having no time for girls. "Maybe we can," she said softly.

Alfred traced the outline of her fingers where they rested on the lush grass. She lifted her hand and he grasped it in his. His hand was warm, and she didn't want to let it go.

Alfred changed the subject and started into the easy conversation that had become so natural between them. He told her that two of the sheep had just lambed, and she should come see the sweet woolly creatures before Master Anderson slaughtered them for Easter dinner. She told him about her garden, and how the radishes were already sprouting. All the while he held her hand, until Sarah presented herself in front of them, sweaty and dirty and out of breath.

"Miss Sarah, would you like to see a brand-new baby lamb?" Alfred asked.

Sarah gave him a bored look. "My father has a whole herd of sheep. I've seen more new lambs than you have, I bet."

"And I still appreciate them every spring," said Alfred. "And . . . I'm late with Mistress Anderson's groceries. I thought if you both come with me, she might not notice."

Sarah rolled her eyes. "Oh, all right." She wiped the sweat off her forehead with her apron.

They walked down Jefferson Street until they came to the Anderson house. Elizabeth ran to meet them. "The mistress is in a fit!" she cried. "Did you walk all the way to Gaithersburg to buy these?" She whisked the sack out of Alfred's hands. "Quick, run to the far field and set to work. I'll try to calm her."

But before Alfred had run two steps, Master Anderson appeared on the porch. "Stop right there, boy," he commanded.

Alfred stopped and turned. Ann's throat tightened.

"I'll teach you to take advantage of my kindness," he growled. "Thomas! Thomas, come here."

Out of the barn came Thomas. He was

older than Alfred, broad-shouldered and very dark. "Yes, Master?" he said. His voice sounded calm, as if he knew nothing about what was happening, but his face told Ann that he'd heard the whole thing and knew full well what he would be commanded to do.

"Tie this boy up, Thomas. And give him thirty lashes. That should teach him to keep my wife waiting." Dr. Anderson adjusted his spectacles, crossed his arms over his narrow chest, and waited for Thomas to obey.

"Master, please . . ." Alfred pleaded.

Thomas grabbed Alfred by the wrists and, though he struggled, overpowered him. He tied his hands together.

"Master, I won't be late again. Please don't whip me!" Alfred cried. He winced as Thomas cinched the rope tighter around his wrists.

"Get on with it," Dr. Anderson ordered impatiently. Then suddenly he noticed Ann and Sarah.

"You, girl." He pointed to Ann. "Get that child out of here."

Ann stared at him, unable to move.

Sarah wriggled her hand free from Ann's grasp. "Ouch, you're squashing me," she complained. "The man says we have to leave." She pulled at Ann's arm.

But Ann felt paralyzed. Her mouth had gone dry as sawdust.

"I said, Get that child out of here!" Dr. Anderson bellowed.

Sarah yanked on her, and Ann felt herself move as if she were swimming through molasses. They started back down Jefferson Street. Ann saw a thicket of bushes that ran in a line toward the barn they'd just left. She pulled on Sarah to duck into the bushes with her. Sarah resisted. "What if someone catches us?" she demanded. She looked a little scared, but also very curious.

"They won't," said Ann, tugging harder.

Sarah followed, saying, "If we get into trouble, I'm blaming it all on you."

They crept along the shrubbery until they were just behind the house and barn. From there they could see and hear everything.

Alfred was already tied, arms outstretched over his head, to a willow tree. Thomas went into the barn and came out with a horsewhip.

"Thirty lashes, you said, Master Anderson?" Thomas asked.

"Yes," he answered, then turned on his heel and went back into the house.

Thomas stood back from where Alfred hung. He raised up the whip and let it fly. It cracked, shattering the still air, and Alfred cried out. One.

Thomas raised the whip again; again it cracked. Alfred moaned. Two.

Ann covered her face. Each snap of the whip jarred her body. Three. Four. Alfred's cries grew louder, more pitiful. Five. Six.

Ann wanted to scream, but the cracking of the whip continued. Seven. Eight. Nine.

Ann heard footsteps and peeked between her fingers. It was Elizabeth, running from the slave quarters toward the barn. She was carrying a pot. Salt water for the gashes, Ann thought.

Crack. Ten. Eleven. Alfred began to moan more softly. Fourteen. Fifteen. Ann held her ears and huddled on the ground. She stopped counting and simply wished for it to be over.

After a time she heard Dr. Anderson's voice from the house. "Thomas, you're going to kill that nigger."

"I've done twenty-five, Master Anderson. You want me to stop now?" Thomas asked.

"No. Go ahead and finish," came the answer.

The last five crisp cracks sounded in the

air. Alfred's moans were faint now. Elizabeth ran to him. Ann looked up to see Elizabeth's hands covered in crimson as she applied the contents of the pot to Alfred's back.

They cut the ropes that held him, and Elizabeth and Thomas dragged his almost lifeless form toward the cabin.

Ann felt the blood drain from her face. Blackness crowded the edges of her vision. "I've got to know if he'll live," she whispered to Sarah.

Sarah's eyes were wide with horror. She simply nodded.

Afraid to stand and be seen, Ann crept along the line of bushes until it ended at the bottom of a little hill. Then, crouched low, she ran as fast as she could to the cabin.

She stood for a moment outside the closed door, terrified of what she would find. She wiped tears from her cheeks and put out her hand to push the door open. Then she heard Alfred's voice.

"Thomas, you are one lousy aim, you know that?"

"Sit still, Alfred." That was Elizabeth. "I'm going to clean this up whether you want me to or not."

"Look who's calling me a lousy aim!"

That was Thomas. "Last time Master told you to whip me, you hit me three times. I call *that* lousy aim."

"Three times no harder than a feather. You hit me — Ouch! Elizabeth, are you cleaning that cut with red pepper?"

Ann's hand remained in midair, next to the door latch. Then, bracing herself, she lifted the latch and opened the door. All three faces turned to her.

Her cheeks were muddy with dirt and tears, her hair was tangled with twigs from the bushes she'd been crawling through, and her eyes were red and wild.

"Miss Ann Maria, I thought you'd gone home!" Alfred exclaimed.

Ann shook her head and took in the scene. Elizabeth stood behind Alfred, a bloody rag in her hand. Alfred sat at the table, his shirt off and the skin of his back stained a clear red. Thomas sat across from him. Although Alfred's back bore the raised scars from past whippings, there was only one place from which he was bleeding: a cut near his right shoulder blade.

"Oh, my Lord, did you watch, Ann Maria?" Elizabeth asked.

Ann nodded.

"How was my performance — pretty

good?" Alfred grinned.

"You sounded like a dying pig, if you ask me," Thomas chided him.

"Will you two hush?" Elizabeth cried. "Can't you see the child is scared half to death?"

Alfred's face fell. "Miss Ann Maria, you thought . . . You didn't know. . . ." He rose from his chair and wrapped his arms around her.

Ann rested her cheek against his chest and sobbed. He was alive and barely hurt. For that she was more thankful than he could know. How they had done it, she still didn't understand.

He held her until she'd quieted. He smelled musky, and a little bit sweet, like berries. That's when she noticed the crushed raspberries in a pot on the table.

"Old Master Anderson, he's more than a bit shortsighted," Thomas explained. "And he doesn't have much of a stomach for whippings, either."

"He usually goes in the house," said Alfred. "So me and Thomas, we practiced and practiced on a tree one spring, cracking that whip just an inch or two away, but not touching it."

"And they put on a show," said Elizabeth, "crying and yelling like cowards, just to make sure the master thinks there's a whipping going on."

"He can't tell the difference between blood and raspberry jam even with his spectacles on," said Thomas. "I wonder what his patients would think if they knew!"

They all laughed, including Ann.

"Where's the white child?" Elizabeth asked suddenly, running to the door and looking around.

"She's up the hill," said Ann. "I need to go to her. She was scared, too." She sniffled and wiped her nose with the back of her hand. "I'll tell her you're all right. But I won't tell her quite how much you look and smell like a raspberry pie."

Alfred tickled her side playfully. "And I won't tell anyone how many of those bushes you're wearing on your head."

Ann reached to pull a twig from her hair, and he caught her hand and held it. It was the memory of the look he gave her then, his round eyes soft and smiling, that she took with her as she left.

Nineteen

There was no travel pass from Master Charles for Independence Day. The summer days grew humid and sticky, with clouds of gnats that swarmed around Ann's head and sometimes got stuck in her eyes. Master Price began to bring groups of slaves into the cellar of the house more frequently. Ann guessed this meant his business was picking up. She had learned, after the evening she'd spent with the first group that passed through, to keep a distance from the slaves. If she talked with them and allowed herself to get to know them, her heart would break each time. So she kept a store of pilfered food in a special hiding place in the larder, and smuggled it to the cellar to supplement the bread Mistress Carol gave her. And she said prayers for each group that passed through. But she never again listened to their stories.

With school out for the summer, Ann

missed her walks with Alfred. Sunday became their one precious day to spend together. On one particularly hot and gnatty Sunday, in the churchyard after services, Alfred asked her, "Miss Ann Maria, will you come to the Rock Creek with me? I'm going to wade and dangle my feet in that nice cool water."

As Ann opened her mouth to say yes, she heard a man deliberately and loudly clear his throat behind her. She swung around and found herself face to face with Jacob Bigelow. He looked as if he would have liked to disappear behind the lilac bushes.

"Miss Ann Maria, I need to have a word with you," he said in a hoarse whisper, "before your master has me arrested for 'mingling with the Catholics' or some other such trumped-up charge."

Ann looked from Mr. Bigelow to Alfred and back again. To Alfred she said, "It's Mr. Bigelow, the man who helped my parents. Will you wait for me here?"

She followed Mr. Bigelow to the side of the graveyard, where tall boxwoods and chirping insects gave them privacy.

"I've offered your master eight hundred dollars for you, and he has again refused to sell you." He looked down at Ann Maria somberly. There was sweat clinging to his bushy sideburns, and his collar looked too tight. "I've come to ask you this: Do you want your freedom — even if we have to steal it?"

Ann's stomach lurched. Images from the gruesome stories she'd heard flashed in her mind. "But they do horrible things to runaways when they catch them. . . ." she whispered.

Mr. Bigelow took out his handkerchief and wiped his face. "We will take great pains to prevent you from being caught. And we will take precautions to protect you if you *are* caught," he said.

Another image crept into Ann's mind — that of Seth Concklin lying dead on a riverbank, his hands and feet in chains, his skull crushed. "But what about *your* safety?" she blurted out.

Mr. Bigelow smiled slightly with surprise. "I am happy to hear of your concern for me, my dear. But you wouldn't be the first slave I've helped find freedom illegally, and you won't be the last. If I'm caught, you needn't feel responsible."

Ann was still reeling from the suggestion, and realized she hadn't yet answered his question. But he had more to tell her.

"I can offer you help to escape to freedom," he said quietly. He rubbed his chin and looked at her sadly. "But I cannot offer you a life with your parents and brothers and sister."

Ann let out a small whimper. What was he saying?

"As a fugitive, you could be hunted anywhere in the States. We'd have to send you north to Canada. I believe you have relatives there."

Aunt Mimi and Uncle William! They'd sent word that the town they lived near was named Dresden. She hoped she'd be able to find them. But how would she ever see her family again if she ran so far away? And suddenly a new thought tugged at her heart: how could she move so far from Alfred?

"You must tell me, Miss Ann Maria," — Mr. Bigelow ducked his head to better see into her eyes — "if you want your freedom under these circumstances. Shall I give you some time to think on it?"

Ann wanted to say, "No, I'll stay here." Stay with what she knew. Stay where she hoped to be allowed to visit her parents soon. Stay close to Alfred and where she knew she would not be putting her life or Jacob Bigelow's life at risk. Stay . . . *in bondage for the rest of her life*. She tossed her head to shake away the temptation. "I do want my freedom," she said. Her voice sounded neither strong nor convincing, but she knew she'd spoken the truth. "No matter what the circumstances."

Mr. Bigelow hesitated, as if giving her a chance to change her mind. "You understand everything I've told you?" he asked. "And you are sure?"

She closed her eyes and nodded. "I'm sure," she whispered.

Mr. Bigelow gave her shoulder a squeeze. "We will do all we can to keep you safe, Miss Ann Maria. For right now, this is what you must do: forget that we have spoken. Forget what you have said to me today."

Ann wiped tears from her cheeks and nodded very slightly.

Mr. Bigelow tipped his hat, as if they'd just been discussing the weather, and bade her good day.

"Miss Ann Maria, are we going to the creek or not?" Alfred called to her.

Ann quickly put on a smile and joined Alfred, who saw right through the fake smile.

"Did that man upset you?" he demanded. He glared angrily at Mr. Bigelow's carriage as it drove past, carrying him away. "I'll have his hide!"

"I think I just got a gnat in my eye, that's all," she said, hoping to deflect Alfred's worry. "Can you get it out?"

Alfred peered into both of her eyes, pulling at the lids and looking very concerned. "Any man ever says a rude word to you, white or black, you let me know and I'll fix his wagon," he muttered as he worked to find the nonexistent gnat.

Ann pulled away and blinked. "I think it's out. Thank you." This time her smile was real.

"Can we go wading now?" he asked. "I'm hotter than a smoked pig."

They walked up the Baltimore Road straight to where it crossed over the Rock Creek on a rickety wooden bridge. They scrambled down to the creek. Ann waded in up to her calves, lifting her dress a bit to keep it dry.

"Look at you, trying so hard to act like a lady," Alfred chided her. He plodded into the creek, trousers and all, and sat down.

"And look at you, acting like a hog in the mud!" she exclaimed.

He splashed her delicately. She splashed him back, and before she could move away, he yanked her hand and she went toppling into the water with him.

She stood up, dripping and with more

than a few dead leaves clinging to her dress. "Alfred, look what you've done!" she cried.

"I've cooled you off, that's what I've done," he said with a grin.

Ann gave an exasperated sigh and began to wash a patch of mud off the hem of her dress.

"I'll help," he offered, and moved closer so he could pick the dead leaves off her back and skirt. She slapped his hand away.

Alfred climbed up on a flat rock in the shade and wrung out his shirt and trousers as best he could while still being in them. Once Ann had cleaned most of the creek mud off her dress, she joined him. Alfred's playfulness had lifted her spirits, and the heaviness of an hour ago, when she stood in the churchyard deciding to leave everything she'd ever known, seemed far away. Suddenly, instead of feeling terribly sad at the thought of leaving Alfred, she grabbed onto a hopeful idea.

She peered into the woods around them, and listened carefully for sounds of anyone on the Baltimore Road. When she was sure they were alone, she spoke. "If I ever have the chance to leave here, would you come with me?" she asked.

"Is Master Charles up and leaving already?" Alfred shook his head as if he didn't believe it. "But you just moved here."

"I don't mean move away with the Prices," Ann said very quietly. "I mean run. Run north to freedom."

Alfred put his hand over her mouth and hastily looked around. The woods were alive with the sounds of summer insects, and the creek rippled over rocks nearby, but there were no other human sounds. His eyes softened and he brushed her cheek with his fingertips. He put his mouth close to her ear. "I will never leave here without you, Miss Ann Maria," he whispered. "And please don't you leave here without me."

She closed her eyes and felt the nearness of his breath. "I won't," she promised. When Mr. Bigelow came again to tell her how she would escape and when, she would make sure Alfred was included in the plans. They would run together.

That evening, as Ann prepared to fall asleep in her usual place in the corner of the kitchen, she heard Master Charles and Mistress Carol arguing in the next room.

"I don't trust the man," said Master Charles.

"That's nonsense. He's a lawyer and a law-abiding citizen," said Mistress Carol.

"Believe me, he hasn't given up yet. I want her where I can see her."

Ann sucked in her breath. Someone must have reported to Master Charles that she'd been talking to Mr. Bigelow in the churchyard.

"Very well, then." Mistress Carol stomped into the kitchen and ordered Ann to gather up her blanket. "You're coming with me," she said, and pushed Ann in front of her toward the door.

All the way up the steps Mistress Carol gave her sharp shoves. When they'd reached the master bedroom, she pointed to the corner of the floor. "There. He wants you where he can see you, so now I'll have no privacy."

Ann simply looked from the floor to Mistress Carol, not comprehending.

"Are you deaf or just stupid?" Mistress Carol clenched her fists. "Go to bed, you wretched girl. Once again, you're causing me more trouble than you're worth!"

Trembling, Ann moved to the corner of Master Charles and Mistress Carol's bedroom and lay down. She pressed herself against the wall, as far away from their four-poster bed as she could get, and wrapped her blanket around herself. She turned her face away and squeezed her eyes shut as she heard Master Charles undressing and getting into bed. He was already snoring when Mistress Carol padded in and joined him some time later.

Ann stared at the ceiling and listened to the loud rumble and snort of Master Charles's snoring. She didn't think she'd ever be able to get to sleep. And she certainly wouldn't ever be able to get away.

Twenty

Ann carefully loosened the soil and pulled out a clump of beets. They were plump and blood-red, with long crisp greens on their tops.

"I could win that dollar if they'd let me enter these," she said aloud to herself.

She put the beets in her basket and loosened another clump. She'd read in the September 11 *Montgomery Sentinel* that there would be prizes for the best vegetables: cabbage, squash, potatoes, turnips, carrots, and, she'd read with special interest, beets. Ann had never seen beets as big and round and red as the ones she grew.

"I could sign you up when I sign up for the plowing contest," Alfred offered when she told him.

Ann sighed. "Mistress Carol says she's not a farmer anymore, and she'll not have me bringing her garden goods to the fair."

"Then come watch me plow, and we'll have a good time anyway. Master Anderson says if I win the race for him, he'll split the two-dollar prize with me. Then I'll share it with you." He smiled so sweetly Ann forgot all about the produce contest for the moment.

The county fair was something of a controversy at the Price household. Mistress Carol said it was loud, smelly, and dirty, which was true, and because the fairgrounds were so close to their house, the noise and dust came right in their windows. She also complained about the evils of the gambling that went on at the fair — the betting on the races. So when Miss Sarah got it in her mind that she wanted to attend the fair, and put on her meanest pout and performed her loudest tantrum, it created quite a problem. Her uncle had no interest in going and her aunt had no intention of being seen around all that gambling and farm produce. That was when Ann stepped in and offered to take Sarah. She pointed out that since children and slaves were not charged the twelve-and-a-half-cent admission fee, it wouldn't even cost anything. That made everyone happy.

The farmers began arriving from all over

Montgomery County with their wagons full of hams, quilts, pies, and preserves, and their best livestock grunting and mooing, squawking and bleating, and — this was the part Mistress Carol disliked the most — dropping manure on the road directly in front of the Prices' house.

Also arriving were the carriages carrying city folk from Washington City and Georgetown. If they brought something to enter in a contest, it was usually a lady's fancy needlework or homemade perfumed soap. But they came to see what the farmers brought, listen to the speeches and the marching band, watch the races and cheer with the crowds, and, of course, bet on the racers.

The night before the first day of the fair, Ann lay awake listening to Master Charles snore. How Mistress Carol could sleep with all that racket, she couldn't understand. She heard the floorboards creak and looked up. Miss Sarah was standing over her in the blue-gray darkness.

"I can't sleep," whispered Sarah.

Ann sat up. "The problem is your eyes. They're afraid to close because they don't want to miss anything," she explained.

Sarah nodded, admitting it was true.

"Tell your eyes the fair won't start until

the sun comes up, so as long as it's dark they should stay closed."

"All right," said Sarah, and she trotted back to her own room.

Five minutes later she returned.

"My eyes won't listen to me," she said.

Ann lifted the side of her blanket. "Here."

Sarah snuggled in beside her. "Will we go as soon as we eat breakfast?" she asked.

"We can go as soon as they open the gates," said Ann.

Sarah clapped her hands and Ann shushed her. Master Charles snorted, shifted in bed, and then resumed snoring at a slightly lower pitch.

"Can we stay all day?" Sarah whispered.

"Yes, we can stay all day," Ann assured her.

Sarah sighed and rolled over, kicking Ann in the process. "I think I can go to sleep now," she said.

"Good."

Ann expected her to get up, but a few moments later she found herself cramped against the wall, with a sleeping Sarah hogging most of the blanket. Ann groaned and tried to find a comfortable position. It didn't really matter, she told herself, because the snoring would keep her awake anyway.

★ ★ ★

She must have dropped off to sleep finally, because it was barely dawn when the moaning woke her up. Sarah's knee pressed into the small of her back reminded Ann that she was sharing her bed, and made it clear where the moaning was coming from. She shook Sarah awake. "You're having a bad dream," she whispered. Fortunately, Sarah had not awakened her aunt or uncle. "Go back to sleep," said Ann.

For a while Sarah looked as if she would do just that. Then her eyes sprang open. "Today is the fair!" she shouted.

There was no sleeping for anyone after that.

Ann had never seen so many people, animals, and flies gathered in one place at the same time. Skinny boys in mended britches chased each other through the mud and dung. Ladies from Washington City in crisp dresses carried parasols and walked arm in arm with men in dark suits. Farm women, both white and free black, in worn gingham, their sleeves rolled up, unloaded hams and homemade fabrics from their wagons. Sweaty-faced men in overalls led sheep and turkeys, oxen and cows, the biggest and the best, to their pens to compete for the coveted blue ribbon.

At about ten o'clock a marching band struck up, and though they were sorrowfully out of tune, they gave the whole place a feeling of Christmas and the best summer Sundays combined.

Miss Sarah wanted to see everything and everyone, so Ann was obliged to be led around from cake table to quilt table, from hog pen to goat pen. Sarah met friends from school, and Ann saw folks from church, and by the time the plowing contest was ready to begin, Ann was very happy to flop down under a shady poplar to watch.

Alfred had only just arrived. He greeted her briefly before taking his place in the field with his team of two horses. He had his own section to plow, and would be judged on speed and the straightness and depth of the furrows he made. Competing against him was Jeoffrey, plowing for his master, Mr. Julius West.

"Come on, Alfred. You can win this!" Ann heard someone shout. She turned and saw Thomas waving his arms.

"Go, Jeoffrey," several men yelled.

The gun was fired, and the horses lunged forward. Alfred took off down his first furrow, his plow splitting the earth like a storm. His bare feet slipped as he marched through the great clods of broken earth.

The crowd cheered, some for Alfred, most for Jeoffrey. Ann saw a man in a top hat slip a handful of paper money to a man with a cigar hanging from his pale lips. *Gambling,* she thought with fascination.

Jeoffrey had pulled out ahead.

"Go, Alfred!" Ann cried. Then, embarrassed, she covered her mouth and glanced around to see if anyone disapproved of a girl shouting. But everyone was cheering and waving, including the ladies in fine dresses. "You can beat him, Alfred!" she yelled as loud as she could.

But Jeoffrey had a large lead. His horses snorted as his plow cut through the earth straight to the end of the marked-off section of ground. Alfred still had a whole furrow to complete.

"I wanted to win that dollar for you," Alfred told Ann when the race was over, wiping sweat off the side of his face with a muddy hand. "I'd have bought you some ice cream."

Ann and Sarah stared at each other, their eyes wide. "Ice cream?" they both asked in unison.

"Didn't you see Mr. Boyle's stand? He'll be making the first batch soon."

Ann could hardly stand still as she waited for Alfred to wash his hands and face at the pump.

"Soda water! Ice cream! Step right up!" Mr. Boyle stood under a canvas awning with glasses and spoons laid out on an overturned crate. He collected money from ladies in silk dresses and men in top hats. Once he'd loaded his pockets with coins, he pulled out a wooden bucket with a hand crank on top, and set it on the crate. He poured cream and sugar into the bucket, cracked a couple of eggs into the mixture, and stirred it briskly. Then he chipped pieces of ice from a great block that stood melting in a bed of straw nearby. Ann touched the ice with two fingers. How amazing, she thought, that a piece of frozen pond could last from winter all the way into September in the icehouse.

Mr. Boyle mixed the chunks of ice with salt in a compartment around the edges of the bucket. Then the cranking began. Mr. Boyle turned the crank himself for a while, then offered up the job. "I'll do it!" Alfred took the crank in his strong hands and spun it until a boy from Sarah's school whined that he wanted a turn. When the boy was tired, Sarah insisted on having a try. She strained, her skinny elbows sticking out like chicken feet, but she could hardly move the crank. Mr. Boyle laughed and took over.

When at last the cranking was done, Mr. Boyle opened the bucket. What had been, a little while before, a soupy, sloshy mixture was now icy thick custard. The small crowd oohed and aahed. Those lucky enough to have paid their money eagerly reached for glasses filled with ice cream.

Ann, Sarah, and Alfred watched the delicacy disappear into the mouths of the ladies and men. It smelled sweet as fresh molasses, and it made Ann's mouth water just to watch.

"I wish Uncle Charles had given me a nickel," said Sarah dreamily.

"I wish I'd won that race," said Alfred.

By the time the first batch was eaten, Mr. Boyle had attracted quite a crowd, and he immediately began collecting the next round of ice cream money.

Ann sighed. "Let's eat lunch," she said.

They found a shady spot and opened their basket. They shared their bread and apples with Alfred, who said he wasn't hungry and didn't need anything, but then devoured everything Ann gave him.

"I want another apple," said Sarah, and opened the basket. But when she reached inside, she pulled her hand back and grimaced. "What are these dirty old beets doing in here? Did you expect me to eat them raw?"

Ann quickly closed the basket. "The apples are all gone," she said. "We can get more at home later."

But it was too late. Both Sarah and Alfred were looking at her, waiting for an explanation.

"Did you see the sorry-looking vegetables on those tables?" Ann blurted out. "They've got lumpy old potatoes, and carrots that look like shriveled-up fingers. And the beets — they're so small the judges will have to put on spectacles just to see them!"

Alfred leaned toward her. "Let's go put yours on the table and show them what real beets look like."

"No." Ann pulled up a sprig of grass and shredded it with her thumbnail. "I'm not signed up, so I can't enter the contest."

But Alfred and Sarah were already on their feet, the basket between them.

"I can't enter without Mistress Carol's permission," Ann objected.

The other two were on their way to the

produce tables. Ann sprang to her feet and followed. "It's not allowed . . ." she called to deaf ears.

"You pretend you're studying what's there," Alfred was telling Sarah, "and when I see no one is looking, I'll quick pull them out the basket and slip them onto the table."

Sarah nodded, her eyes twinkling.

Ann leaned against a table of baked goods, hoping no one would think she was part of the mischief going on at the produce table. She hid half her face with one hand. A moment later, Sarah and Alfred ran to her, laughing and victorious.

"You have to come see," said Sarah, breathless.

Reluctantly, Ann let them lead her to the table where prize beets lay like red and green jewels. Each entry had a tag with a name tied to it. Each, that is, except one. And that one, judging by size and roundness and deep red color, should, by all rights, be the winner.

Ann grinned. She knew her "entry" would be disqualified, and no prize money would come her way, but inside she felt as proud as if she'd won. The next thing that happened caught her completely by surprise. Alfred slid his hand onto the back of her neck, leaned over, and kissed her. His soft mouth left the sweet taste of apples on her lips.

Sarah giggled, and before Ann knew whether to feel embarrassed or annoyed or happy, Alfred took her hand and dragged her toward the speaker's podium. "They're going to start one of those talks where half the words are so highfalutin you wonder if he's speaking Latin like the priest," he said.

The Honorable Andrew Stevenson, a statesman of Virginia, was just being introduced. "Ladies and gentlemen," Mr. Stevenson began, "the Agricultural Society of Montgomery County, Maryland, has not only nobly accredited the wisdom and patriotism of its founders, but has spread over the whole state a new zeal in favor of agricultural improvement and high farming, and added fourfold to the productions of the greater portion of the cultivated lands of Maryland. . . ."

Sarah tugged on Ann's skirt. "Who's that?" she asked.

"Some statesman from Virginia," said Ann.

"Not him, *him*," said Sarah.

Ann looked to where Sarah was pointing. Her eyes met the steel-blue eyes of a grimy-faced man standing several yards away.

"He's staring at you," Sarah whispered.

Ann could see that, and when the man saw her look directly at him, he broke into a brown-toothed grin. He ran a dirty hand through his shock of blond hair, turned away to spit a stream of tobacco juice onto the ground, then turned his gaze back to her.

Ann's stomach churned.

"Do you know him?" Sarah asked.

"Of course not," Ann said crossly. "Let's go home. *Now*."

"You promised we'd stay all day," Sarah whined.

"We *have* stayed all day!" Ann informed her. She bade a hasty good-bye to Alfred, and dragged Sarah toward the fairground gates. As they left, Ann kept glancing behind. She was relieved to see that the strange man did not follow them.

That night, lying awake as usual, Ann's thoughts buzzed with the excitement of the day. She wasn't sure what was more at fault in keeping her awake — Master Charles's snoring or her memories of Alfred's gentle kiss — but she longed more than ever for the quiet of her kitchen corner. Fortunately, Miss Sarah had given her an idea.

Soon after Mistress Carol came to bed, Ann began to moan, at first softly, then louder. She kept it up until the mistress sat bolt upright and announced, "Wake up this instant!"

Ann stirred, pretended to awaken, and asked sleepily, "Yes, Mistress Carol? Shall I get you a glass of water?"

"No," she answered angrily. "Go back to sleep."

Ann waited until Mistress Carol's breathing slowed in sleep; then she started the moaning again.

This time the mistress got out of bed and shoved Ann with her foot. "I don't know what you children ate at that fair today, but it is causing the most wretched nightmares. Pick up your blanket and go back to the kitchen."

Ann happily gathered her bedding and tiptoed down the steps. In the peaceful quiet of the kitchen, she fell asleep.

Later that night, Ann was awakened by the sound of the floorboards creaking. She sighed. Miss Sarah must be suffering from excitement again, she thought. She was not pleased with the prospect of sharing her bed. She didn't even turn over, but waited for Sarah to come to her.

The soft footsteps approached. Suddenly there was a thud beside her. A large hand came down against her mouth. Her breath caught in her throat.

"Don't make a sound or I'll knock you over the head to keep you quiet," a man's gravelly voice whispered in her ear.

Terror seized her. Ann could not move to struggle as the man hoisted her over his shoulder like a dead possum. Stealthily, he opened the back kitchen door and carried her down the steps. He need not have told her to keep quiet: panic had frozen her voice. He threw her into a carriage, banging her head on its door in the process, and tossed her blanket in after her.

"Stay hidden under that blanket, do you hear?"

In the moonlight she'd seen who he was. It was the man from the fair.

She heard reins slap against a horse's back and felt the carriage move beneath her. The horse's pace changed quickly from a walk to a trot to a canter, and the rickety carriage bounced and bumped over the rutted road. Under the blanket, her breath came in short, tight bursts.

As the road sped by under the carriage wheels, she felt herself disappearing. There would be no trace, no way to find her — just a sad message sent the next day to all who cared: Ann Maria Weems was kidnapped last night.

Twenty-one

The carriage traveled for hours, and in that time Ann managed to calm herself enough to think. If she jumped from the coach, she would either be mangled by the wheels or, if she managed to run, easily caught by her captor. If she simply obeyed his orders, she would be taken to a slave pen somewhere, sold for his stolen profit, and passed on south where no one from Maryland would be able to track her down. She had made the difficult choice between remaining a slave near Alfred and her family or living free far from them. But to be held as a slave far from those she loved — that would be too much to bear. She decided that, even though she might be killed in the attempt, she would wait until the carriage stopped and then try to make her escape.

The sound under the wheels changed, and Ann realized they must have entered a city. They had left the dirt road and the wheels now rattled over cobblestone. She peeked out from under the blanket and saw the eerie light of gas lamps. Though she'd never been there, it seemed the place must be Baltimore. Could this man be stupid enough to bring her to the city where her own master did his slave trading? If she could only slip away and hide, surely she could find Master Charles before a week had passed.

She touched the lump on her head. She hoped she would not be too dizzy to run. The carriage slowed and turned. Once again the sound under the wheels was of dirt. There were several more turns, and the horse slowed to a walk. Ann tensed, like a lion ready to spring.

The horse stopped. In an instant, Ann threw off the blanket and grasped the handle of the carriage door. But the man had leaped so quickly from his seat, he was already standing over her.

"I told you to stay covered!" He threw the blanket over her head and lifted her in it, his arms tight as a vise around her chest.

Ann's mouth bumped against something bony — his shoulder? She opened her mouth wide and, blanket and all, bit him as hard as she could.

The man yelped and dropped her. She

landed on her rump and struggled to get untangled from the blanket. He grabbed her again and, this time with no blanket to cushion him, she bit down on his arm.

A door opened and a slice of yellow light brightened the dark street.

"Help!" Ann cried.

But the blanket came down over her head again.

"Are you mad?" It was another man's hushed voice. "The constable patrols this street every hour all night!"

"The wench bit me!"

Ann found herself being held tightly by two pairs of strong hands.

"Just get her inside."

She heard a door shut and as it did, her heart sank. She was trapped.

"You've scared her half to death, is what you've done."

"I got her here, ain't I?" came the voice of her captor.

The blanket was lifted off her head. A hand grasped hers and helped her to her feet. She blinked, uncomprehending. She was standing in the foyer of a narrow row house. One candle flickered on a table nearby. In the dancing light she saw the stubbly face of the tobacco-chewing man from the fair. He was calmly picking his teeth. When she turned to see the other man who'd helped him drag her inside, she let out a yelp and stepped back, her hands covering her mouth. It was Jacob Bigelow.

"Welcome to my home," said Mr. Bigelow.

Ann took in a sharp breath. "You're . . . I mean . . ." She pointed to the other man. "He's . . ."

Mr. Bigelow smoothed her sweaty hair away from her forehead. "There will be time for explanations," he said. "Are you in one piece?"

She nodded.

Mr. Bigelow handed the man a fat wad of paper money. "You got her here safely. Now be off before the constable comes by to find out why there's a brawl going on in my foyer at three a.m."

The man tipped his hat to Ann and slipped out the door.

"I apologize for his conduct," said Mr. Bigelow, "but often it's only the roughest sort who are willing to do such risky work. And I'm sure you understand why we had to do it this way."

Ann screwed up her face. "I don't think I understand anything," she said, bewildered.

Mr. Bigelow helped her to a chair in the

parlor, carrying the candle with them. She sat stiffly and uncomfortably. It was the first time she'd ever sat in a parlor.

"We had to steal you from your master this way," he said.

Ann felt a quiver go from her throat to her belly as it dawned on her what had actually happened this night.

"You see —" Mr. Bigelow adjusted his spectacles. "If you'd known that you were escaping, you would not have played the part so convincingly. But as it was, if you'd been taken up by the sheriff, what would you have told him?"

"That I'd been kidnapped!"

"Exactly," said Mr. Bigelow. "And you would have been returned to your master without harm or suspicion."

Ann's eyes widened as the plan began to make sense.

"And if anyone has seen you, the rumor mill will serve us well. You were not seen running away. You were being carried away against your will."

Ann rubbed the bump on her head — what a small price to pay for a clean escape! "Thank you," she said. She held her hands together toward him in a gesture like prayer. "Thank you so much."

Mr. Bigelow pressed his fingertips together. "Ah, yes," he said. "A lawyer by day, a lawless kidnapper by night. It's a wonder I get any sleep at all."

There was the sound of footsteps in the street. They stopped briefly outside the door, then moved on.

"That's Sergeant Orme on his patrol," Mr. Bigelow said quietly. "I'd better show you to the guest quarters now."

He led Ann into the hallway and, with one wiry eyebrow raised, pointed to the ceiling. "There you are," he said. "The most comfortable lodging in town for kidnapping victims."

The candlelight flickered and Ann squinted at the place where he'd pointed. All she could see was wide ceiling boards that fit tightly together. Was he playing a joke on her?

Mr. Bigelow hummed as he opened a nearby closet and pulled out a ladder. Then he climbed up and pushed carefully on the ceiling. Ann's mouth dropped open as a piece of the ceiling lifted up and he slid it aside.

"Up you go," he said, stepping down off the ladder. He gave her the candle.

Ann climbed up until her head entered a stuffy, attic-like room. She lifted the candle and saw a pitcher of water, a dish of corn bread, a straw mat and quilt, and a chamber pot over in the corner. She looked down at Mr. Bigelow. "No one will know I'm here!" she exclaimed.

"My thoughts exactly," he replied.

Ann scrambled up, then lay on her stomach to peer down before closing up the opening. "May I know his name?" she asked. "The man who brought me here?" He had given her several hours of terror and a rather large bump on her head, but he had, in fact, been her savior. She wanted to remember him.

Mr. Bigelow rested one foot on the bottom rung of the ladder. "The Powder Boy," he answered. "He takes both gunpowder and fugitives on his sailing vessel. Of course, that's not his real name, but that is how he's known on the Road — and since you are now a passenger on the Road, that is how you should know him."

The Powder Boy. She would never forget. She looked quizzically at Mr. Bigelow. "The road?" she asked, shaking her head slightly.

"The Underground Rail Road. You have just begun to ride it, my dear. I am one of the conductors, and this is your first stop. It runs all the way to Canada."

Canada. She felt the quiver run through

her again. She could not turn back now. And Canada was so far away.

They said good night, and Ann slid the ceiling boards back into place. They fit perfectly. The hiding place must have been built, she thought, like a hidden closet behind one of the upstairs bedrooms.

When she blew out the candle, the room went quite dark. Her stomach had been through too much this night for her to eat the corn bread, but she drank thirstily from the pitcher. The air was hot and close. Sweat dripped down her neck as she lay on the mat. Her heart pounded in her ears with a new rhythm — one she'd never heard before. It said, "I'm free, I'm free, I'm free. . . ."

Twenty-two

When Ann awoke, she saw light leaking in through a small opening at one end of the narrow room. It wasn't quite as hot as it had been the night before, and when she peeked out of the hole, she saw why. Great storm clouds covered the sky. She ran her finger over the edges of the hole. It had been roughly chiseled from the wall, large enough to let in a little light and air but small enough so as not to be detected from the street below. She was not the first fugitive to be hidden in this secret room.

The hole gave her a bit of a view. Down below was a dirt road, much wider than the streets in Rockville. As she watched, a horse and carriage passed by, then a boy herding a small group of cows, then a chicken squawking as if it had lost its way. Across the road was a two-story frame house with a neat yard, but on either side of the yard, as far as her peephole would let her see, grew tall grass and brambles. And out there, somewhere beyond the brambles, was her family's home. Now that she was so close, she longed more than ever to see them.

Her stomach growled and she remembered the corn bread. It sat on a dainty blue and white china dish, with a line of ants happily serving themselves. Ann brushed the ants away. "That's mine," she told them.

As she ate the corn bread and drank from the pitcher, a loud crack of thunder startled her. The rain started with a few drops pattering, then grew quickly to a torrent. It reminded her of nights in the sleeping loft back home in Unity, when late-summer storms would blow through the cabin, leaving puddles on the floor and making the roof sound as if it would fly off at any moment. She smiled, remembering how it was always Joseph, the youngest, who would tell the rest of them not to be afraid of the storm.

Thunder cracked again, but farther away this time. The rain settled to a constant thrumming. The room soon cooled, and the sound of the rain comforted her. She lay back down on her mat. By now they would know she was gone, she thought.

Master Charles would be furious, no doubt, to find he'd been robbed. And Miss Sarah would want to know who would walk her to school and who would cook her breakfast now. Ann wondered if Mistress Carol would simply be relieved, and demand that her husband buy her some experienced household help for a change. Whatever they were thinking and feeling, they felt far away from this snug attic room, which was so removed from the rest of the world.

After what seemed like hours of looking up at the ceiling, she drifted off to sleep. It was dark again when she heard a door open below. "Miss Ann Maria, are you there?" asked Mr. Bigelow.

Where else would she be? she wondered. "Yes," she answered.

She heard knocking and fumbling as he set up the ladder. "I'm sure you're ready for a good meal," he said as he helped her down. "And I must apologize, because you won't get one as long as you rely on me as your cook."

Ann smiled. "The corn bread was fine," she said.

Mr. Bigelow shook his head. "Baked by the wife of a good friend, and all gone." The curtains were drawn, and the small sitting room was lit by an oil lamp. "I would employ servants, but I'm afraid any one of them, white or black, might be tempted to turn in a fugitive to collect the reward money. And so I manage on my own. Let's see what I have in the kitchen."

He led her to the back of the narrow house and began rummaging through his cabinet.

"Cabbage," he said, pulling out a wilted bundle of pale leaves. "There should be no one searching for you for a little while, as the newspaper ads won't appear for a few days yet. Carrots, though they're sprouting lovely flowers and they're rather brown." He plopped the vegetables on the table. "So you might as well get a bath and a hot meal, because once the ads are out you'll be in hiding round the clock. Turnips. They've gone mushy. But I did pick up a nice piece of beef on my way home." On the table he placed a brown-paper parcel with blood leaking through at the edges. He sighed. "But when I get through cooking it, it will be tough and stringy, I guarantee."

Ann eyed the package. Fresh beef was something she'd seen only when a cow was slaughtered on the farm in Unity, and it was not something that was ever shared with the slaves. "I could make a good stew," she offered.

"Nonsense. You're a guest, not a servant."

Ann squinted, not sure she'd heard him correctly. Her, a guest of a white person? It was all so new, and she'd been so bored lying up in her room all day; she was anxious to have something to do, and longed to put her hands to the familiar rhythms of her old work. "I'd like to cook," she said.

Mr. Bigelow finally agreed to her offer, admitting that they'd both get a better meal that way. But he insisted on helping. Ann had to hold back a smile as he rolled up his shirtsleeves and prepared to chop vegetables. She'd never seen a man cook before, and here was a white man, dressed in a fine suit, ready to make stew. She thought he looked as out of place as a goat in a henhouse.

As they chopped, Ann worked up her nerve to ask the question that had been on her mind ever since she'd learned she was in Washington City. "Will I see my family soon?"

Mr. Bigelow kept his eyes cast down at the turnips he was hacking at. "That's a delicate matter," he said slowly. "You can't go to them. The home of a colored person can be searched any time of the day or night without a search warrant. If they were to come here, that would raise suspicion about my involvement with your disappearance; then you, and I, would be in danger."

Ann felt herself crumple inside with disappointment.

"But I know how much it means to you." He stopped working and looked directly at her. "I will work out a way if I possibly can."

Ann fought against a lump in her throat. Might she really have to travel on to Canada without seeing them? She let out a ragged sigh. She'd known how dangerous the whole journey would be when she told Mr. Bigelow yes to the escape. She would see her family in heaven if she could not see them before then. It was little comfort, but she forced herself to accept it.

As if to take her mind to other thoughts, Mr. Bigelow began to explain more of his plans for her. "I thought it best not to take you across the Mason-Dixon Line — that's the border between the slave states and the free states — until after all the uproar about your disappearance has died down. So you'll be my guest for a while."

Ann looked up from the chopping board

where she was slicing the beef into chunks. "How long?" she asked.

"Weeks, at least. Possibly a month or two. We'll have to see how much fuss Mr. Price makes over you."

Ann ducked her head over her work so Mr. Bigelow wouldn't see the look of dismay on her face. Months of lying in that stuffy room, staring at the ceiling? She hadn't counted on freedom being so . . . so *boring*. She clenched her teeth and resolved to get through it without complaint.

As if reading her mind, Mr. Bigelow said, "Once things have settled down somewhat, you'll be able to come down for meals and such." He looked apologetic. "To tell you the truth, it's the first time I've had to keep a child hidden for so long."

Ann rose and dropped the meat into the pot hanging in the hearth. It sizzled loudly. "I'll be fine," she said as lightly as she could. She stirred in water, the vegetables, salt, pepper, and sage, and put on the lid to start the pot boiling.

Mr. Bigelow brought paper, pen, and ink into the kitchen. He lifted the pen high into the air and, in a tone of mock formality, announced, "And now I must draft a letter to your former owner, offering him that sixteen hundred dollars he was demanding for you."

Ann let out a tiny gasp. "Just to frustrate him?" she asked, amazed.

"Yes," said Mr. Bigelow. He dipped his pen into the ink. "And to throw him off a bit." He drew the pen across the paper in graceful, curving lines. Ann watched carefully. She'd only ever printed on a slate with chalk. The quill pen and paper fascinated her, as did Mr. Bigelow's flowing cursive.

"When he set the price for you so high, we would have liked to simply pay the cash and skip all of this dangerous mess," Mr. Bigelow explained as he wrote. "But the Vigilance Committee cannot give in to the exorbitant prices slave owners demand when they know a person's freedom is at stake. If we did, we would open ourselves up to blackmail, we'd soon be paying five thousand dollars a head, and our stores of money would be exhausted in no time."

Ann stirred the bubbling stew. She pictured Master Charles reading the letter offering him $1,600 for her, and exploding in anger because he no longer had her to sell. She couldn't help letting out a laugh.

"Did we make funny stew?" Mr. Bigelow asked.

Ann giggled some more, covering her mouth. "No," she said. "I think we made good stew."

After a delicious dinner, Mr. Bigelow dragged a bathtub to the middle of the kitchen floor and hung a pot of water in the hearth to boil. "I hope you'll excuse a gentleman for preparing your bath, but, as you can see, I have no wife to do the service."

Ann didn't mind.

"And here is a change of clothes, which has been waiting for you for quite some time." He handed her a parcel.

Ann untied the string, folded back the paper, and held up the first item of clothing. It was a sunflower-yellow dress with a white collar, tiny white buttons down the front, and a sash around the waist. Her mouth hung open in awe. It was made of smooth cotton — the kind of cloth white people and free colored people wore — and though it was well worn, the yellow was still vibrant. She could scarcely believe it was hers to wear.

There was also a long white nightgown of cotton so soft Ann touched it to her cheek to feel its smoothness. There was a slip to go with the dress, and a pair of bloomers, which she tucked discreetly back into the paper wrapper. All of the clothing was neatly mended and patched, and freshly cleaned. At the bottom, wrapped in another layer of paper, were black stockings and a pair of black shoes with laces all the way up the front. She crinkled up her nose. Everything else was a dream come true, but she didn't like the idea of stuffing her feet into something so stiff and tight as a shoe.

"Those are all things that Catharine outgrew," said Mr. Bigelow.

Ann's heart leaped. Her hands began to shake. She hugged the parcel to her chest, then buried her nose in it and inhaled. The smell was of her mother's soap, the stitches in the mending were by her mother's and her sister's hands, done as they sat by the fire with her father. And Catharine had been the last one to make this dress move with grace. These clothes would help her feel their presence even if she could not be with them.

Twenty-three

The days of coming down from the attic for meals were short-lived. Within the week, runaway notices appeared, Mr. Bigelow told her, in the *Montgomery Sentinel* and the *Baltimore Sun*. The reward offered was $500, and the city was crawling with slave catchers looking for her. Mr. Bigelow handed food and water up to her in the hidden room, emptied her chamber pot, and spoke with her briefly in the evenings when he came home from his job as a lawyer for the Washington Gas Light Company.

Then one evening, Ann heard a pounding on the front door and a man's angry voice declaring that he had a search warrant and was here to find that "blasted Weems girl." Mr. Bigelow greeted the man as "Sergeant Orme" and calmly invited him to have a look around. Ann listened from her hiding place, scarcely daring to breathe. Sergeant Orme went stomping through the house opening closets and shoving furniture around. Ann prayed he would not figure out that she was just one thin wall away, behind a bedroom chest of drawers.

"What's this ladder?" Sergeant Orme shouted when he opened the closet nearest her trapdoor. "What the hell are you doing with a ladder in the house?"

Ann's heart pounded hard and she hugged her knees. *How could we be so stupid as to leave the ladder right there?* She bit down on a knuckle to keep from groaning in despair.

Mr. Bigelow's reasonable voice was the next thing she heard. "I'm not a particularly tall man, Sergeant Orme, yet my company does expect me to inspect a gaslight here and there. If you can suggest another way for me to reach the lights other than with a ladder, a way that would not irritate you so, then I'd like to hear about it."

Ann bit down harder on her knuckle, waiting to hear Sergeant Orme's response.

The Sergeant grunted and shut the closet door.

"If you don't have the wench here, I think you know where she is," he said menacingly.

"I wish I did," said Mr. Bigelow. "I've

been trying to buy her freedom for quite some time."

"So I've heard," the Sergeant growled, with disdain.

Ann was relieved when she finally heard the door shut behind him. When the house was quiet, Mr. Bigelow rapped three times on the trapdoor — their signal that all was safe. Ann lifted the board and peeked down through the opening.

"Just a short visit from our friend Sergeant Orme," said Mr. Bigelow. "He was bound to come sooner or later."

"Is he gone for good?" she asked.

Mr. Bigelow reached up and touched her hand comfortingly. "My dear, just make sure you are in your room when he comes."

Ann rubbed the deep red tooth marks she'd made in her knuckle. She hoped Sergeant Orme would not come to visit again.

"The trouble is that huge reward Mr. Price is offering for you," Mr. Bigelow said. He took off his spectacles to clean them on his handkerchief. When he looked up at her, his eyes had an unfocused gaze. "Every man and his uncle wants a piece of that five hundred dollars. You must have been very important to them. Were there children you cared for?"

"One," said Ann. "A little girl."

"That's it, then," he said. "If there's one thing slave owners can't abide it's their children's bawling when they've lost a nurse and have to get used to a new one."

At first, Ann couldn't imagine Miss Sarah feeling sad about her leaving. She herself had missed the child but thought Sarah's heart too closed for her to care much. Then she remembered how Sarah had snuggled in close with her that night before the county fair, and how she'd been so happy to help enter Ann's beets in the contest. Sarah had grown attached to her, after all. She was probably giving the master and mistress fits. Five hundred dollars' worth of fits.

That night Ann was sorry she'd thought about the fair. She'd worked so hard to keep that day out of her mind — the memories of the picnic under the trees with Alfred, and of his gentle, apple-laced kiss. What plagued her most was the promise she'd made to him the day they'd gone to the Rock Creek. "I will never leave here without you, Miss Ann Maria, and please don't you leave here without me," he'd said. And she'd promised him she wouldn't. Would he ever know it hadn't been her choice to leave without a word?

The days seemed to go on forever. She ate each meal slowly, alone in the stuffy room, trying to make it last as long as possible. And she took a long time dressing, changing into her nightgown each night and into the beautiful yellow dress each morning. It seemed a shame to wear the best clothes she'd ever owned with no one to see her in them except the spiders hanging in the corners.

The rest of her time she spent looking through the peephole, watching the street outside with its lazy procession of people, horses and carriages, sheep, goats, chickens, and cows. They were near the corner of Seventh and E streets, Mr. Bigelow said, just a few blocks away from Pennsylvania Avenue, where President Pierce lived in the White House.

How strange, she thought, to be free and yet to be a prisoner. She would gladly have made herself busy with washing and cooking and sweeping. Anything would be better than this boredom.

One evening, during a talk with Mr. Bigelow, while he stood on the second rung of the ladder and she rested her chin on her hands at the edge of the trapdoor, she looked into the living room at the walls lined with bookshelves. The books were fat and black, some with gold lettering on their spines.

"What are all of those books about?" she asked.

"Ah. Those are my law books. They are there to give off a musty odor and convince all my visitors that I am, indeed, a very educated man."

"There must be a lot of laws to fill so many books," she said.

Mr. Bigelow gazed at his library and scratched a sideburn. "Strange, isn't it? I am a man of the law, and yet, by the law, I am a criminal and deserve to be thrown in prison."

They were both silent for a time.

"Well, enough lamenting for me. It's time for bed," said Mr. Bigelow, and turned to step off the ladder.

"Wait," said Ann urgently. She didn't think she could stand another day of staring alternately at the ceiling and out the peephole. "Your books — might I borrow one to read?"

"Why, my dear child, I had no idea you could read!" he said, astonished. "But those books . . ." He looked at the long black rows. "They're no more interesting than watching ice melt." He gave a perplexed sigh, then suddenly brightened. He marched over to a low corner shelf and pulled out a small red book. He blew dust off it and brought it back to her. "I saved this from when I was a boy, in case I ever had a son of my own."

Ann held the book and read the title embossed in silver on the front cover: *Robinson Crusoe.*

"It's really a story for boys, but it's the best I can offer," said Mr. Bigelow.

Ann turned the book over in her hands, feeling the smoothness and coolness of it. Mr. Bigelow must have seen the look of excitement and longing on her face, because he said, "I suppose now you'll want a candle."

"Oh, could I?" She could scarcely believe her good fortune.

He gave her a very short, stubby candle. "This is to make sure you get *some* sleep tonight," he explained.

She thanked him profusely, and gladly retired to her bed. There, by the light of the candle, she opened the book. She ran her hands over the silky pages, then turned to the text and began: "Chapter 1. I was born in the year 1632, in the city of York, of a good family. . . ."

She was carried away to the world of a young man's decision to seek adventure on the high seas, a terrible storm, and his narrow escape from a sinking ship. She read until the candle flickered, sputtered, and died. But even in the dark, images of grand ships and raging storms lasted in her mind until they mixed with her dreams.

Twenty-four

The peephole gave Ann just enough light for reading. Each day she looked forward to discovering where Robinson Crusoe would find himself. In the evenings she showed Mr. Bigelow the words she hadn't been able to sound out and the parts she couldn't understand, and he helped her with them. When Mr. Crusoe was captured and became a slave of the Turkish ship captain, Ann was perplexed.

"Isn't he a white man?" she asked Mr. Bigelow.

"Yes," he assured her.

"And he's a slave?"

"My dear," said Mr. Bigelow, "men have made slaves of each other for thousands of years, and men of every race on earth, and their wives and children, have found themselves under the yoke of slavery."

Ann was relieved when Crusoe escaped from his master. He traveled to a land filled with dense jungles and wild beasts. Ann and Mr. Bigelow discussed whether or not Crusoe had done the right thing when he shot the great lion, who was simply sleeping in the shade. Ann thought it was cruel, and that Crusoe should have gone looking for water someplace else and left the poor beast alone.

Whether she approved of Crusoe's actions or not, his story kept her rapt attention. Her hidden room had been transformed into a place of adventure, and she no longer felt like a prisoner in it.

Weeks passed, and by late October, although her runaway notice was still appearing in the papers, Mr. Bigelow said the worst of the furor had died down. He decided it would be safe for her to come down for meals again.

He kept the front door tightly bolted, the heavy curtains drawn, the trapdoor open, and the ladder set up and ready. If there was a knock at the door, Ann was to climb to the attic and stay there until he gave the three-knock signal for her to come down. In the meantime, she was glad to be able to stretch her legs walking around the house, get another bath, and insist on cooking.

One Sunday morning, as she was frying bacon and boiling porridge for a late breakfast, there was a loud knock at the door. She froze and for a moment couldn't move. Then, quickly, she ran to the ladder. Her foot slipped and her shin slammed into one of the rungs. Mr. Bigelow came to hold the ladder steady for her. "Stay calm," he said softly, "and *quiet*."

Shaking, she climbed up, then fitted the boards into place. She heard Mr. Bigelow slide the ladder into the closet.

The front door opened, and she heard muffled voices from outside. The voices moved inside and she heard them more clearly.

"We're mighty glad things have settled down — you know — and that we could come," she heard a man say. As soon as she heard the voice, she wanted to cry and shout and jump all at once. But she held her breath and waited for the three knocks from Mr. Bigelow. A baby cooed. The three knocks sounded. Ann flung open the trapdoor and without even waiting for the ladder, swung down through the hole and landed on the floor like a sack of flour.

"Papa!" She jumped into her father's arms.

Her father squeezed her tightly. "There's my baby girl," he said softly, caressing her hair with one large, rough hand. She clung to him until he said, "Your mamma's here too."

Ann let him go and reached for her mother. She let herself be folded into the softness of her mother's arms, breasts, and belly. She choked on tears, then let them flow as if she were a small child again. "It's all right," her mother said, rocking her gently. "You're with us now."

Ann lifted her head and caught a watery glimpse of Catharine with a child on her hip. She stretched out her arms to include both of them in an embrace. "My new brother!" she exclaimed. She laughed through her tears as the baby caught a clump of her hair and gave it a yank. "Ow!" she cried. "He's strong, like his daddy."

Mr. Bigelow brought Ann a clean handkerchief and ushered them all into the sitting room. First they just wanted to look at one another — all dressed in freedmen's clothes of smooth cotton and rough wool. Catharine's face had grown round, and Ann noticed that in the time they'd been there her sister hadn't coughed once. Her father had more gray hair peppered in with the black, and her mother's waistline had quite expanded since the last time Ann had seen her.

Ann tapped on her mother's large middle. "That John Junior must have been a big one," she teased.

"He was not." Arabella lifted her chin proudly. "It's a new one. Due to arrive this winter."

Ann's eyes grew wide. Another baby brother or sister! She touched her mother's belly again, this time with awe, then felt a twinge of sadness as she realized she would probably never even see the child.

They talked about Catharine's school, and how Arabella was attending a freedmen's school in the evenings to learn to read and write. Ann proudly shared with them her own ability to read and write.

"You can write to us when you get to Canada!" Catharine declared.

But Ann didn't want to think about Canada now; she just wanted this day with her family to go on forever. She was thankful when her father changed the subject. "We've brought one of Arabella's famous apple pies, so let's eat."

The bacon and porridge had long since burned. Mr. Bigelow threw them out the back door, and they started over with fresh bacon and potatoes to fry. John Junior sat on his mother's lap to eat, stuffing potatoes into his mouth with tiny fists.

The light coming through the heavy curtains became brighter with the afternoon, then began to fade as the day slipped away. They talked about Joseph, Addison, and Augustus, and how they were still trying to locate them. Ann wondered what her brothers were doing on this Sabbath — if they'd found new people to fish with and go to church with. She hoped they weren't too lonely or mistreated.

"We'll find them," her father said, gazing at the curtains as if he could see through them. "I feel it in my bones."

Even though Ann wished it wouldn't, the conversation drifted back to talk of Canada. Her parents spoke in encouraging tones of Aunt Mimi and Uncle William. Of course, no one dared write to tell them of her coming; she was far from safe, and a letter could be intercepted. But her parents had heard more news: The Bradleys had had another child, a son. And her uncle had been able to buy land, and they had built a small house on their homestead.

"Just like he always dreamed of!" Ann breathed.

Her father nodded. "And they'll be happier than pigs in mud to have you come live with them."

"You'll be able to meet our new cousins,

Ann," said Catharine.

The talk about her aunt and uncle should have made her feel hopeful, Ann knew, but it only made her feel how far away her parents, brothers, and sister would be. Mr. Bigelow must have seen the look in her eyes, because he interrupted: "But we won't be sending her on for a while yet. We want Mr. Price to give up searching before we risk all that travel."

Finally, sadly, it was time for her family to leave.

"They ring those firehouse bells at nine," said her father, "and Negroes and children have one hour to get themselves indoors or the constable comes after you."

Ann was stunned. Even in Unity, when they were slaves, no one had insisted they be indoors by ten.

"City laws," Catharine explained.

"If all remains quiet, we'll see you here again next Sunday, then?" Mr. Bigelow asked.

"A mountain of snow couldn't keep me from visiting my baby girl," said her father.

They hugged each other tightly, just in case worse things than snow happened before the next Sabbath.

Twenty-five

The next few Sundays brought joy-filled visits for Ann with her family. She baked real bread and stewed a chicken for them, to show how she'd learned to cook since they'd seen her last. John Junior, who hadn't paid much attention to her on his first visit, took to crawling up on her lap and trying to eat the buttons off the front of her dress. And no one mentioned Canada. It was as if they had all decided secretly to pretend that these Sunday visits would go on forever. And that was the way it felt.

One Monday evening Ann rested on her mat in her hiding place, imagining a life for herself in Washington City: how she would go to school with Catharine and help her mother with John Junior and the new baby when it arrived; how she would be here to welcome her brothers when they came home to freedom. The sound of the front door opening, and then the familiar three knocks, pulled her back to reality.

"Miss Ann Maria, please come down," said Mr. Bigelow.

Ann roused herself from her dreamy state and lifted the ceiling boards.

"I need to move you to a new hiding place," said Mr. Bigelow.

Ann's stomach twisted. She'd grown so used to her life in the tiny room, with her reading and daydreaming, and Sundays with her family. She'd all but blocked out of her mind that soon things would change. She climbed down the ladder and smoothed the front of her dress.

"Where am I going?" she asked.

"Remember what I said about how I don't hire any servants because of the risk?" Mr. Bigelow asked. His spectacles had slipped down a bit, and his eyes looked huge behind them.

She nodded.

"I've changed my mind," he said, fumbling with the package he was holding.

Ann gave him a quizzical look. He had a strange hint of a smile at the corner of his mouth.

"Here are some new clothes for you," he said. He pushed his spectacles back up.

"But I love the dress Catharine gave me, I —"

"Just take a look." That corner of a smile was beginning to twitch and look as if it were about to break out over his whole mouth.

Ann took the package from him and laid back the brown paper. Inside she found new clothes — brand-new clothes.

She fingered the crisp fabric of a starched white shirt. The newness was exciting, but the colors were disappointing. Along with the white shirt was a black wool jacket with big brass buttons. There were black leather gloves and a brand-new pair of shiny black shoes with brass buckles. At the bottom of the package, she picked up what she expected would be the black wool skirt to go with the jacket. Instead, she found herself holding a pair of *britches*.

By now Mr. Bigelow was grinning. "And here's the hat." On her head he placed a carriage boy's black hat with a brim.

She wanted to tell him she was thoroughly enjoying the boy's book he'd loaned her, but saw no need to also dress like a boy.

"But —" she began.

"This is your new hiding place," Mr. Bigelow said simply.

Ann gaped at the clothes she held.

"Quickly, go change and we'll work on the rest of your disguise."

Ann climbed back into her old hiding place. Slowly, she took off the dress Catharine had given her and replaced it with the britches, black stockings, white shirt, and black jacket. She even put on the shiny new shoes. How strange, she thought — now she had two pairs of shoes, and she didn't want to wear either one of them. She climbed down the ladder, feeling very foolish and awkward.

"Very good," said Mr. Bigelow. "Now let's see how you walk."

Ann walked across the sitting room and back. The shoes made a hollow thumping sound on the floor, and the britches swished softly. Mr. Bigelow knitted his brow at her and shook his head. "You need to look more like you've been on a horse all day. Like this." He demonstrated an exaggerated rolling gait.

Ann frowned, and walked across the room again, trying to imitate Mr. Bigelow. She thought she must look more like a rag doll than a boy, swinging her arms like that.

"Good!" Mr. Bigelow proclaimed. "Much better. Now try sitting."

Ann dropped down gently on the settee,

knees together, hands resting on her knees, back straight. Mr. Bigelow sighed heavily.

"Think slovenly," he commanded. "I want you to lean back — slouch. And you've got britches on now, so let those knees flop north and south."

Ann gave him a pleading look. Couldn't she just stay in her old hiding place? But she concentrated, and tried to remember how Alfred sat. She relaxed her back, lounged a bit to one side, and, against her better judgment, let her knees flop apart.

"Yes!" Mr. Bigelow gave her a round of applause. "And remember to slurp your food, and burp after drinking."

Ann covered her mouth and giggled.

"And no covering your mouth when you laugh."

She gave him a perturbed look.

Mr. Bigelow cocked his head to one side and gazed at her as if he were examining a painting. "I'll have to cut your hair," he said thoughtfully.

Ann reached up and tugged at her unbraided hair. It was too long for a boy's, certainly.

"And you'll need a name," he said.

So she would have a new name, just like the Powder Boy and Uncle William. A name for the Road. But how would she choose one, she wondered? "Do you have an Underground Rail Road name?" she asked Mr. Bigelow.

"In all my letters to other conductors, I am William Penn, after the freedom-loving Quaker who founded Pennsylvania," he said.

"Might I have a Quaker name as well?" Ann asked.

Mr. Bigelow rubbed his chin, thinking. "William and Phebe Wright are good Quakers and friends of the slave. They live in Pennsylvania, not far from York — that's where we'll say you're from. Would you like to share their name?"

Ann smiled. "Then I'll be Phebe Wright," she said, satisfied. She liked the sound of it.

Mr. Bigelow leaned forward. "Phebe is a very odd name for a coach boy," he said.

Ann glanced down at her britches and jacket, then up at Mr. Bigelow. She grimaced. "You mean I'd be *William* Wright?" she asked, still not quite believing it.

He raised one eyebrow at her.

Ann sighed. "I'd like to pick another given name, then, so my family doesn't think that everyone who goes north to Canada becomes a William."

Mr. Bigelow waited patiently.

"I'd like to be called Joseph," she said finally. "I want to be as brave as my brother Joseph."

Mr. Bigelow offered his hand to shake hers, man to man. "I'm honored to meet you, Joe Wright," he said. "My name is William Penn."

They shook hands, pleased with their shared secret.

"Now, one more thing," Mr. Bigelow said.

Ann looked at him expectantly.

"I need to teach you to drive."

Twenty-six

"Pull in a little. No, he thinks you want him to stop; you just want him to slow. Better. Now have him speed up; slap those reins. Whoa! Not too fast . . . watch this turn. Cattle have the right of way, so pull in hard and let this herd pass."

Ann held the reins in her leather-gloved hands and watched as a boy followed a small herd of cows across the mud street. She squinted her eyes almost shut, but still the sunlight sent stabbing pains through them. It had been over two months since she'd been outdoors.

"I think you're ready for Pennsylvania Avenue," said Mr. Bigelow, who sat next to her in the driver's seat.

He directed her onto the cobblestones of the wide avenue. The loud clatter of the carriage wheels over the stones was suddenly familiar to Ann. "The Powder Boy took me along here!" she said loudly over the noise.

Pennsylvania Avenue was filled with scores of other carriages, wagons, and horses, one flock of sheep, and clouds of dust billowing around them all. Ann had to dodge a large omnibus, overflowing with passengers, pulled by an entire team of horses.

"I think we'd better go back to the side streets!" she shouted to be heard.

"Not until I show you where Franklin Pierce lives," said Mr. Bigelow.

"The President?" Ann asked in amazement.

"That's where you'll be leaving from — directly in front of the White House. Sometimes the best place to hide is the last place anyone would expect to find you." Mr. Bigelow took the reins himself to guide the carriage. He nudged her and pointed as they approached a magnificent building. It was white with tall, slender pillars, set far back on a grassy lawn. A bronze statue of a man stood proudly looking out at them. All around the lawn was a black iron fence, its sharp posts pointed skyward like a thousand spears.

"The statue is of Thomas Jefferson," said Mr. Bigelow. "So we have one President on the outside of the White House, and another President on the inside."

Ann stared in awe. She blinked and squinted harder, hoping to catch a glimpse of Franklin Pierce on his veranda.

Mr. Bigelow took her past other important buildings. They passed the hulking Treasury Building, which had more tall columns than Ann could count, and the Capitol with its mountains of white marble steps, pillars, and huge wooden dome. On their way back to Mr. Bigelow's house they passed the General Post Office, with its towering gray marble walls and black iron fence.

"Decisions for the whole country are made in this city," said Mr. Bigelow.

The sheer size of the buildings had made Ann feel the importance of the decisions made inside them.

As they rode the last couple of blocks, Mr. Bigelow went over their plan one more time. A professor from one of the medical schools in Philadelphia would come to fetch her as soon as his Thanks Giving vacation started. His Underground Rail Road name was Dr. H. They would meet in front of the White House and, with Ann acting as his driver, they would cross the Mason-Dixon Line into Pennsylvania. He would accompany her first to Philadelphia and then to New York City, where she would be delivered to members of the New York Vigilance Committee. Ann's life was beginning to change very quickly again, and she didn't feel the least bit ready for all of it.

Back in the humble row house, Ann blew into her hands to warm them. With the curtains drawn, her eyes felt much better.

"Let's have tea," said Mr. Bigelow.

They both went to the kitchen. Ann filled the kettle with water she'd fetched earlier, and Mr. Bigelow rummaged in the cupboard for biscuits.

Suddenly there was a loud pounding on the front door. Ann jumped like a startled cat. She dropped the kettle and ran to where her ladder should have been. It was gone. In a panic she rushed back to the kitchen and clutched Mr. Bigelow's arms. "Where shall I go?" she whispered hoarsely.

Mr. Bigelow loosened himself from her grasp. Out of a closet he brought a groom's box and handed it to her.

"You are Joe Wright, my coach boy," he said calmly. "Where you will go is outside to curry and brush my horse, as soon as you have served our guest."

Ann tried to calm her breathing. Mr.

Bigelow opened the door to an angry Sergeant Orme.

"You could have hidden five fugitives in the time it took you to come to the door!" Sergeant Orme shoved his way into the house. He was wide and burly, with straight red hair that stuck out from under his policeman's cap.

"Pardon me. I was in the back of the house, in the kitchen, making tea," said Mr. Bigelow.

"It's been reported that the Weems family is here night and day." Sergeant Orme narrowed his eyes. "That missing Weems girl can't be far away."

"I am friendly with the Weems family. They've been visiting me on Sundays," said Mr. Bigelow. "Would you like some tea? Or a glass of water, perhaps?"

"Water," Sergeant Orme grunted.

"Joe, get the officer a glass of water. And get it fresh, mind you," Mr. Bigelow said to Ann, who had been standing like a statue holding the groom's box in both hands.

Ann set the box down and went through the kitchen and out the back door to the water pump. Though the air was cold, she felt sweat drip down her back. She pumped a fresh bucket of water and carried it into the house. Her hands shook terribly as she filled a glass with the icy water and handed it to the officer. He didn't even look at her.

"Get back to your work now," said Mr. Bigelow.

Ann was thankful to leave the house. She patted the horse on the nose, and he snorted at her. He nuzzled her hand, looking for a treat. "If you stand still for a good grooming, I'll bring you a carrot," she told him.

The rhythm of the curry comb against the horse's warm back calmed her. She brushed him all over and picked out his hooves. When she was done, she said, "That miserable Sergeant Orme isn't gone yet, but you deserve your carrot."

She took a deep breath and marched up to the house. Inside, she was shocked by what she heard and saw.

Sergeant Orme had Mr. Bigelow by the collar. "I think you know where that Weems girl is, and when I prove it, I'll have you thrown in prison for so long your own mother won't recognize you when you get out." He thrust his rubbery face to within an inch of Mr. Bigelow's nose, then shoved him away. He cast an indifferent glance at Ann and left.

Ann was horrified. "Did he hurt you?" she cried.

Mr. Bigelow adjusted his collar and straightened his tie. "No harm done," he said briskly.

"But . . . what if he figures it out?" she whispered. What if Mr. Bigelow was sent to prison — or worse — because of her?

"My dear, that man is such an imbecile he can't figure out which shoe to put on first in the morning."

Ann twisted her hands and said nothing.

"Don't be so worried," said Mr. Bigelow. "*Whom* was he searching for?" He gave her an amused look. "And *where* was she?"

Ann tried to see the humor in the situation, but she was still quite shaken.

Mr. Bigelow held her shoulders firmly and looked at her hard. "You will face guards and sheriffs and constables from time to time on your journey." He went to his desk and pulled out pen and ink. "Let's do this immediately. It will help you remember who you are."

He took an official-looking piece of paper out of an envelope. It had printing on it, and a raised seal. He mumbled as he wrote on the paper, "Name: Joseph Wright. Place of birth: York, Pennsylvania. Description . . ." He glanced up at her several times as he wrote, "Light-skinned, slender, freckles . . ." He signed the document with a flourish and folded it back into its envelope. "Your freedman's papers. Don't let them off your person."

Ann slipped the forged document inside her jacket. Freedman's papers — just like her father's. Only they were for her other self. Her Underground Rail Road self.

"And let's hope all the constables from here to Canada are as stupid as that Sergeant Orme," Mr. Bigelow said. He pulled back the curtains and peeked out front. "How is my horse doing? Still confused from breaking in a new driver?"

"Oh!" Ann suddenly remembered the carrot. "I promised him a treat."

She went to the larder, found a carrot, and held it up with a smile as she passed Mr. Bigelow on her way out the front door. She broke the carrot into pieces and shared it with the horse, then rested her cheek against his jaw and listened to the hollow crunching as he chewed. The sky grew red with the sunset, and the words "from here to Canada" echoed in her mind. Thanks Giving was in just eight days. Dr. H. would be coming for her soon.

Twenty-seven

"If I didn't know better, I'd think I had a new son!" said her father.

Ann showed off her newly acquired talent of walking, sitting, and moving like a boy. It made everyone laugh, and the levity helped her forget for the moment that this was their last Sunday together.

Arabella took Ann's cap off and examined Mr. Bigelow's handiwork. "A new son with the crookedest haircut I've ever seen," she said.

"Oh, dear. My failings as a barber have been discovered," said Mr. Bigelow, looking sheepish.

"Give me the scissors and I'll fix it," said Arabella.

Ann watched more of her hair fall to the floor. How fitting, she thought, to have her mother cut her hair the same way she used to cut Joseph's. "Now I'll look even more like Joseph," she said.

When she was done, Arabella stepped back. "Yes, sir," she said with satisfaction, "you'll blind the eyes of anyone looking for that 'fleeing girl of fifteen.'"

"What 'fleeing girl of fifteen'?" Ann asked.

"It's just the advertisements about you, Ann," said Catharine. "They've been running for months in the papers. Haven't you seen them?"

"Advertisements about *me? I'm* the 'fleeing girl of fifteen'?" Ann's voice trembled.

Mr. Bigelow reluctantly pulled a newspaper out of a pile on the floor. "I didn't think you particularly wanted to see them," he said apologetically. "But since you'll soon be on safe soil, you might as well read one."

Ann jutted out her jaw as she held the paper and read,

$500 REWARD. Ran away on Sunday night, the 23rd instant, before 12 o'clock, from the subscriber, residing in Rockville, Montgomery county, MD, my NEGRO GIRL "Ann Maria Weems," about 15 years of age, a bright mulatto, some small freckles on her face, slender person, thick suit of hair, inclined to be sandy. Her par-

ents are free and reside in Washington, D.C. It is evident she was taken away by some one in a carriage, probably by a white man, by whom she may be carried beyond the limits of the State of Maryland.

I will give the above reward for her apprehension and detention so that I get her again. C. M. Price.

Ann's thoughts swam with confusion. About *fifteen* years of age? Had she miscounted? Had Richard lied? Could she have been wrong in figuring her age all this time? Her throat tightened and she looked up into the worried eyes of her parents and sister. She decided to simply blurt it out. "But I thought I was *thirteen!*"

The group surrounding her all began talking at once.

"That stupid Mr. Price doesn't know anything," said Catharine.

"Whatever Master Richard told you about your birthday was right," said her mother.

"He obviously didn't want it to look as if he'd mistreated a child enough for her to run, so he made you older to save his reputation," said Mr. Bigelow.

And finally, her father gave her the best evidence yet. "Baby girl, you've been walking around here looking for all the world like a boy, isn't that right?"

"Yes, Papa," said Ann.

"Well, you won't pass for a boy once you've turned fifteen, you mark my words."

Ann looked from Catharine's shapely form filling out her pale green dress, to her own flat chest under the black jacket. When she looked up again, Catharine was grinning at her.

Arabella shifted in her chair. "Ann Maria, I never would have known how important a birthdate could be to a child if it hadn't been for you. So John Junior and this new one will always know — now that I've got the time to tend to more than just keeping hunger and sickness from our door."

John Junior sat at Ann's feet, playing with a spoon and a wooden bowl. Ann bent over and kissed the top of his head. His baby curls felt soft on her lips. "Thank you, Mamma," she said.

The light behind the curtains faded, and when it had been dark for some time, they all began to feel it. There was an uneasiness, then long breaks in the conversation, and finally silence — except for the sound of the clock ticking toward nine.

Ann felt it first as a tightness in her throat. Then, when her father rubbed his forehead with one trembling hand and said softly, "Those curfew bells will be ringing soon," she felt as if her whole body wanted to shout "No!"

Her mother stood and held out her arms to Ann. But Ann refused to go to her. "Don't make me go," she said, clutching her chair. She turned to Mr. Bigelow. "Please don't make me go," she begged.

Mr. Bigelow's shoulders slumped as if the weight of her sadness rested on him.

"Let me stay here — I'll live as a boy. No one will ever know." Her words tumbled over each other. "Joseph and Addison and Augustus will be home soon — they can protect me. Master Charles will give up searching for me — he won't hunt me forever . . . then I can live with you." She looked searchingly at her parents. "You can tell everyone I'm . . . a nephew. Please . . . let me stay here." She didn't even try not to cry. Her shoulders shook and she hung her head, letting tears drip onto her lap.

She felt her mother's arms wrap around her shoulders, holding tightly and rocking. "Shhh . . ." Arabella whispered.

"Please let me stay here. . . . Let me stay

here. . . ." Ann chanted it to the rhythm of the rocking, wanting the words to make it come true.

Suddenly she felt her mother push away. She was startled by the fury she saw on Arabella's face.

"That bastard Price!" Arabella cried. "Who is he, to rip this child away from us?" She swayed, and John caught her under the elbows to steady her. His face twitched with anguish.

"You're going to a new world, baby girl," he said softly.

Ann could feel the time slipping away. When she'd told Mr. Bigelow yes to freedom, she had set in motion a wheel that would not — could not — stop turning until she arrived in that new world.

"Will you —" She swallowed, trying to form the words around her tears. "Will you come visit me?"

Her father pulled her from her chair and clasped her so tightly it hurt. "I will save every penny — and in a few years, if it's not enough for train fare to Canada, I'll jump a freight car to come see you," he vowed.

"Me, too," said Catharine, and she wound her thin arms into the hug so that she could hold Ann as well. Ann closed her eyes and breathed in the mingling smells of her father's wool waistcoat and the rosemary oil in Catharine's hair.

"Learn enough in school for both of us, all right?" she said to Catharine.

Catharine tipped her head back to gaze at Ann. "I will," she said solemnly.

When Ann embraced her mother, they stood silent for a moment. Then Ann whispered, "Will you visit me, too, Mamma?"

Arabella nodded into the nape of Ann's neck. "Give these babies some time to grow up. Then we'll *all* jump that freight car!"

Ann sighed, knowing it was only a dream that they would ever be able to come, but remembering that Uncle William's dreams had come true. She gave her mother a squeeze — and felt a tiny shove from her mother's belly. She jumped back. "I think she's telling me good-bye!" she said.

"I believe she is," said Arabella.

John Junior tugged at Ann's skirt, begging to be picked up, and she gave him a good-bye kiss. "You grow up healthy, you hear?" she said to him. He patted her nose.

"We'll write to you and tell you everything — when you get a new sister or brother, and when your brothers come home," said her mother.

"You be good, and take our love to Uncle William and Aunt Mimi," her father said.

The curfew bell rang. Ann's parents, sister, and brother hurried to take their leave. As the bell clanged in the crisp night air, Ann felt that it announced the end of her time as a daughter and a sister within this circle of her family.

The next day, the sun rose cold and clear. Ann washed and dressed in her coach boy's clothes. She took a last look around the sitting room, which had been her bedroom since she became Joe Wright. She rolled up her straw mat and folded her quilt. Mr. Bigelow peeked in on her. "Ready?" he asked.

Ann straightened her cap. "Thank you . . ." she began, but then felt there were no words to express how grateful she was.

Mr. Bigelow held out both his hands to her, his head cocked in a way that showed he understood. Ann reached past the hands and went right to a hug around his middle. He pressed Ann's head against his chest briefly, then held her away to look at her. "Whom will I discuss *Robinson Crusoe* with when you're gone?" he asked sadly.

"Maybe you should get married and have that son you were saving the book for," Ann said.

Mr. Bigelow chuckled, but said he would consider her suggestion. "And now let's be off," he said. "Dr. H. will be waiting for us."

Mr. Bigelow rode inside the carriage. Ann drove expertly down the wide dirt streets of the city and turned onto the cobblestones of Pennsylvania Avenue. She found herself immediately in the path of a huge omnibus with passengers hanging off the sides and a full team of horses huffing as they pulled the heavy thing up the avenue. A month ago, she might have panicked and let go of the reins, but today she turned right, avoided another carriage and a man on a horse, and continued to her destination: the White House. There, waiting for them in front of the black iron fence, was a tall, slender man with a pointed nose and sandy brown hair.

Ann, now playing the part of a servant, was not introduced. While Mr. Bigelow and Dr. H. chatted and exchanged comments about the weather, she climbed down from Mr. Bigelow's carriage and mounted Dr. H.'s carriage. Dr. H.'s black horse twisted his head around to get a good look at his new driver.

Ann held the reins, ready to go. Inside her leather gloves her hands turned clammy with sweat, but she kept her face expressionless and calm. "I'm Joe Wright," she told herself, "and no one is chasing me."

When Dr. H. had climbed back into his carriage and it was time to go, Ann turned to see Mr. Bigelow one last time. He lifted his chin, as if telling her to be strong, and gave her a lingering look, his eyes soft with fatherly affection. Ann pressed her lips together to keep from smiling too broadly. She didn't dare wave or call good-bye, but after she'd slapped the reins against the horse's back, she briefly swept one hand in an arc that appeared to passersby as if she were shooing away flies, but to Mr. Bigelow was meant as farewell.

They drove down Pennsylvania Avenue, turned onto F Street, and followed the road past the last few row houses, past the boggy places near the Potomac River, and out into the countryside. When they were a good way from the city, Dr. H. stuck his head out of the carriage. "Tell the horse whoa," he said.

There, without a house in sight, he climbed out of the carriage. "Is my horse treating you well?" he asked. He shaded his eyes and squinted at her.

Ann thought he seemed pale, as if he spent more time reading medical books than out in the sunshine. "He's been very good," she said. "Except he has given me a few worried looks, wondering who I am."

"I'd like to switch places with you," said Dr. H. "He's very used to me, and I'll feel better if I drive most of the way."

Ann was relieved. She'd never driven for more than an hour or two, and she knew they would be traveling all day. Dr. H. reached up to help her down. She was surprised by the gentleness of his hands. He had slender fingers with delicate skin — good for a doctor, she thought. They would be very soothing on a feverish brow or an aching belly.

"It will be a two-day journey to Philadelphia," he explained. "My horse will need to eat tonight, and we'll need to sleep. We'll stop in with old acquaintances of mine who, unfortunately, are slaveholders. But it's safer than stopping at a tavern." He opened the carriage door for her, like a gentleman.

Shortly after sunset Dr. H. stopped the carriage. The air had turned quite cold, and Ann was glad to hear they had only about a mile left to go.

"These people knew me as a young man," said the doctor. "They thought I had very strange ideas." He rubbed his hands together to warm them. "When I argued that blacks should be treated as equals with whites, they thought I'd gone mad." He gazed into the distance. Then he kicked the dirt once and said, "I think it's best if tonight we make them think I have matured, seen the error of my youthful ideas, and now agree that slavery is a fine institution."

Ann nodded. It sounded like a good way to keep the doctor's friends from becoming suspicious.

"And you, Joseph, must play the part of my free black servant."

Ann blinked, startled to be called Joseph.

The doctor gave her instructions on how to act and what to expect: "You'll have your supper in the kitchen, not in the dining room and not in the slave quarters. You'll be served by the slaves. *Don't* talk to them, or their owners may think you're enticing them to run away to Pennsylvania. Don't look the master or mistress in the eye, but don't act too cowed, either. Remember, you're a *free* servant."

Ann listened intently. When Dr. H. was finished, he asked her, "Ready?"

"Yes, sir," she said, sounding more confident than she felt. She took the reins and they rode on toward the distant light of the farmhouse.

Ann was thankful for the warmth of the kitchen, where she ate her supper while Dr. H. joined the family in the dining room. She nodded her thanks to the stoop-shouldered slave woman who served both her and the white folks, but did not say a word to her.

Ann easily overheard the discussion in the dining room. The farmer spoke about a black man in the area, a farmer as well, who owned slaves.

"He's got eight or ten head of slaves on that place, and he rides around checking up on their work like he thinks he's a white man. It just don't make sense," the man said, his voice rising, "a nigger owning slaves like that."

"No," said Dr. H. "It makes no sense at all."

Ann smiled to herself, knowing what the doctor really meant by his words. But the next thing she heard made her chest turn cold. It was the farmer's wife who spoke.

"Your boy can sleep in the cellar with our male slaves tonight. There have been so many runaways in the area — with us being so close to the line, you know — we keep them chained at night. I'm sure we can find an extra chain for your boy."

Ann sat rigid, listening.

Dr. H. cleared his throat. "Ma'am, if he were to run away, he simply wouldn't get paid this week. I don't think the chains will be necessary."

"Oh, dear, how silly of me," said the woman. She laughed nervously. "I forgot how it is you-all do things in Pennsylvania."

Still, Ann did not relish the idea of sleeping in the cellar with a group of men and boys she'd never met.

"My health has been poor," the doctor was saying. "I suffer from dizziness at night. I would like the boy with me, to tend to my needs if necessary. Simply give him a bed quilt and he will fare well enough in a corner of the room."

The farmer and his wife readily agreed to the request, and Ann breathed a sigh of relief.

Snug and warm in a corner of the bedroom, wrapped in the soft quilt, with the doctor sleeping in his bed nearby, Ann relaxed. As she drifted off to sleep, she was thankful for many things, including the fact that Dr. H. did not snore.

Twenty-eight

They were up before dawn, and on the road by first light. "I want you safe at William Still's house, and me safely reported to my wife, by nightfall," said Dr. H.

At Havre de Grace they boarded the ferry to cross the Susquehanna River. The ferryman, pushing with his pole and spitting tobacco juice from between brown teeth, stared at Ann, narrowing his eyes. Ann moved around to the other side of Dr. H.'s horse, putting his black bulk between herself and the ferryman. She stroked the horse's neck and talked to him as if he didn't like ferry crossings and needed calming.

"You don't see many with freckles like that," the ferryman said.

Ann's knees almost buckled and she grasped the bridle to steady herself.

"I beg your pardon?" said Dr. H.

"I say, there's one escaped, got a five-hundred-dollar reward on its head, what got freckles like your nigger," the man said.

Ann heard the doctor say, "I see," and nothing more. The horse threw his head up and yanked against her grasp. She realized she'd been nearly hanging on the bridle. Her hands shook as she stroked his neck to quiet him.

They traveled in silence, listening to the splash of the river against the ferryboat. As the opposite shore got closer, Ann began to panic, wondering what they would do if the ferryman wanted to report her to the sheriff at Perryville.

"Good God, man, are you always this slow?" Dr. H. said impatiently. He paced back and forth on the boat and pulled out his pocket watch several times. "First the colonel kept me talking this morning, like a farmer who has all day to get his work done, and now I've got the slowest damned ferry in the state." He stopped, stood over the ferryman, and glared at him. "Do you realize I have patients waiting, some of whom are extremely sick?"

The man apologized to the doctor and rowed furiously. As soon as they disembarked on the opposite shore, Dr. H. ordered Ann into the driver's seat and joined her. He handed Ann his hat and slapped the reins hard until his horse was galloping over the rutted road, Ann was bouncing wildly, and the doctor's hair was flying in the wind.

When they'd left the ferry far behind, Dr. H. slowed his horse to a walk, then pulled him to a stop. "Would you like a more comfortable seat inside the carriage?" he asked. There were beads of sweat on his forehead, and his hair had flopped into his face.

"Please," Ann said. She'd gripped the seat so tightly her fingers were numb. She gave the doctor his hat. "Thank you," she said. *Thank you for keeping me safe,* she thought.

Dr. H. smiled at her, raked his hair back out of his face, and put his hat on. He jerked his chin toward the horse. "He likes to go fast," he said.

Ann climbed into the carriage and bundled her hands and legs under the blanket. For a long time she watched the landscape go by — clear-cut farmland, forest, small creeks. She swung around to look behind several times to make sure no one had followed them. No one had.

After a while the motion and warmth made her sleepy. She dozed, half wondering what Philadelphia would be like, half dreaming that she was back in Rockville, walking hand in hand with Alfred on a bright summer day.

Suddenly she became aware that the carriage had stopped. She rose up out of her dream state like a swimmer rising to the surface of a lake. They were in a heavily wooded area, cut through by the road. Between the naked branches she could see the sky, white and drab with heavy winter clouds. She sat motionless. Had the ferryman followed them, after all? Was there a sheriff barring their way? She dared not move.

Dr. H. hopped down from the driver's seat and opened the carriage door.

"Is something wrong?" Ann asked quickly.

He looked at her with a calm smile. "No. I just thought you might like to stretch your legs. We passed the Mason-Dixon Line a while back. You are on free soil."

"Oh!" Ann jumped out of the carriage and dropped to her knees on the frozen mud of the road. She broke off a clump of red earth and crumbled it in her hand. "Pennsylvania . . . no one holds slaves here?" she asked.

"Not since about 1847," said the doctor, "so it has been eight years or so."

Ann rose and walked a little way into the woods. Free soil, free trees, free sky, free blanket of dry leaves under her feet. What moments before had looked like a colorless winter landscape now was a beautiful tapestry of muted hues — gray bark, brown leaves, white sky, and ruddy soil.

"Six years ago," said the doctor, "all you would have needed to do was set foot in a free state, and chances were you could have lived free with no one to trouble you. But that Fugitive Slave Law changed everything. Now every sheriff is bound by law to help return runaways."

"That's why I'm going to Canada," said Ann softly.

The doctor nodded.

"So this soil is not really free for *me*." She brushed off her hands and rubbed the streaks of red dirt from the knees of her britches.

"You have several hundred miles to go before you reach truly free soil," said Dr. H.

Ann smelled Philadelphia before she could see it. It began with the odor of things burning. Soon they were close enough to see the redbrick factories and the smokestacks billowing black smoke. They drove onto the muddy, rutted streets between row houses crowded together like jars in a cupboard. Here the odor was also of things rotting. In the alleys behind the houses were piles of garbage and poor shacks made of wood scraps. She saw a group of pasty-faced boys in torn jackets huddled around a fire. A particularly large pile of garbage had both a little red-haired girl and a hog rooting through it. As Ann's carriage passed, several fat rats came scuttling out of the pile and across the road, startling the horse.

The sides of some buildings had signs painted on them: "Superior White Ash" and "C. Souder, Bootmaker." And everywhere there was traffic: horse-drawn carts filled with barrels, men on horseback, raggedly clothed children playing on doorsteps, women hurrying along the muddy sidewalks with packages from the day's marketing balanced in their arms.

Dr. H. sat with her and directed her driving. They turned onto Locust Street and then onto Twelfth Street. Here there were fewer houses, all of them well kept, less traffic, and more lawns. In front of a tidy two-story frame house, Dr. H. told her to stop. "This is Mr. William Still's home," he said. "Reveal your true identity to him *only*. To everyone else you are Joe, from

York." Ann promised to do as he said.

A black woman with cheerful eyes and a kind smile opened the door to the home. "Why, Doctor, how good to see you," she said.

"Mrs. Still, I wish to leave this lad with you a short while, and I will call in two days and see further about him," said the doctor. With that, he left in a hurry.

"Come into the kitchen," Mrs. Still said to Ann. "With only a few days left until Thanks Giving, we're all busy as can be with the baking."

The kitchen was steamy and warm and smelled like nutmeg and pumpkin. Besides Mrs. Still, there were two other women up to their brown elbows in flour and sugar. One of the women was young, about Hannah's age. The other was older and plump as a baked apple. Ann learned from introductions and from their conversation that the young woman was a hired girl working for the Stills, and the plump one was a fugitive, Laura Lewis, from Kentucky, who was staying with the Stills on her way north. The group was stirring and kneading, talking and laughing. Ann watched for a while and realized she wanted desperately to join in, to put her hands to work at old, familiar tasks, to feel part of this group of women, rather than lonely and separate.

"I would love to help," she announced cheerfully. "I'll just wash my hands, and —"

The women's laughter stopped her short. "Oh, dear, no!" said Mrs. Still. "I could never abide a boy in the kitchen."

Ann looked down at her britches, dismayed. "But I'm not actually . . ." Her voice trailed off as she remembered the promise she'd made to Dr. H. She could reveal her true identity only to Mr. Still. The women's eyes danced with amusement. "I'm not actually very good at baking," she said quietly.

"I should think not!" said Mrs. Still.

The three of them went back to their work, and Ann sat idle at the kitchen table. She wished for Mr. Still to arrive very soon. The light outside grew dim with the evening, and lamps were lit.

"He worries me so when he stays late at the shipyard," said Mrs. Still. "I tell him his customers should call on him in the daylight hours so that he can get home safely."

"Those gangs are getting rougher and meaner every day," said the hired girl.

"Gangs?" Ann asked, not sure what they were talking about.

"Mmm-hmm," said Laura. "It's mostly the Irish who just got here. They're poor as mud and angry as snakes." She began listing off the names of the gangs, counting them on flour-dusted fingers. "They've got the Moyamensing Killers, the Blood Tubs, the Death Fetchers, and the Smashers."

"Don't forget the Bleeders and the Tormenters," the hired girl chimed in.

"When they're not fighting each other, they've been known to pull respectable black citizens from their beds and beat them to death," said Mrs. Still. "And a black man walking alone after dark is not the least bit safe." She peered out the window at the darkening sky and clucked her tongue.

"They paint nasty words everywhere, too," said Laura. "All over fences and on the sides of buildings."

There was a noise at the front door. Mrs. Still cried, "Mercy!" and went to greet her husband.

"The doctor has been here and left this young boy," she said as she led Mr. Still into the kitchen. "He said he would call again in a couple of days to see about him."

Mr. Still was chestnut-skinned, with broad cheeks and serious eyes. He was wearing the kind of tailored suit that only fine gentlemen wore. "Ah, you must be the person the doctor went to Washington after, are you not?" he asked Ann.

Ann glanced at the three women, who were all looking at her. She swallowed hard, and said, "No."

"Where are you from, then?" asked Mr. Still.

"From York, sir," she said. But as the words left her lips, she heard her father's gentle voice in her head: "No good ever came out of a lie, baby girl."

Mr. Still was saying, "From York? Why, then, did the doctor bring you here? He went expressly to Washington after a young girl, who was to be brought away dressed up as a boy, and I took you to be the person."

Ann didn't know what to do. She didn't want to lie again, but she'd been forbidden to tell the truth. Without saying another word, she got up and walked out of the house.

Ann stood on the front porch, looking up into the cold, starry sky. She wondered if the gangs were out prowling tonight, and if they came up onto porches to grab people. She was thankful when the door opened and Mr. Still poked his head out.

Ann stood on tiptoe to peer behind him. He was alone.

"I *am* Ann Maria," she whispered. "The doctor told me not to tell anyone but you."

"Good gracious!" exclaimed Mr. Still. "You *did* have me confused. Come — my wife and the others can be trusted."

Back in the house, Mr. Still revealed Ann's true identity to the three women. They laughed at how thoroughly they'd been fooled. "And to think we let her sit there twiddling her thumbs when there was work to be done!" said Laura. They let Ann join in with the rest of the cooking.

After a fine dinner, Mrs. Still offered Ann a bath. Ann was surprised when, instead of pulling a washtub into the middle of the kitchen floor, Mrs. Still led her upstairs to a small room that already had a sink and a bathtub in it.

"But isn't it a lot of work to carry the water up here, bucket by bucket?" asked Ann. "And then to empty it, we'll have to carry it all back down the steps and outside. . . ."

Mrs. Still smiled at her. "You've not been to a large city before, then?"

Ann shook her head.

Mrs. Still leaned over the tub and fiddled with some brass knobs at one end of it. To Ann's utter amazement, water began to flow out of a brass spigot into the tub.

As Ann stared, wide-eyed, Mrs. Still explained. "Thanks to Kensington Water Works, we now have running water."

But suddenly the brass spigot began to sputter and spit, and the water coming out of it turned brown, then black, then stopped coming out at all. Mrs. Still put her hands on her hips, annoyed, and called to her husband, "William, the water gave out again."

"Use the well," he called from the parlor.

She turned off the useless spigot. "You can either get a bath the old-fashioned way, or we can try again tomorrow."

Ann chose to wait, both because she was fascinated by the thought of a modern bath in a "bathroom," as she learned it was called, and because she was so weary she'd rather simply go to bed.

"You'll bunk in with Laura," said Mrs. Still. She carried the candle down the hall to a bedroom with a four-poster bed, two wooden chairs, and a dressing table. "I presume you didn't bring a nightgown away with you, so you may borrow one of mine."

Ann was glad to take off the britches and jacket, which by now smelled quite like the horse she'd been driving. She put on the soft nightgown, gathered up a quilt she found folded at the foot of the bed, and chose a corner of the room in which to bed down for the night.

As she drifted off to sleep, someone padded into the room in stocking feet. She opened one eye and saw Laura hold a candle high, making the shadows of the chairs move and shift on the walls. Then she padded out.

"Where did Ann Maria go?" she heard Laura ask.

"She went to bed," said Mrs. Still.

"She ain't there," said Laura.

Both women returned to the room. "She's gone!" cried Mrs. Still. "William!"

Ann sat up sleepily in her corner. "I'm over here," she said in as loud a voice as she could muster.

Laura marched over to her and shook her head. "Lord, Lord."

Soon Mr. and Mrs. Still were also standing over her, looking upset.

"Did I do something wrong?" Ann asked. "Is this your quilt?" She lifted a corner of the quilt toward Laura.

"So this is what they teach children in the South?" Mrs. Still's voice rose in anger. "That they're fit to sleep on the floor like dogs?" She reached to grasp Ann's hands and pulled her up.

"Come on, girl," said Laura. "You've got a lot to learn about living like a free person."

Mr. Still left discreetly, and the two women walked Ann to the four-poster bed. Mrs. Still folded down the covers. "Up you go."

Ann touched the bed, but didn't move. "But . . . it's got sheets on it . . ."

Laura sighed. "Lord, would you get in? I'm tired as an old plow horse." Laura climbed in on one side of the bed. Her large form made a deep indentation in the mattress.

Mrs. Still bade them good night. Ann climbed hesitantly onto the soft bed and sat there, feeling the cool smoothness of the linen sheets against the soles of her feet.

"Lie down," Laura ordered.

"But I've never —"

"Stop talking, lay that skinny body of yours down, and go to sleep," said Laura.

Ann scooted under the covers and slowly laid herself down on the bed. The softness enveloped her shoulders like a hug.

"In Kentucky I used to sleep on the bare dirt, with ants and spiders and all," said

Laura sleepily. "Never again."

Ann's tired muscles relaxed into the comfort. Laura's breathing grew deep and rhythmic next to her, and she felt herself sink down into sleep.

Twenty-nine

The next day was the oddest day Ann had ever spent. First, she was awake before the rest of Philadelphia used up all the clean water, so she got a modern bath in the "bathroom." And when she was done, Mrs. Still showed her the hole in the bottom of the tub, through which the water drained away to some unknown place, so she didn't have to cart all that water down the steps after all. Ann was very impressed. She dressed in her britches and jacket and went down to breakfast.

Odder still was that after breakfast, kind, well-dressed people — both black and white — began arriving for one purpose: to meet her. They wanted to hear her story of escape, learn about her family and former owner, and marvel at how well she played the part of a boy.

"I never would have guessed!" said a tall, homely woman in a Quaker dress and bonnet.

"She fooled me!" said a spectacled man with a double chin.

These were members of the Philadelphia Vigilance Committee and "stockholders" in the Underground Rail Road, Mrs. Still explained to her. They were the people who donated money, clothing, food, time, and often a spare bedroom or attic hiding place to help fugitive slaves like her. They were part of the secret network, and they'd all known about her escape and had been waiting expectantly for her to arrive safely in the north.

Ann was very surprised to find she had become someone whom white folks and well-to-do black folks wrote letters about and talked about by name. It was a strange feeling, though no more strange than sleeping in a real bed or watching water drain out of a tub with a hole in the bottom.

Some of the Vigilance Committee members spent the morning with them, others came later and spent the afternoon, and when several more arrived for supper, Ann began to wonder if they would ever stop coming. In all the days she had spent working in the garden, kitchen, stables, and tavern from before dawn until after dark, she had never had a day as tiring as this one, spent sitting in the parlor talking to polite, enthusiastic strangers.

After supper, fortunately, Mrs. Still noticed Ann's weariness. She politely reminded the admirers that Ann was still a child, and hurried her off to bed. The soft mattress felt like a cloud; Ann was instantly asleep.

Dr. H. came to see about her before sunup the next day. Mrs. Still shook Ann awake in the chilly morning darkness. "It's time for you to go," she said softly.

Ann groaned and sat up. "But I've only just gotten here." The Stills had been so warm and welcoming. And now she had to leave to meet new strangers.

She dressed hurriedly in the cold bedroom. Laura opened one eye. "Where you going so early?" she asked.

Ann sighed. "Dr. H. is here. I suppose I'm going to New York."

Laura let out a low whistle. "Mercy. You stay close to that Dr. H. I hear the ruffians in New York walk around with knives in their teeth — make the Philadelphia Blood Tubs look like old ladies."

Ann's face went slack. New strangers and new hoodlums all in one day.

Downstairs in the foyer Mrs. Still gave

Ann a chunk of warm buttered bread for her breakfast and handed Dr. H. a package of food for their trip. She adjusted Ann's cap on her head. "You're so young to be going all alone . . ." she began, her eyes sad. Then she caught herself and brightened. "Our prayers will keep you safe," she said.

Mr. Still came down the steps with his collar and tie not yet fastened. He rested a hand on Ann's shoulder. "We would have liked to have you stay for Thanks Giving," he said. "But it's best to send you on quickly."

Dr. H. glanced at his pocket watch. "The roads between here and New York are better than those in Maryland," he said, "but we'll still be hard pressed to reach New York in one day."

Ann suddenly felt the urgency that had been making Dr. H. pace impatiently since he'd arrived. She thanked the Stills for all they had done to help her and said her last good-byes. Then she climbed back up to her perch on the carriage driver's seat to begin the next part of her journey.

In the countryside between Philadelphia and New York, Ann noticed the changes. There was less clearcut and more forest.

The snow began as a sprinkling on the ground, and became deeper as they traveled north. By the time they neared New York City, there were several inches of snow on the fields, the forest floor, and the road, and clinging to the branches of the towering pines.

As they rode the ferry across the Hackensack River, the sun set behind gray clouds. The ferryboat splashed through the icy water and made Ann seasick. By the time they boarded the ferry to cross the Hudson River, they had only the moon to light their way. It was not a small ferry, like the one they'd shared with only the ferryman on the Susquehanna. It was a large, flat boat with a huge paddle wheel and a smokestack to power the wheel, and was crowded with other carriages, horses, and passengers. Many of the people were dressed richly. Ann had never seen so many tall top hats and finely embroidered shawls. A stiff wind rippled the water, making the moon's reflection glitter and dance. Ann pulled her cap down as far as it would go and huddled close to Dr. H.'s horse.

When the ferry neared the shore, Ann could see in the moonlight that the harbor was teeming with other boats. Some were sailing vessels, with their ghostly white sails bulging in the wind, and others were steam-powered, with their smokestacks spewing the black smoke of coal fires.

Onshore the din of crates and boxes being thrown onto the docks combined with the shouts of the workers. Dr. H. helped her lead the horse onto dry land, then mounted the driver's seat with her and took the reins. He had to dodge other carriages, pedestrians, wagons filled with barrels, and fast-trotting horses just to get to the street. Ann glanced up at the sign: Barclay Street.

Dr. H.'s carriage continued to weave in and out of the rushing traffic. The streets were lit everywhere with gas lamps, and in their amber light the life of New York City seemed to be going on as if it were midday. Tall buildings, some as much as eight stories high, rose on either side of them. Ann saw men in wide-lapeled suits, with stiffly waxed mustaches that stuck out like sheep horns under their noses. She saw ladies in colorful dresses, with feathers in their bonnets. Walking along the same sidewalks were people dressed in torn and dirty rags.

The noise was deafening. There was the sharp striking of many horseshoes against the stone pavement, red and yellow omnibuses clattering along their iron rails, the rattling of boxes in the bumping wagons, and everywhere the shouts and curses of drivers and pedestrians as people and horses and vehicles came close to colliding.

Ann rubbed her eyes. They stung from the coal smoke. She also began to cough, both from the smoke and the stench. It smelled as if all the chamber pots had been emptied directly onto the street.

They rounded a corner, and there was a bit less traffic. Ann heard what at first sounded like several babies wailing at once, then realized it was a choir of cats. Groups of men loitered on the sidewalks. Ann overheard conversations and drunken songs in the same Irish brogue she'd first heard in Philadelphia, and in another strange language Dr. H. said was German. They passed several houses where ladies with scarlet shawls draped over their bare arms stood outside, while inside it sounded as if a band was playing! Ann stared at it all, wide-eyed as an owl.

They pulled onto a street that seemed almost quiet compared to what they had just driven through. There, in front of a four-story brownstone building, Dr. H. stopped the carriage. "Here," he said. "The home of the Reverend Charles Bennett Ray. He's a colored minister from the Congregational Church. He's expecting you."

"Reverend Ray!" Ann exclaimed. "That's who my father met with when he came to New York." She felt suddenly as if she were about to meet a friend, not another stranger.

As Dr. H. walked her up the steps, Ann exclaimed, "What a big house the Reverend has!"

Dr. H. chuckled. "It's an apartment building. The Reverend just has rooms on the third floor."

Reverend Ray greeted them and took Ann's hands in his.

"You *do* look like your papa," he said. He had bushy sideburns with some gray in them, and a round, friendly face.

Ann was very happy to hear someone talk about her father. She glanced around the small apartment and imagined her father sitting on the couch, drinking tea from one of the teacups hanging in the kitchen, looking out the window at the street below.

"I'll leave you, then," said Dr. H. "I must find an inn before too late. Shall I consider the parcel from Mr. Bigelow safely delivered?"

"Safely delivered, indeed," said Reverend Ray.

What parcel? Ann wondered.

Ann thanked Dr. H., and once again felt how small her words were in the face of the risks he had taken to bring her across the Mason-Dixon Line and this far north into the free states. Dr. H. nodded modestly. "I consider it my duty," he told her.

Ann expected to be shown a place to sleep in Reverend Ray's home, but instead the Reverend put on his coat and hat. Ann followed him down the steps and out to the street, where she held the horse's bridle as Reverend Ray hooked up his wagon.

"We'll deliver you to Mr. Tappan right away and put his mind at ease," he said. "He's been waiting for this package as well. We expected you to arrive some time ago, so the Tappans have been worried to distraction."

Ann was dismayed. She wasn't carrying the package Dr. H. had mentioned and that Reverend Ray now was so intent on delivering to Mr. Tappan. Had someone forgotten to give it to her?

"Sir, I'm so sorry," she said. "But I don't have the package."

Reverend Ray gave her a puzzled look, then burst out laughing. "*You* are the package!"

"Me?" Ann asked in surprise.

"It's the way we speak and write our letters," the Reverend explained. "We refer to you, and others in your situation, as the 'parcel' or 'article' or 'item' or 'package.' That way, if a letter is intercepted or a conversation overheard, it simply sounds as if we're sending little gifts along for one another's wives. It's a sort of code, I suppose."

Reverend Ray patted his horse's flank and held out his hand to help Ann onto the rickety wagon. They rode down the street, then turned onto an iron-paved road where the wagon wheels made a hollow-sounding racket. As they traveled, Ann noticed that many of the people walking, riding horses, and driving wagons in this part of the city were Negroes. *Freedmen,* she thought with satisfaction.

Before long they came to a modest stone house with warm yellow light glowing from the windows. Here they stopped, and Reverend Ray led Ann up the front steps. A white woman, her brown hair pulled back tightly in a bun, met them at the door.

"Sarah." Reverend Ray beamed at her. "Here is the parcel from Washington."

"At last!" Sarah Tappan cried. "Come, my husband is in the parlor."

Lewis Tappan greeted Ann with a broad

smile. He was a kind-looking man with a great bulbous nose and a head that was bald on top and framed around the sides by a mass of brown and gray hair. "You've certainly been a long time coming, haven't you?" he said to Ann. "I think it was almost two years ago Jacob Bigelow first wrote to us about you."

Mrs. Tappan offered Ann a late supper, which she was ravenous for, and the adults sat with her and sipped tea while she ate. She recounted her story between mouthfuls, and they told her their side of it — the meetings with her father and the letters back and forth between themselves, Mr. Still, and Jacob Bigelow, alias "William Penn."

When they retired to the sitting room, they each carried with them a straight-backed chair from the kitchen, at Mr. Tappan's suggestion. He apologized for the absence of comfortable seats. "I can't afford to replace all of the furniture at once — just one piece at a time, as funds allow."

Reverend Ray leaned over to explain this to Ann: "The Tappans had a visit not long ago from some of their neighbors who don't like abolitionists. They dragged all of their furniture out of the house and set it on fire."

Ann sucked in her breath. "Was anyone hurt?" she asked.

"No, no," Mrs. Tappan assured her. "Just the chairs and tables and a couch."

Ann studied the faces of these three brave people, two white and one black, and wondered which required more courage: to be a fugitive, or to be the one who helped the fugitive reach safety.

As Sarah Tappan tucked Ann in to bed that night she told her, "Tomorrow is Thanks Giving, so we'll hide you here. But the next day we'll deliver you to the Reverend A. N. Freeman. He's the pastor of the Siloam Presbyterian Church in Brooklyn. He will take you to Canada."

Ann was beginning to see why they called her the "parcel" and the "package." She was, after all, being delivered quickly and efficiently from doorstep to doorstep.

The next morning at breakfast, Mrs. Tappan made a startling announcement. "A man will be here tomorrow to take your daguerreotype, Miss Ann Maria."

Ann's spoonful of porridge stopped on its way to her mouth. Only presidents and rich people had their daguerreotypes taken.

Mrs. Tappan continued, "Reverend Ray

said Mr. Bigelow has written saying your mother requested it. They want the picture taken before you change back to your rightful sex, and it will be kept as part of the Underground Rail Road records."

Ann was even more astonished. Her mother? Here she was, in this faraway city of New York, and a message had been sent from her *mother*. So this was the magic of writing letters.

Around midday, Sarah Tappan explained that it would be best if Ann stayed upstairs, since their Thanks Giving guests were not all abolitionists and could not be trusted with the knowledge that there was a runaway in the house. She took Ann to a room on the third floor. It had a fire in the fireplace, and, over in one corner, a wooden chair and a desk with an inkwell, a quill pen, and papers.

"I want you to lock the door," she told Ann. "I'll be up later with your turkey and plum pudding, and to see how you're faring."

But Ann had her eye on the desk. "I'd like to write to my family," she said.

Mrs. Tappan stared at her a moment, surprised. Then she went to the desk, opened the inkwell, and pulled out several sheets of blank paper. "Of course you may, dear. But please — don't mention the name of anyone who has helped you get here, and do keep the letters well hidden until you reach Canada. It would not be safe to post them before you cross the border."

Ann promised she would.

Mrs. Tappan left to tend to her guests, who were already beginning to fill the parlor downstairs, and Ann locked the door securely. She sat down at the desk and ran her fingers over the smooth cherry wood. She picked up the quill pen. It felt strange in her hand. She had only ever formed letters on a slate with a crude piece of chalk. She dipped the pen in the ink and moved it toward the paper. A dollop of ink dripped onto the page, making an ugly dark blotch. She sighed. She dipped the pen again, then tapped it lightly on the edge of the inkwell. This time it didn't drip.

"*Dear . . .*" She drew the pen over the paper, printing her letters the way young Miss Sarah had taught her. Her writing wasn't beautiful, like the graceful cursive she'd seen Mr. Bigelow use, but she could print out the words the way she remembered them from newspapers and books. She smiled, bit her lip, and continued slowly: *". . . Mother, Father, Catharine, and John Junyor. I miss you all more then I can say."*

She dipped and wrote, and felt in the movement of her hand that she was touching her family. It was not a solid touch, like an embrace or a kiss, but a caress, like feathers or wind. She saw her thoughts appear on the page, and hoped that when her family read her words, they would feel that she was close rather than so far away. *"They will take my dagerotype befor I leve, and send it to you. I do hope that it will not be the last time you see my face befor we meet in Heven. I send all my love. Yours, Ann Maria."*

She wiped the tears quickly off her cheeks, so they wouldn't splash down on the page and ruin the ink. As she wrote, she felt another strong tug on her heart. She pulled out a blank sheet of paper and began:

"Dear Alfred. I never ment to leve you without a word. . . ."

Thirty

The next morning Ann scarcely had time to eat breakfast before members of the New York Vigilance Committee began arriving. They praised her for her courage and pressed gifts into her arms: girl's clothes to change into once she was safe in Canada — a warm cape and bonnet, knitted brown mittens and scarf, a dress made of deep green wool, bloomers, stockings, a slip, and a small leather suitcase in which to pack it all. "You'll need everything you can carry to keep warm in Canada," said a round, pale woman in a widow's black dress.

Ann's stomach had begun to do little flips with each mention of Canada. In a very short time the Reverend Freeman would come to get her and start the journey.

"And don't you let that suitcase out of your sight," said the widow, her gray eyes narrowing, "or someone is liable to step off the train with all your possessions."

Ann's stomach did a tremendous flip. The *train?* In Philadelphia she'd watched a train rumble wildly along its tracks, spewing black smoke like an angry monster. And Laura had told her about the gory accidents, when at night folks didn't see the engine's lamp, didn't hear the warning whistle, and got torn to pieces by the monster. She didn't want to get near a train, let alone get on one.

Sarah Tappan interrupted her thoughts. "Ann Maria, the man is here to take your daguerreotype."

Ann found herself being hurried over to a chair. Lewis Tappan brought her cap and placed it carefully on her head. Sarah Tappan smoothed her lapels and straightened her tie. "We want you to look like a boy, but a nice neat boy," she said.

A lanky white man stood next to a large black contraption on stilts. He told her to sit very still: then he disappeared behind the contraption. Ann smelled something that reminded her of the orange iodine Mistress Carol used on Miss Sarah's knees when she skinned them. After a few minutes, the man told her she was free to move. As he tinkered with a thin copper plate, the air filled with the odor of rotten eggs.

"We'll send the plates to your parents as soon as they're developed," said Mr. Tappan.

A loud knock sounded at the door, and Mrs. Tappan hurried to answer it. A tall, thin-shouldered gentleman entered. He had a long face and a straight nose that made him look as if he had Indian blood in his veins along with the African blood. Everyone from the Vigilance Committee seemed to know him, and there was hand-shaking all around. When he came to Ann, he said, "You must be the guest of honor. I'm Reverend Freeman. I understand we'll be traveling to Canada together."

Ann's hands went clammy. "Yes," she said softly. All the way to Canada. Today. On a train. She did not feel the least bit ready, but knew there was nothing she could do but follow her journey to its end.

The final good-byes from the members of the Vigilance Committee, the drive through the gathering dusk in the Tappans' carriage to the train station, her first close-up view of a monster train sitting idle, spitting steam — it all felt like part of a dream. She could just as well have been watching it as living it.

Ann climbed up the steep steps into the train car. She figured it was better to be inside a train rather than outside, near the dangerous tracks. She took her seat next to the Reverend Freeman in the car reserved for colored passengers. As she looked out at the night, the train lurched, hissed, and started its slow chugging. The motion quickened and gathered speed, until they were flying through the darkness with the wide black Hudson River on their left and short jagged cliffs and forest on their right. The train jostled her, shoving her back and forth relentlessly. She felt the miles fly past with more speed than she'd ever experienced, and felt the distance growing between her and everything she had ever known. And as the rhythm of the train vibrated her bones, it meshed with an old familiar rhythm inside her, a rhythm that spoke. As she listened, it said, "Good-bye, good-bye, good-bye . . ."

Thirty-one

The train rumbled through the night. The conductor came through the car from time to time, calling out towns — Albany, Utica, Syracuse — like the names of long-lost sons. When Ann got up to find the privy, she found it difficult to walk, the car jostled so. She wondered if there were any other fugitives on board. The car was almost full, with either passengers or piles of luggage taking up every seat. A few children lay sprawled across their mothers' laps, both child and mother asleep. One young mother slept, her head tilted back, with a baby nursing at her breast. There were men in fine suits and men in torn, threadbare coats, all of them bumping from side to side with the motion of the train.

Sometimes Ann slept, then awoke with her neck stiff and her back aching. Reverend Freeman sat next to her, sometimes dozing, sometimes looking out the window into the darkness. She'd hardly spoken to him, but he seemed to understand her silence, and remained a comforting, quiet presence.

It was still dark when the train stopped at yet another town, and the commotion of passengers leaving and getting on awakened both Ann and the Reverend. He caught her eye and smiled.

"How are you holding up?" he asked.

Ann rubbed her sore neck. "I'm all right," she said. "Are we close to Canada yet?"

"Getting there," he answered. Then he pointed out the window. "Look at the mills."

The massive brick buildings stood silent, their rows of tall, dark windows staring into the night like hollow eye sockets.

"Sixty years ago," said the Reverend, "slavery was dying out. It looked as if folks were about to come to their senses and end the whole thing. But then the cotton gin came along, and folks up North here realized they could use lots of raw cotton for the mills. The only place to get raw cotton is the South, and the only way to grow it cheaply is with slave labor. Slaves growing cotton in the South meant that mill workers in the North would keep their jobs, so both Northerners and Southerners decided maybe slavery wasn't such a bad thing after all. We got a hundred new mills and thousands of new slaves."

The train started up again and carried them past the town and its mills, into the countryside. In the east the sky began to turn pink, and the snow took on a rosy glow.

"Is it time for breakfast?" Reverend Freeman asked.

"It must be," said Ann.

He opened the bundle Sarah Tappan had packed for them: slices of cold bacon between thick chunks of bread, apples, and a flask of water. They ate as the sun rose, small and white-yellow.

Ann had fallen asleep again by the time the conductor marched through their car and called, "Next stop, Buffalo!" She rubbed her eyes and sat up straighter.

The Reverend leaned close to Ann. "After Buffalo is Niagara Falls," he said quietly. "Many of the trains don't go across the suspension bridge to Canada, so we may need to get off this one and wait for one that does."

It sounded simple enough.

"The suspension bridge is the most likely place for slave catchers to be waiting," Reverend Freeman said.

Ann's stomach tensed.

"This will be our plan," said the Reverend. His voice was calm and reassuring. "We will act as if you are very ill. I will support you as if you barely have the strength to stand. Even a slave hunter will be afraid of catching a bad case of cholera or consumption. Lord willing, we'll be left alone and a train will come soon to take us over the bridge."

This sounded like a good plan. Why shouldn't it work? She'd come too far to be caught now, she decided. She watched the early-afternoon sun make the snow glitter with multicolored points of light.

At Buffalo more passengers got off than got on. Ann guessed that not many people went to the small town of Niagara Falls, and even fewer were going across to Canada.

"Next stop, Niagara Falls!"

She gripped the arm of her seat and waited. As the train pulled into the station, passengers gathered their food baskets, coats, and luggage. Reverend Freeman checked the latches on his suitcase. Ann held hers in her lap and hugged it. Outside on the platform passengers waited, their bags at their feet, their breath freezing in the cold air. Many people wore hats and coats made of fur instead of wool.

A white man in an official-looking uniform stepped onto their car. "Papers. I need to see your papers," he said.

The passengers rummaged in sacks and pockets, pulling out their documents. One man even ripped the lining out of his coat in order to retrieve his. The Reverend took his freedman's papers from his suitcase, and Ann reached inside her shirt to get hers. The uniformed man read each document carefully, checking to make sure the printed description matched the person. As he read Ann's, he looked from the paper to her, and back to the paper again. She knew he was reading a description very similar to the one in her runaway notice: thick hair, light skin, slender build, freckles. And she knew that the description, combined with the girl's clothes in her suitcase, could easily betray her. She hugged her suitcase more tightly. Then she relaxed her grip as the man handed her documents back to her and moved on to the next passenger.

After the man left the car, the train still showed no signs of moving, and no conductor came to announce the next stop. Reverend Freeman rose and began to gather their belongings. "Looks like we'll have to change trains," he said. He fixed his eyes on Ann. "We'll do just as we said."

Ann picked up their bundle of food and hoisted her suitcase, but the Reverend reached for it. "I'll take that," he said. "Remember, you're too weak to carry it."

She was ready to stumble off the train looking as sickly as she could manage. The fact that her papers had passed inspection gave her confidence, and she'd begun to think that acting ill might be rather interesting. Then she heard the dogs.

It was the sound of bloodhounds on a hunt — of "nigger dogs" in hot pursuit of a runaway. The sound froze them both, and out of the train window they saw a well-dressed man being led away in shackles. Ann's breath caught in her throat. He had made it this far — almost to Canada! And now he would be sent back. She shut her eyes and her mind against what would happen to the man once he was returned to his master.

A conductor moved through the car, asking for tickets. When he looked at theirs he said, "Clear through to Canada, eh?"

Reverend Freeman nodded.

"Sit down, then. This car goes across."

Ann sat down, trembling, and greatly relieved. The bloodhounds used one of two things to find a runaway: the scent from an item of their clothing, left behind, or the scent of fear. Dogs were not fooled by well-forged papers or elaborate disguises. Ann felt quite certain that if she'd had to walk by those hounds, they would have smelled her terror.

Ann willed the train to start and get her out of this land where innocent people could be beaten and maimed for simply wanting their freedom. Outside her window she saw the man who had checked her papers talking with the two men holding the hounds. The dogs were restless, pacing to the end of their straps, straining, being yanked back, and pacing again. Almost without thinking, Ann reached into the food bundle and pulled out a chunk of bread and bacon. She remembered, what seemed like a lifetime ago, running up a hill in the moonlight to feed Master Charles's hounds. It was one of those important things her parents had taught her, like remembering to say "sir" when speaking to one's master, or remembering to keep one's skirt away from the flames in the hearth. *Remember to have food in your hand when the hounds are near.* She pressed her fingers around the bread and bacon and rested her forehead against the window, wishing those men would leave, or the train would start, or both.

She glanced at Reverend Freeman in his seat next to her. He sat silently, his eyes closed and his head bowed. She saw his lips move in prayer. Suddenly it struck her that he was in more danger than she, and her chest went cold. If they were caught, she, at least, would be sent back alive. Would the Reverend Freeman receive his trial and sentence and punishment right here on the cliffs overlooking the Niagara River? She shuddered, and touched his hand lightly. As he opened his eyes to look at her, a dog's yowl startled them both. The sound did not come from outside on the platform. It came from behind them, at the end of their car. Ann jumped up to kneel on her seat to see. The three men she'd seen talking together, and the two hounds, had just entered their car.

"One more search before we go over the bridge," the man in the uniform said.

The hounds yelped and strained at their collars. Two of the small children began to cry. A woman swatted at one of the dogs with an umbrella, and the dog's owner threatened to hit her.

"You have checked our papers. Why are

you molesting us with these hounds?" Reverend Freeman's voice boomed above the mayhem.

"If your papers are real, then you have nothing to worry about, now do you, boy?" the uniformed man snapped.

Ann took calm, slow breaths. She blocked the fear out of her mind. If only her own safety had been at stake, she might not have been able to keep the terror at bay, but she must not — *would* not — be the cause of horrible things happening to Reverend Freeman. The bread felt sweaty in her palm.

The dogs moved down the aisle, rowdy and excited, but not yet locked into a scent that said "fugitive." Ann wished she could tell Reverend Freeman how important it was to stay calm, but there was no time.

The dogs yelped, yanked on their straps, and raced the last few paces to the Reverend's seat, dragging their owners with them. They barked viciously at the Reverend, baring their teeth, their owners barely able to restrain them.

"Call your dogs off," Reverend Freeman held up his hands to protect his face. "Call them off, I say!"

"I think we have something here," one of the men said, grinning. With one hand he held his dog back, and with the other he grasped Reverend Freeman's arm. "You're coming with us, boy." He jerked his chin at Ann. "You, too. Let's go."

Reverend Freeman yanked his arm out of the man's grasp, and at the same moment, Ann shot her hand inside the breast of the Reverend's suit. She pretended to fumble around, and when she pulled her hand out she revealed the bread and bacon.

"Uncle," she found herself saying calmly, "why do you always keep your lunch in your coat like that? You're driving those poor dogs crazy."

She broke the morsel in two and threw one to each of the dogs. Then she quickly found the rest of their bread and bacon and continued throwing bits to the now well-distracted hounds. "Your dogs seem mighty hungry, sir," she said as amiably as she could muster, tossing the last of the food at the snapping mouths. "They wanted that bacon real bad."

The dogs sniffed the floor, the seats, and Reverend Freeman's breast pocket; they pulled to get at Ann to sniff her hands. But they were quiet. They no longer cared about leading their masters to a fugitive and her escort. Their only interest was in more food.

The men scratched their heads.

"I told you we wasn't feeding them enough," one of the men said, and punched his partner in the arm.

"I know, I know." The other man rubbed his arm, annoyed.

They led the hounds off the car. As they left, Ann heard one of them say, "Stupid nigger — keeping that greasy old bacon right in his coat pocket. They don't know nothing about living like civilized people."

Ann and the Reverend looked at each other. She smiled shakily. He took out his handkerchief and mopped his brow with trembling hands. The train gave a rumble and a hiss, and slowly began to move. Ann gasped. "We're going!" she cried.

The train picked up speed, and within minutes it left the solid earth. It snaked its way onto the suspension bridge hanging between the States and the free land of Canada. Hundreds of feet below, the emerald-green Niagara River wound through the gorge. Here and there on its surface, flecks of white rapids glistened in the sun. On either side stood tall, steep cliffs. Ann watched as the far cliff, the one called Canada, came closer and closer.

As the river below disappeared and the train once again rejoined solid earth, Reverend Freeman reached for her. "Thank God!" he cried. He clasped her hands in his. "We are safe in Canada!"

Thirty-two

Ann couldn't stay still in her seat. She pushed past Reverend Freeman's knees into the aisle and would have danced a jig there, except that the jostling of the train nearly knocked her over. She leaned almost onto the lap of a very large woman so she could get a good look out of the other side of the train.

"We're in Canada!" she told the woman exuberantly.

"I know it, honey." The woman clutched her purse and eyed Ann curiously. "Now, you just sit down and look out your own window, you hear?"

Ann grinned at her and happily went back to her seat, though she still wriggled with excitement. "Look!" she cried, pointing. "The trees are different. The sunshine is different. *Everything* is different — even the clouds and the sky!"

The Reverend laughed, but didn't tell

her that it was she who had changed, not the sun and trees and clouds.

"This is *mine*," she continued, watching out the window, taking it all in. "Here I belong to no one but myself, so this all belongs to me." She had her face so close to the window she kept fogging it up, and then had to wipe it with her sleeve.

Reverend Freeman nodded along with the motion of the train. "I suppose it does, Miss Ann Maria. I suppose it does."

The conductor came through calling, "Next stop, St. Catharine's."

The Reverend hurriedly opened his suitcase and took out paper, pen, and ink. "I want to write a few lines to our friends in New York to let them know we've arrived safely," he said. "I'll post them in St. Catharine's."

Ann imagined the joyful news spreading from the Tappans and Reverend Ray in New York, to the Stills and Dr. H. in Philadelphia, to Jacob Bigelow and her family in Washington City, and even to the Powder Boy, wherever he was. All the risks they'd taken and the work they'd done had been well worth it. She was safe, and free, in Canada.

She remembered her own letters and reached under her shirt to retrieve them.

The ink had run a little from being close to her skin, but the addresses were still legible. "Would you post these, too?" She handed them to Reverend Freeman.

When the Reverend stepped off the train in St. Catharine's, Ann watched him with satisfaction. In a few days her family would receive her letter. They would learn that she was well, and feel her love for them through her written words. And in a few days Alfred would receive a letter, too. He would take it to one of the free blacks in Rockville who could read. At last, he would learn that she had not left him so abruptly on purpose, that she cared deeply for him and always would, even though they would not see each other again on this earth.

The afternoon sun sank low as the train rumbled across the flat, snowy landscape. They pulled out their food basket and ate the last of the apples.

The train stopped at many small towns, and Ann dozed between stops. It was dark night and Ann was quite groggy by the time the conductor came through calling, "Chatham! Next stop, Chatham, Canada West."

Reverend Freeman nudged her. "That's our stop," he said.

As she stepped off the train, icy air bit her nose and cheeks. She shivered. For once, she was glad to be wearing shoes.

A black man with a mustache and a dark, heavy coat approached them. "Evening," he said. "Are you in need of a boardinghouse?"

"Yes," Reverend Freeman answered.

The two men walked and talked and Ann walked behind them, listening. The man was Sherwood Barber, owner of the Villa Mansion, a boardinghouse nearby where colored folks were welcome. His wife, Martha, would be happy to fix them a hot meal.

"Is it possible to go to Dresden tonight?" the Reverend asked. "We have relatives there."

"I'm afraid not," said Mr. Barber. "There's no moon, the road is rough, and there's no conveyance can be got tonight. You're welcome to stay with us, though."

Reverend Freeman accepted the offer.

"Is that your son?" asked Mr. Barber, glancing around behind him at Ann.

"No," said Reverend Freeman. "Do you know a man by the name of William Bradley living in Dresden? This is a relation of his."

"I know him well. Is that his brother?"

The Reverend hesitated. "No — not exactly a brother," he replied.

Mr. Barber gave him a puzzled look, but didn't ask any more questions.

The boardinghouse had a cozy sitting room filled with a lively group of boarders and friends of the Barbers. Mr. Barber began the introductions, but before he could include Ann, she slipped to a seat in a corner near the fire. She was too tired to play her role as Joe Wright, too bone-weary to talk to anyone.

She warmed her hands and feet at the fire. All she really wanted was supper, a place to sleep, and the light of day to return so they could go to Dresden to find Aunt Mimi and Uncle William.

Ann noticed Reverend Freeman talking quietly with Mr. and Mrs. Barber. She turned her face to the fire and hunched toward it. If someone would just offer her a piece of cold cornbread and a blanket, she could leave this crowded room. She flinched when Martha Barber laid a hand on her shoulder.

"I'm sorry I startled you," said Mrs. Barber. "But I'd like to show you to your room."

All right, Ann thought, she would go to sleep without supper. Her stomach grumbled, but a place to lie down sounded just as good as food, so she followed willingly. So did every single one of the women from the company. They took her upstairs to a bedroom and closed the door.

There was a lot of whispering among the ladies, but Mrs. Barber spoke directly to Ann. She was a small woman, with soft brown eyes and skin the color of ripe walnuts.

"We've been told you might like to change your clothes," she said.

Of course! There was no longer any need of a disguise.

Ann had never imagined having so many handmaids. The women all wanted to help. They gave her water to wash with, and as soon as it touched her skin she felt better. They fastened on her petticoat, buttoned up her dress, and combed her short hair, all the while chattering about what a daring escape she'd made and how pleased they were to have her here. The green dress was beautiful, with a flowing skirt that made Ann feel graceful and feminine.

When the ladies decided Ann was ready, they walked her down the steps like a queen surrounded by her court. "Gentlemen," Martha Barber said in a loud voice. All heads turned. "I would like you to meet Miss Ann Maria Weems."

Reverend Freeman must have explained what had been going on upstairs, because the group broke into cheers and applause. Ann half hid her face in joyful embarrassment as she was pulled into the room by exuberant people who wanted to congratulate her on her successful journey. A few of the men even slapped her on the back, seeming to forget that she was actually a girl and not the boy she'd come in looking like. The group quieted and listened intently when Reverend Freeman told the story of their encounter with the dogs. Several other people chimed in with their own stories of escape, from Virginia, Georgia, and Delaware. Some had ridden steamboats; others had traveled much of the way on foot. Two of the people there had stopped at William Still's house on their way north.

"There are about three thousand fugitives right here in Chatham," said one of the men.

Ann realized that she had entered a community in which people would understand what she'd been through. They would also understand her homesickness, because they felt it, too.

Martha Barber fixed them a late supper

of boiled turnips and salt herring. Toward bedtime, Ann excused herself and slipped away from the group into the backyard, in the direction of the privy. Before she got there, she stooped down and cleared away a patch of snow with her hands. Underneath was the frozen ground. She scraped at it with chilled fingers until she'd managed to dig up a small chunk of earth.

"There," she said. "This is free soil for *me*."

Thirty-three

The next day was Sunday, and in order to keep the Sabbath there could be no traveling. Ann was impatient, but thankful for the day of rest after the long, wearying train ride.

Very early Monday morning, they left in a wagon borrowed from Mr. Barber, with Ann in her green dress, cape, bonnet, and mittens. She offered to drive, but Reverend Freeman just laughed and took the reins. They rode through the town of Chatham, with its low-slung, unpainted houses, and out into the countryside.

The land was flat, with roads straighter than any Ann had ever seen. In some places the road was merely a slice through dense forest. In other places the land had been cleared for farming and the wind swept over wide, flat fields. They saw only a few houses and passed just two other wagons. It had warmed up a bit. The melting snow mixed with the mud of the road and made for a treacherous and slippery journey.

It was afternoon when Reverend Freeman spotted two black men on the road ahead, one on horseback and one on foot. "I'll stop and ask directions," he said. "We must be very close."

As they approached the men, Ann, eager to act like a proper young lady after weeks of acting like a boy, discreetly turned her head so that her bonnet hid her face.

"Hello," called Reverend Freeman. "Can you tell me how far it is to Mr. Bradley's?"

"Not much more than a mile," said one of the men. "That way, over Little Bear Creek. But I reckon I am the one that you want to find. My name is Bradley."

Ann swung her head around and saw, atop a dapple-gray horse, her uncle William.

As soon as Uncle William saw her face, he cried, "My Lord! Ann Maria, is that you? My child, is it you? We never expected to see you again!" He jumped down from his horse and Ann scrambled from the wagon. She leaped into his arms.

They held each other and Ann wept. Her journey had finally ended.

"We had given you up," said Uncle William. He held her away from him and took a long look. "Oh, what will your aunt say? She will die!"

Ann wiped tears from her cheeks. "She'll probably say, 'I *told* you to say good-bye to your uncle before you ran off with your brothers!' "

Her uncle laughed and clasped her to his chest again. "I was on my way to Malden, but I can't go now. I'll go on ahead of you back to the house, and open the gate and have a good fire to warm you."

He galloped off, the other man tipped his hat to them, and Ann and the Reverend started up their horse again. That last mile felt like the longest mile she'd yet traveled. Finally they approached the cleared fields, barns, smokehouse, and one-and-a-half-story frame house of her aunt and uncle's homestead.

Aunt Mimi stood at the gate, wringing a handkerchief in her hands. "Ann Maria, is it you? Oh, Ann Maria!" she cried.

Ann ran to her, with cape flying and bonnet thrown back and bouncing on her shoulders. She fairly threw herself into her aunt's outstretched arms.

"We were talking about you today, and saying we would never see you again, and now here you are with us!" Aunt Mimi cried. She squeezed Ann tightly.

Ann rested her cheek on her aunt's soft shoulder and breathed in the old familiar smell of lye soap. Then she pulled her head back and stared at Aunt Mimi in alarm.

"What's wrong with your shoulder? Aunt Mimi, what happened to you?" she asked. There must have been some kind of accident to make Aunt Mimi's shoulder droop so low.

Aunt Mimi glanced at her own shoulder and moved it in a shrug. "Nothing happened, child. I'm just fine."

Ann studied her aunt. It wasn't just the one shoulder, it was both of them. In fact, her entire aunt was much lower than she should be. Suddenly Ann burst out laughing, and could hardly catch her breath to explain. "It's *me*," she said finally. "I must have grown!"

Aunt Mimi herded them all inside, out of the cold. Ann wanted to touch everything — the wooden chairs, table and cabinets her uncle had built, the dishes and flatware they'd bought with wages earned as free people, the curtains her aunt had sewn, the dried herbs hanging from the rafters, herbs they'd grown on their own land. It was theirs — the house and farm of her uncle's dreams — and now it was hers as well.

Aunt Mimi insisted that Reverend Free-man stay for supper before traveling back to Chatham. Ann helped her chop cabbage to fry and mix up a batch of corn bread. The commotion woke the babies from their naps, and Ann was introduced to her new cousins. Margaret, the older of the two, climbed into Ann's lap and gazed at her with happy curiosity. The parts of her hair that were long enough to braid were in neat plaits, and the rest of her black curls ringed her chubby face. Aunt Mimi changed baby Elias's clothes, which were soaking wet, and then handed him to Ann. He stuck his fingers in her mouth and she, obligingly, kissed them.

Over a supper of fried cabbage, pickled beets, and corn bread, Ann recounted her story, with Reverend Freeman chiming in on the last chapter. That got him talking, and he told them about the abolitionist work he'd done when he was pastor of the Abyssinian Congregational Church in Portland, Maine.

"We'd hide the fugitives in the vestry of the church," he said, his eyes alive with the memories. "We'd have a ship waiting to take them to Canada or some other safe port, and a group of us ready to surround them as a kind of bodyguard so they wouldn't be seen while going between the church and the harbor." He leaned forward. "We would wait until nightfall. . . ." He shoved back his chair. "Then we'd rush from the church! Run down to the harbor! The fugitives would scurry up the gangplank onto the ship. The crew would pull in the gangplank before anyone could say, 'What's going on here?' and the ship would be off." He sat back with a look of satisfaction.

Ann and her aunt and uncle were very impressed, and Uncle William added his stories about escape to the ones already told. In between, Ann answered questions about her parents, her brothers, Catharine, Hannah, and David. And every once in a while, Aunt Mimi clasped her hands together and cried out, "My child, you are here! Thank God, you are free!"

Thirty-four

The next day Aunt Mimi took out her needle and thread, some linen she'd bought to make a summer dress with, and cornhusks saved from the fall harvest, and in a couple of hours she'd made a brand-new bed for Ann. Soon Ann was sharing not only the bedroom but also her new bed with her young cousins, who found every opportunity to snuggle in with her. Reverend Freeman had left Ann with five dollars to help her get started in her new life. Ann had never held that much money before, so she immediately gave it to Aunt Mimi, who said she'd buy material to make her a nightgown and, come spring, a cotton dress.

This new life as a free person took a little getting used to. Sometimes, half awake in the morning, with rays of sunlight already filtering through her window, Ann had a moment of panic, thinking she had overslept and would get a beating from

Mistress Carol. She welcomed the delicious flood of relief when she remembered where she was.

Ann fell naturally into working beside her aunt and uncle, making soap, baking bread, feeding Elias, bathing Margaret, milking their one cow, carrying the slop to the barn for the pigs. She had assumed that this would be the rhythm of her life now — doing the work she'd always done, only doing it now as a free person, with time for rest, and the joy of eating anything and everything they grew on the farm. There was milk for the children, butter and cheese they made from the milk, real bread every day instead of only on Christmas, eggs from the chickens, and, when Uncle William decided it was time for a treat, candies bought from the grocer in Dresden. They even had meat on most Sundays, either from their collection of chickens and pigs, or brought home from a day's hunting by Uncle William. Ann felt contented working beside her aunt and uncle. Then, one day, Uncle William made an announcement that changed everything.

"I've talked to the Wallaces, and it's all worked out," he said. It was late afternoon, and the sunset had turned the snowy fields to orange. "You'll start school Monday morning."

Ann dropped the comb she'd been using to fix Margaret's hair. It clattered to the floor. "School?" she asked, not sure she understood.

"It's nothing fancy, mind you — just a group of children in the Wallaces' kitchen — but Mrs. Wallace does a fine job of teaching. Now, the white children, they have a schoolhouse and a hired teacher and new books. We can complain all we want — and we *have* — but they're not going to let the colored children into that white school. . . ."

He continued to talk about the unfair education laws, and the poor-quality ink that was all the Wallaces' school could afford, but Ann was hardly listening. *School.* In Rockville she'd always had the door slammed in her face, and the most she could do was stand under the window to hear snatches of what the teacher said. But come Monday, she would be welcomed inside as a student. She stood on tiptoe and hugged her uncle around his neck. "Thank you, Uncle William," she cried. "Thank you so very much!"

It made sense, Ann decided, that the

school in Dresden was in the Wallaces' house. The seven Wallace children made up half the class. Ann was given a book — a reader — which was as tattered and worn as her uncle had warned her it would be. But it would be hers until school let out in the spring, and that was all that mattered. Mrs. Wallace was impressed with how well Ann could cipher numbers, read, and write already, and promised she would help her do even better.

The first person Ann noticed was Priscilla Wallace. She was tall and thin, with her hair in neat braids, and, as Mrs. Wallace pointed out, was about the same age as Ann. When class was let out for the day, Priscilla sidled up to Ann shyly. "Mum says I can walk you partway home, if you'd like," she said.

Ann agreed happily, and they walked out into the brisk air.

Priscilla filled Ann in on the gossip about the children in the class: her older brother Samuel, who was nice but shy; her younger sister Helena, who once knocked over the inkwell and got a good paddling in front of everyone; and little Philip from up the road, who was always wetting his trousers and being sent home to change.

Ann enjoyed Priscilla's stories, and decided she would never do anything that would earn her a paddling in front of the class.

"I'll be fourteen next September, the twelfth," said Priscilla. "When will you turn fourteen?"

Ann hesitated, then answered as best she could. "In the spring."

"So you're a little older than me. What day in the spring?" asked Priscilla.

Ann felt a tightness in her throat. "At corn-planting time," she said very softly. She felt her face burn red and wished she hadn't said anything at all.

"Don't you remember when your birthday is?" Priscilla said loudly, teasingly.

Ann stopped walking and jutted out her jaw. "I don't have a birthday," she snapped. She turned and stomped down the road, leaving Priscilla startled and confused.

"Wait!" she called after Ann, running to catch up. "Everyone has a birthday. If you don't know yours, let's pick one for you."

Ann gave her a suspicious glare. "Pick one?"

"My pa plants his corn around the first part of May. Pick a date, and you'll have a birthday." Her expression was sincere and friendly.

But Ann shook her head. "I don't —"

Priscilla interrupted, "How can we celebrate if we don't have a date?"

Ann blinked. Celebrate? The way
Richard Price had celebrated the year he
turned eleven?

Priscilla continued, "You could pick
May third, or May sixth, or —"

"May sixth," Ann said quickly. There,
she'd done it.

Priscilla grinned. "We'll still be in
school. I'll ask my mum to bake a cake for
you."

A thrill went up Ann's spine. There was
so much newness about living as a free
person. What would be her next surprise?

At the post office in Dresden, Uncle
William picked up a brown envelope ad-
dressed to "Miss Ann Maria Weems, c/o
Mr. William Bradley, Dresden, Canada
West." Ann held it in her hands, almost
afraid to open it, lest she break the spell of
joy she felt when she read the return ad-
dress: "Mrs. Arabella Weems, c/o E. L.
Stevens, Duff Green's Row, Capitol Hill,
Washington City, USA."

"Open it before I die from the sus-
pense," said Aunt Mimi.

"Go ahead. It won't bite," Uncle William chimed in.

Ann opened the envelope, being careful not to tear it, and read her mother's careful, flowing script. " *'My dear daughter . . .'*" She shared the news with her aunt and uncle as she read, "They're so thankful I made it here safely, and they send you both their love. Oh! She had the baby! It's a girl, she's healthy, and they've named her Mary."

"Thank the Lord," said Aunt Mimi.

"And . . ." Ann's face lit up. She flapped one hand as if she'd touched something hot. She was barely able to get out the next words. "They've found Addison and Joseph in Alabama! They've found them!"

Ann clutched the letter and jumped up and down as she hadn't done since she was a small child. Margaret jumped with her, giggling, and Elias clapped his hands.

"Keep reading. Keep on reading, now," Uncle William said, trying to calm her.

Ann stood still and focused on the letter again. "Their owner has agreed to turn them over to my father once the price has been paid for them, and the Vigilance Committee has already raised the money. Oh, Aunt Mimi, Uncle William — they're going to be *free!*"

Aunt Mimi was dabbing her eyes, and Uncle William put his arm around her.

"This whole family is going to be free," Uncle William said with conviction. "What does it say about Augustus?"

Ann read further and her joy dimmed. "They've still not found Augustus, but they will keep searching." Then she crumpled with dismay. "Oh, no . . . oh, no," she whispered.

"What is it, child? Tell us!" Aunt Mimi grasped Ann's hand and gave it a little shake.

"She heard from Cousin David that Master Charles has had himself appointed postmaster in Rockville. He intercepted a letter I sent there. He saw the postmark from Canada."

"That snake . . ." Uncle William began.

"So now all of Rockville knows I'm in Canada, and Master Charles won't come after me, and he'll give up having me hunted." The words she spoke were happy, even glorious, but her feelings were of despair.

"What is it, Ann Maria?" Aunt Mimi asked. "There must be something you're not telling us."

Ann shook her head slowly. "She says I won't be able to write to Hannah and David in Rockville because he'll likely grab any letter from Canada West, hoping to find proof of who helped me get here . . ." Her voice trailed off. "My letters won't get through."

"That's no problem," said Uncle William. "You won't return, and he won't cross into Canada to get you."

Aunt Mimi nodded, but her eyes were still on Ann's crestfallen face. "There's something either in that letter or in your head you're not telling us, and I want to know what it is this instant before you worry me into my grave."

Before Ann dissolved into tears, all she was able to blurt out was "Now he'll never know!"

Thirty-five

Aunt Mimi helped Ann go over every piece of why she felt so sad about Alfred. First, that she'd left without a word after she'd promised not to.

"A slave's word is no good — not because of the slave, but because of the slavery," said Aunt Mimi. "You would have kept your promise if you could, child. He'll know that in his heart, even without a letter."

Second, she sorely missed him. Her aunt smiled and said she understood. Then she added, "But there are plenty of handsome young boys right here in Dresden. Once you take a shine to a new boy, you won't miss Alfred so much."

Ann frowned.

And last, she felt awful that Alfred was still in slavery and she was not. "There is not a thing you can do about that," said Aunt Mimi. She told Ann how many of the fugitives in Dresden, in Chatham, and farther south in Buxton had left wives and children, or husbands, behind in slavery and there wasn't anything they could do except hope and pray that someday their loved ones would be free.

"And do they get married again here in Canada?" she asked.

Her aunt shook her head. "Sometimes. But if you ask me, that's wrong. Most times they don't. They just wait to be reunited in heaven."

Ann rested her chin on her fist. "Then I won't ever get married," she said.

"What do you want to go and decide that for?" her aunt asked, surprised.

"Because Alfred was going to ask me to marry him when I turned fifteen. That's as good as being married."

Aunt Mimi smoothed Ann's hair away from her face. "Child, you've got lots of years left to meet a boy and fall in love and —"

"I'm not ever going to love any boy except Alfred," Ann said emphatically.

Her aunt pursed her lips, but didn't argue.

Everyone said this winter, the winter of 1856, was the coldest they'd had in years.

The snow lay deep and quiet. Uncle William changed the wheels on his wagon to sleigh runners so he could still get into Dresden to pick up mail and groceries. By February 22 the temperature had dropped to minus fourteen degrees Fahrenheit, and school was canceled for a week because it was too cold for the children to walk to the Wallaces' house. Ann helped her aunt sew a new dress for Margaret, who was growing fast, and a pair of tiny britches for Elias, who had started walking. In the evenings, she helped Uncle William make plans for the garden, which would be bigger this year because of Ann's arrival.

It was April before the snow started to melt. With the warm weather came the mud, and flies, and birdsongs. Also, with the warmth, came the fugitives. Hardly a day passed that they didn't hear the church bells ring out their news: another former slave had arrived from the States.

"Before 1833, when Canada still had slavery, Canadian slaves often escaped into the United States to freedom," said Uncle William. "Now Canada is returning the favor."

On May 6, Mrs. Wallace brought out a walnut cake for the children at school to share in honor of Ann turning fourteen.

That evening Aunt Mimi surprised Ann with a most wonderful gift: a new summer dress of sky-blue calico. "I told you I'd make you that dress someday," said Aunt Mimi.

The weeping willow tree in the yard had sprouted buds, then tiny leaves, then a curtain of leaves that provided privacy for Ann and Priscilla when they climbed up into its branches to talk.

"My brother Samuel keeps asking about you," said Priscilla one warm, breezy day.

The soft willow branches swayed, then settled.

"Hmmph," said Ann. Samuel had been spending more time at school staring at her than tending to his studies lately, and had gotten rapped on the knuckles for it more than once.

"I think he likes you. Do you like him?" Priscilla asked innocently.

Ann sighed. Samuel was handsome enough, tall and lanky with curled-up eyelashes and a disarming smile. He was two years older than she, but shy as a minister's son. "He's nice. . . ." Ann began, but couldn't say more than that. How could anyone understand? All the other boys seemed like shadows compared with her memories of Alfred. There was that first Christmas they'd danced, his hand pressed against the small of her back. There was the way he asked her how she was faring each time he met her on their walks to and from Sarah's school, and how she'd begun to feel that he was part of her family once he knew all the best stories about her life in Unity. There was the sparkle in his eyes when they sat on the grass and talked in the warm Maryland sun, and of course, there was that soft, apple-scented kiss. . . .

"He's very nice," Priscilla was saying. "He's not vulgar like some of the boys."

"I know." Ann was still at a loss for words.

She was relieved to hear her uncle call, "Ann Maria, where are you?"

"I have to go," said Ann. "Uncle William wants the whole garden hoed before the Sabbath."

The two girls swung down out of the willow, and Priscilla headed home.

"Ann Maria, you've got a package!" Uncle William called.

Ann ran to meet him. It was a large, fat envelope that bore the familiar return address from Washington City.

"Let me go find your aunt so we can hear the news together," said her uncle.

She brought the package inside, and her aunt and uncle waited expectantly while she pulled out a letter, along with the June 7 issue of the *Montgomery Sentinel* newspaper. Elias grabbed for the papers, and Uncle William picked him up, out of reach. Margaret climbed into Ann's lap as she read.

"She says the baby, Mary, had the croup but she's better now. John Junior talks all the time, and his favorite word is 'Papa.'" Ann held up the newspaper. "The copy of the *Montgomery Sentinel* is so I can read news from home. She says my runaway notice stopped running in it a while ago."

"Hallelujah!" said Uncle William.

"Papa is working hard, and, my goodness . . ." Ann's eyes widened as she read. "Catharine has decided she wants to become a nurse! She is saving her wages to pay for the schooling."

"Wonderful!" exclaimed her aunt. Her uncle hummed his approval.

Ann opened the newspaper and glanced over the front page. But remembering her responsibilities, she turned to her uncle. "Did you want me to finish the hoeing today?"

"That old garden can wait. You go enjoy your paper."

Ann returned to the willow tree. She hoisted herself up, got comfortable with her back leaning against the trunk and one leg dangling down, and settled in to read.

She turned first to the page that held the ads — advertisements for jobs, notifications about auctions, and runaway notices. Sure enough, her own runaway notice was not there. But what she did find startled her so profoundly that she nearly fell out of the tree. "Aunt Mimi!" she shrieked.

Her aunt came running out of the house. "Good heavens!" she cried.

Ann clambered down to the ground, scraping her arm in her haste. "Aunt Mimi, look!" She ran to her aunt and shoved the newspaper under her nose.

"Gracious child, I thought you'd fallen out of that silly tree. You know I can't read without my glasses. What is it?"

Ann tried to catch her breath long enough to speak the words, "It's a runaway notice.

" '$100 reward. Ran away from the subscriber, living in Rockville, Montgomery County, Maryland, on Saturday 31st of May last, Alfred, 22 yrs. 5'7" dark copper color and rather good looking. He had on when he left a dark blue and green plaid frock coat of cloth and lighter colored plaid pantaloons.'

It's signed by Dr. Anderson!"

Aunt Mimi grasped Ann's hands, closed her eyes, and began to pray. "Dear Lord, protect this boy. Let the slave catchers walk right by him without seeing him. Send him safely to a place where he can be free."

Thirty-six

Ann hummed as she dried the last of the breakfast dishes.

"You sound like your heart is filled up with sunshine," said her aunt.

Ann smiled. "I suppose it is."

Her aunt eyed her. "And my guess is, it has something to do with a boy."

Ann felt herself blush. "You can't blame me for feeling good, now that I know Alfred got himself out of slavery."

Aunt Mimi clicked her tongue. "You still got *that* boy on your mind?"

Ann looked down at the floor. "Yes, ma'am."

"You've got to pray for him, that he doesn't get caught, and then put him out of your head."

"I've been praying," said Ann, "and I know he'll be safe. He'll outsmart those slave hunters, I just know it. So I'm happy for him." She shrugged. "I can still think about him if it makes me happy, can't I?"

Her aunt gave an exasperated sigh and wiped her brow with her apron. "Lord, the sun is barely up and it's hot as a frying pan already. Why don't you take a walk over to Priscilla's house and spend some time with her in the shade. We can get our chores done this evening."

Ann laughed. "Aunt Mimi, if you think this is hot, you've forgotten what Maryland was like!"

"Indeed I have," said her aunt, and wiped her brow again.

Ann knew why she was being sent to Priscilla's, though, and it wasn't to spend time in the shade. It was to give Samuel a chance to come out of his shyness long enough to speak to her.

"It doesn't feel hot to me. I'll go pull up some radishes for dinner."

"No, you won't either," said her aunt. "I don't want you fainting from heatstroke. Now go on and visit with the Wallaces." It wasn't a suggestion. It was an order.

Reluctantly, Ann removed her apron. She walked through the gathering heat into town and to the Wallace house. Timidly, she raised her hand to knock on the front door.

At that moment several of the smaller

Wallace children, all girls, came running around the corner, squealing and laughing. After them came Samuel, arms outstretched, fingers bent claw-style. He growled menacingly and the girls shrieked and huddled together. Samuel looked up, saw Ann watching him, and nearly collapsed with embarrassment.

"I — uh — we were playing. Um. Priscilla is —" He stumbled over a few more syllables, then stopped talking altogether and simply gazed at Ann.

"Priscilla is . . . here?" she asked. His gaze made her uncomfortable, just as it had during the final few weeks of school before summer vacation.

"Uh . . . yes. Out back. Hanging the wash."

The three little girls giggled. "Be the bear again, Sammy!" cried Dolly, the smallest.

Samuel shook his head. Ann could feel his eyes follow her as she walked around to the backyard to find Priscilla.

Priscilla, too, seemed to be suffering from the heat. She wiped a sweaty cheek on her sleeve as she lifted her father's heavy work trousers to hang them on the line.

"You want some help?" Ann offered.

Priscilla blew at the cloud of gnats surrounding her head. "I'm just finishing up," she said.

"My aunt told me to come over here and sit in the shade with you. Why she thought you'd be sitting, I don't know," said Ann.

Priscilla huffed as she lifted the empty laundry basket to her hip. "Can we go to your house? If we stay here, my mum will put us both to work."

Ann nodded agreeably.

On their way back to her house they passed a group of older boys from town. Ann had seen two of them at church.

"Hello, girls," one of the boys called. "Are you going swimming? Maybe we'll come watch," he taunted.

"Then we can steal their clothes!" another blurted out.

The group of them hooted and slapped each other on the back.

"Leave us alone!" Priscilla clenched her fists and scowled at them.

"Oooh, look out. She's going to fight us," another boy teased.

Ann rolled her eyes and took Priscilla by the arm to lead her away. "They're like babies," she said. "Come on."

The girls walked away, and the boys lost interest and headed toward town.

"I told you some of the boys around here are vulgar," said Priscilla.

"I know, and your brother is not like them," Ann said in a tired voice.

"It's true," said Priscilla defensively.

"It's just that he's so *quiet*," said Ann. "Don't you have to be able to talk with a boy if you want to get to know him?"

"Yes," said Priscilla. "So you could come to my house for supper one evening, and you two could sit out on the porch together. Then he'll talk to you."

Ann sighed. "Maybe," she said.

As they neared Ann's house, Priscilla groaned. "Lord, it's hot. I don't even think the willow will be cool today."

"We could go dangle our feet in the river," Ann suggested.

Priscilla said that sounded perfect.

"I'll go tell my aunt and uncle where we're going," said Ann.

The Sydenham River was not like the rivers back in Maryland, with their rocky banks, clear, fast-running water, and straight courses. The Sydenham wound lazily through the flat plain, with so many turns and curves that Ann thought it seemed as if it had lost its way. The water was deep, muddy, and slow-flowing. With its steep banks and narrow course, the river looked like a filled-up bathtub. Willow, ash, and elm trees crowded one another for space along its banks and provided a thick curtain of privacy for anyone who wanted to sit there. One bend in the river wound right onto the edge of Uncle William's land, and Ann thought of it as her own piece of the Sydenham.

Ann plopped herself down on the bank and sank her feet into the cold water. Priscilla did the same. Their movements sent ripples out in all directions. Ann leaned back and looked up at the sky between the canopy of branches overhead. "This is better than doing the wash, eh?"

Priscilla grinned. "Except I want to get all the way in."

Ann covered her mouth and giggled. "Priscilla!"

"Why not?" Priscilla splashed one foot in the water.

"What if those boys come find you — and your clothes?" Ann warned.

"They're all the way to town by now," Priscilla assured her. "You said yourself this is part of your uncle's farm. No one will bother us."

Ann's eyes widened. "*Us?* I'm not taking my clothes off out here in the middle of . . ."

"Of nothing," said Priscilla. "Shhh. Listen."

They sat very still. The slow-moving water made a very soft swishing sound around their bare legs, and the only other sounds were the larks and whippoorwills.

"No one will even know. I promise," said Priscilla. She sounded in urgent need of a partner to join in her daring idea.

The two girls exchanged one mischievous glance. Then, suddenly, they were both on their feet. Calico dresses, slips, and bloomers fell to the ground, and they leaped off the bank into the welcoming river.

Ann felt the rush of icy water over her body. When she popped her head up, she could scarcely breathe, from both the excitement and the cold.

"Isn't it glorious?" cried Priscilla, her black hair wreathed in shiny beads of water.

"Glorious and cold!" Ann tossed her head and sent silver droplets flying.

Priscilla splashed and swam easily into the middle, where the water was deepest. Ann's toes found the mucky bottom close to the steep bank, and she grabbed on to some roots for balance.

"I'll teach you how to swim," Priscilla offered.

But before Ann could answer, they both heard it: male voices, and twigs snapping underfoot.

"Help!" cried Priscilla. "It's the boys — they'll steal our clothes!"

Panicked, Ann scrambled up the bank and onto the shore, with Priscilla close behind her. They pulled on bloomers over muddy feet, and yanked their slips over their heads.

"They were coming out here to dangle their feet in the water." It was Uncle William speaking.

"You've got a right nice piece of land here, Mr. Bradley," came another voice.

"Quickly, Ann — here!" Priscilla thrust Ann's dress at her and frantically pulled her own calico on.

But Ann had stopped, transfixed. She held her dress up under her chin, but made no effort to put it on. She had heard that voice before. . . .

Uncle William stepped out of the thicket, and when he saw Ann in just her slip, he cried, "Good gracious!" and politely turned his back to her.

He grasped the shoulder of the young man who had stepped out of the trees with him, and tried to turn him around as well. But the young man, too, was transfixed.

His eyes rested on Ann, her bare arms drying in the dappled light, her blue calico clutched in her hands.

Ann barely found her voice. She whispered, "Alfred!"

Ann and Alfred were married in the Buxton Settlement in Canada by the Reverend William King. Their wedding was a large, joyous celebration, befitting the free people they were.

Ann Marie's
Route to Freedom

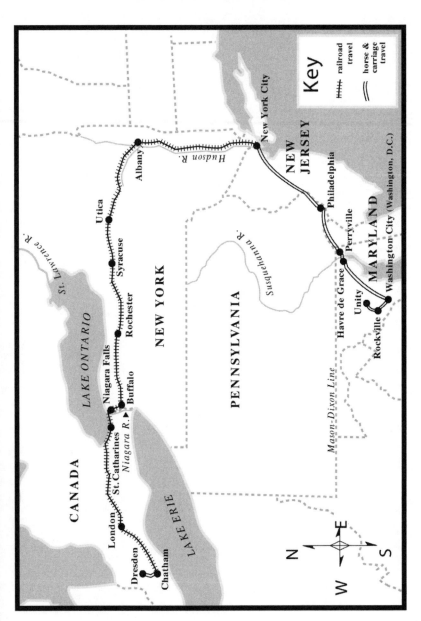

Author's Note

In writing about Ann Maria Weems, I wanted to both tell the story of this brave young girl and paint a vivid picture of life in the mid-1800s.

In order to paint this picture, I had to know as much as possible about everything I put in the story, whether it was farming methods in the 1850s or what Washington, D.C., streets looked like in 1855. I felt that every detail I could gather would help me better create a time travel experience, and so I spent five months doing full-time research and detail gathering before I started writing, and then continued my research during the two years I wrote and edited the book.

Probably the most helpful resources for this book were the thousands of pages of slave narratives I read. These first-person accounts of slavery breathed life and blood into the concept of "slave." They gave me details about clothing, food, and culture, but more than that, they gave voice to the intense emotions of slavery.

Because every character in the book is a real person, I was able to dig up actual records to uncover some of the facts of their lives. For example, I went to the land records and copied down everything Charles Price, Ann Maria's master, bought or sold from about 1840 to 1860. That's how I knew he had a roan gelding named Bob and a bay mare named Sally! I went to the District of Columbia archives and found records on Ann's sister Catharine. That's how I discovered that she had asthma and that she had gone to nursing school. Canadian census records showed me that Ann's mother, Arabella, and Aunt Mimi had learned how to read and write.

I also researched details about the land, cities, towns, and artifacts that are included in the story. I interviewed Mrs. Givens, an elderly resident of Unity. She told me about the huckleberries in the woods near where Ann lived. I went to Oakley Cabin, a restored slave cabin in Montgomery County, and lay down on the cornhusk mattress so I could capture the feelings and sounds (*crackle, crackle!*) of rolling over on it. I convinced a very nice maintenance man to let me into historic St. Mary's Catholic Church so that I could climb up into the loft, which used to be reserved for slaves and free blacks, and imagine what it must have been like when Ann worshiped there.

Sometimes the best way for me to find out what Ann herself experienced was to act out the things she actually did. When I wanted to find out why she didn't like to wrap her feet in rags during the winter, I wrapped one of my feet in rags, left the other one bare, and went outside and walked around my yard until I felt I understood. In late November, the same time Ann traveled to Canada, I bought myself a ticket on a train that followed Ann's route to Chatham (although my train ride started in Washington, D.C.). Instead of getting a sleeper car for the twenty-hour trip, I got a seat, the way Ann did, so I'd see what she saw out the windows and so I'd know what it felt like to travel for that long sitting up. (My research revealed that twenty hours in a train seat makes you bone-weary and gives you a headache!)

Of course, I wasn't only researching details, I was also piecing together Ann's story. It seems that Ann became somewhat of a celebrity in Underground Railroad circles in her day, though she has been all but forgotten today. Her story was available, but quite hidden and obscure. With the help of Anthony Cohen, Alice Newby, Bryan Prince, and Gwen Robinson, I was able to put together the bits and pieces of Ann's story from microfilmed newspaper articles, old letters found in boxes in Philadelphia and Ohio, rare books, census and land records, wills, and graveyards. Little by little, the sequence of events began to take shape.

Stealing Freedom takes literary license to make Ann's story flow well. The first part of the book, up until Ann's escape, is really a condensed version of events that happened over a period of about five years. It was necessary, for the sake of the narrative, to change some of the specifics of the events, but the essence remains true. In order to make the story full and real, I used a combination of what really happened and what *could have* happened. The latter part of the book, beginning where Ann is made to sleep in Charles and Carol Price's bedroom, actually follows her life quite closely. There are even a few places where the dialogue is taken directly from letters and accounts written a few days after the incidents occurred.

After I was done with the writing, I continued to do research so that I'd know what happened to Ann, her family, and the other people in the book. Here is some of what I found out:

Joseph and Addison were freed in 1857. The Vigilance Committee gave John Weems the money to buy his sons. By then, donations were coming in from England as well as the United States, and the Reverend Henry Highland Garnet was helping to raise funds in Scotland for the Weems family. Legally, John Weems became Joseph and Addison's owner. Then, once the boys were home safe in Washington, D.C., John Weems had manumission papers drawn up for each of them. Manumission papers were legal documents that set a slave free. Addison got a job as a laborer, and Joseph became a foreman at the Treasury Department. In 1870, Addison shared a home in Washington with Joseph, Joseph's wife, Eliza, and their two sons, three-year-old Eugene and baby Ulysses.

Augustus was the last member of the family in slavery, but finally in late 1857 his owner in Alabama agreed to sell him. Arabella wrote in a letter to William Still, "I have just sent for my son Augustus, in Alabama. I have sent eleven hundred dollars which pays for his body and some thirty dollars to pay his fare to Washington." Augustus was manumitted in 1858.

After all of her own children were free, Arabella Weems continued to work with Jacob Bigelow, William Still, and others to help enslaved people reach freedom. At some point, Uncle William, Aunt Mimi, and Ann must have convinced Ann's parents to give Canada a try, because by 1861 John and Arabella had moved with young John Junior and Mary to a rented farm near Uncle William's homestead. They farmed there for a while, but by 1870, after the end of the Civil War, the Weems family had moved back to Washington. Uncle William and Aunt Mimi stayed in Canada and raised their children there.

Sadly, by 1861 there is no longer any trace of Ann Maria herself. We can only guess that she either moved, changed her name, or died. Alfred's life as a free man is also a mystery. He and Ann had lived near each other in Rockville and Alfred passed through William Still's house a few months after Ann did on his way to Canada. One book published in Canada has led us to believe that the two were reunited and married, but I have not been able to find them in the census records of either the Canadian settlements or Washington, D.C. It is hoped that further research will solve the mystery of what happened to Ann and Alfred.

Catharine completed nursing school and worked as a nurse in Washington for many years. She became a home-owner when the parents of a former patient expressed their gratitude to her by giving her a frame house in the city. She never married, but shared the house with her youngest sister, Mary, and Mary's husband, James A. Savoy.

John Junior became a carpenter and by 1870 owned his own carpentry business in Washington.

Jacob Bigelow continued to help slaves reach freedom, either by legally purchasing and manumitting them or by helping them to escape. Several times, authorities sent blacks as decoys to ask Mr. Bigelow to help them escape, with the intention of trapping him in this illegal activity and throwing him in jail. But Mr. Bigelow was, somehow, never fooled, and he pursued his work with the Underground Railroad without being caught.

Since *Stealing Freedom* was first published in 1998, one very exciting piece of information has been revealed: the identity of the mysterious Dr. H.! A reader from Arizona happened upon a book published in 1897 that confirmed that Dr. H. was Dr. Elwood Harvey, dean of the Female Medical College of Pennsylvania. It was also fascinating to learn about one of the doctor's motivations for helping Ann Maria escape: The Medical College had no dissection manikin, and there was no money in the treasury for the purchase of a manikin. Because the journey was so dangerous, Dr. Harvey was paid three hundred dollars for transporting Ann Maria to the north — *a lot* of money in those days. He used that money to buy the first dissection manikin for the Female Medical College of Pennsylvania.

Richard Price attended the University of Maryland medical school, became a doctor, married a woman named Elizabeth, and had several children.

A few years after Ann left Rockville, Charles Price purchased a building on Duke Street in Alexandria, Virginia. In this building and an adjoining jail, he and several other men, including his wife's brother, ran a flourishing slave-trading business, Price, Birch, & Co., until it was closed down by Union troops during the

Civil War. The three-story brick house is now owned by the Urban League of Northern Virginia, and contains a small museum dedicated to the slaves who passed through its doors.

Unity, Maryland, is a smaller town now than it was in 1853. It has only a few houses and no businesses, not even a post office. The home of William Price, which was the tavern and the inn, is now a private home.

St. Mary's Catholic Church is still standing in Rockville, although the graveyard has many more headstones than it did when Ann lived there, and instead of a few carriages rolling by each day, heavy traffic zips by on busy streets. Rockville has grown into a city. Michael and Cecilia Fitzgerald (the couple who looked at their grave sites with Father Dougherty) are both buried at St. Mary's, along with their son, Edward, and his wife, Molly, and Edward and Molly's son F. Scott Fitzgerald, the author of *The Great Gatsby* and other well-known American novels. You can visit their graves at St. Mary's Church in Rockville.

In Washington, D.C., cattle and sheep don't wander down the streets anymore. The boggy areas have been filled in, houses and offices have been built on the empty lots, and Washington has grown into a major U.S. city. The buildings Ann saw — the White House, the Capitol, and the Treasury Building — are still there, but the Capitol now has a marble dome rather than the wooden one it had when Ann drove past it.

William Still's house in Philadelphia was torn down in 1992. A blue plaque marks the place where it stood on Twelfth Street.

The willow tree in the backyard where Ann lived near Dresden is still standing.

Acknowledgments

I would like to thank Anthony Cohen, whose book *The Underground Railroad in Montgomery County* introduced me to Ann Maria Weems, and who gave enthusiastic support throughout the researching and writing of this book. I would also like to thank my editor, Tracy Gates, for her invaluable guidance.

My gratitude goes out to the librarians and research assistants at the following historic sites and facilities: the Montgomery County Historical Society; the Maryland State Archives; St. Mary's Catholic Church in Rockville, Maryland; the Rockville Office of Land Records; the Agricultural Museum of Montgomery County; Mount Olivet Cemetery of Washington, D.C.; Martin Luther King, Jr., Public Library, Washingtoniana Division, in Washington, D.C.; the District of Columbia Archives; the Library of Congress; Loudon Park

Cemetery, in Baltimore; the Northern Virginia Urban League, of Alexandria, Virginia; the Alexandria Office of Land Records; the Historical Society of Pennsylvania; the City Archives of Philadelphia; the New-York Historical Society; and in Ontario, Canada: the Ontario Historical Society; the Raleigh Township Centennial Museum; and the Chatham Office of Land Records.

Special thanks go to Alice and Duane Newby, Bryan and Shannon Prince, and Gwen and John Robinson, all of Buxton, Ontario, who fed me, gave me a place to sleep, drove me all over Chatham, Dresden, and Buxton, and greatly contributed to my research into Ann's life in Canada. I was honored to meet with and learn from two descendants of Reverend A. N. Freeman: Madeline Wheeler Murphy, his great-granddaughter, and Christopher M. Rabb, his great-great-great-grandson. Several people also helped with oral histories and questions about farming, crops, livestock, and hundreds of other matters. They were: Mrs. Givens, Charlie Lake, Mike Heyser, Mike and Lisa Corbitt, Sally Davies, Mary Ella Randal, Uma Krishnaswami, and Monica Mundstuk.

And finally, I would like to thank my

family: Rachel, always a first reader; Daniel, always supportive and enthusiastic; and Jim, who not only helped with the editing but convinced me I could do it.

About the Author

Elisa Carbone makes her home in Montgomery County, Maryland, where Ann Maria Weems lived in the 1850s. Ms. Carbone has lectured about Ann's life to teachers and historians.

Elisa Carbone is also the author of *Starting School with an Enemy*, *Sarah and the Naked Truth*, and *Storm Warriors*.

The employees of Thorndike Press hope you have enjoyed this Large Print book. All our Thorndike and Wheeler Large Print titles are designed for easy reading, and all our books are made to last. Other Thorndike Press Large Print books are available at your library, through selected bookstores, or directly from us.

For information about titles, please call:

(800) 223-1244

or visit our Web site at:

www.gale.com/thorndike
www.gale.com/wheeler

To share your comments, please write:

Publisher
Thorndike Press
295 Kennedy Memorial Drive
Waterville, ME   04901